# FIRST
## ON

Frank Gotch saw the metal box with a life-support system attached to it along with a two-way radio from which he had heard the cries. Through the transparent plastic front of the box was visible a live human baby, sleeping peacefully now.

Breathing hard in anger and despair, Gotch checked the indicators on the box. The baby had adequate air pressure, oxygen, and warmth. Then he read the legend painted in bold letters across the top of this ingenious extraterrestrial crib:

*Timothy Davis Barlow, born here, Mars date July 43, Second Annual Cycle After Manned Landing. He shall be great!*

Gotch wondered what was the cause of this lunacy: a baby on Mars, this wild, desolate, barely settled planet. What could the parents, now both dead, have been thinking?

Then the kid started squawking again. "All right, little guy," Gotch said, "yell if you must. But I've got to get you out of here before this storm claims your life too."

# SKYCLIMBER

**Raymond Z. Gallun**

TOWER BOOKS ▮ NEW YORK CITY

**A TOWER BOOK**

Published by

Tower Publications, Inc.
Two Park Avenue
New York, N.Y. 10016

# 1

Frank Gotch slowly got some awareness back. The memory of when he had been able, really, to think before, seemed as distant as some other life, with an eon of dazed misery between then and now. Mostly, he kept his aching eyes closed. But he knew that he was flat on his back, somewhere. For a while his wits remained a blurred, unsorted jumble of incidents, impressions, names. Marie. Everett. Bessie. Where did they all belong?

Sometimes he was far from sure that the ordeal was over. Often he still felt a fearsome urgency, toward terrible, puzzling, necessary effort. Such spasms would smother in his weakness and confusion. Then his mind might drop into his far-lost past. To Dakota wheatfields, awave in a summer breeze, to a distant horizon. Or to the feel and slap of a basketball as he dribbled it down the floor. In high school! What good in recalling such remote stuff? Or, from a little later on, to the sounds of city traffic, the wink of lighted signs, and being on an apartment-house rooftop at night, bare-eyed, or with a little telescope, tripod-mounted.

There, there was some clarity. Particularly for a ruddy spark, high in the southeastern sky. While he had ached and yearned in his lonesome, restless gut, that craved more than food and company—to stand tall on top of distant mystery and danger. The blessing, or foolhardy curse, of a few like himself.

Then he had been at the University, absorbing much diversified but coordinated knowledge. After that, he had sweated and prayed his way to top honors in the special exams; he had passed his physical and the probings of his personality for defects equally well. He had gotten signed up for training, and through it, with joy and impatience, yet with scare that he wouldn't be among the leading four of the fifty finalists who had won out from hundreds of eager candidates. Well, he had won there, also: inclusion in the first live crew to be hurled toward Mars.

Uhuh, trite old Mars, wearied by thousands of fantastic tales from more than a century ago, before there was any intrusion into outer space at all: Romantic guesses that had been killed by since-discovered facts. But still Mars by fact, and by default of any better goal —if one discounted the airless, but very near, terrestrial Moon, and the artificial satellite stations, and the habitable cylinder worlds, long in prospect, and already under prototype testing. Such fabrications were of another category—man-made.

There was a shortage of natural planets at all suitable for easy human habitation, not sun-blasted Mercury, pressure-and-heat-smothered Venus, or Jupiter and the other gas-giants, or their many satellites deep in cryogenic freeze, or the even colder and almost lightless Pluto. As for the stars, man's spiritual goal, they were so far away that reaching them at all might remain fantasy.

Mars was less harsh, but not very promising, either. It was at last rejected as a place to attempt a human settlement, after considerable argument. Still, to satisfy a common curiosity, it should be visited briefly by actual explorers. Public opinion about space programs, often uneven, but just then strong, favored this. But

6

second thoughts about the great expense finally reduced the numbers of ships to be sent from three to one. Surely enough to satisfy pure science!

Gotch was remembering better now: There had been the long ride out, Everett Holsten and Bessie Blythe to stay with the ship in Mars orbit, Marie Manning and himself to descend to the surface.

Mated pairs, not necessarily married, but both couples were—though the women chose to keep their own family names—had been judged the best arrangement for harmony on long missions. Of course, all four of the crew had contraceptive implants under their skins.

Gotch recalled the landing: yes, he of the funny name and face, and that petite clutch of energy, courage, enthusiasm, and cuteness—Marie. Beauty and Beast? Plummeting together in the descent-vehicle, into personal contact with fact, beyond what all the complex, robotized probes could show!

To there, everything had gone with the smoothness of a computerized sequence, riding a wave of supportive enthusiasm on Earth. Down past the lofty, swirling fringes of the south-polar vapor hood, thousands of kilometers across, to a preselected touchdown spot at 54 degrees south-latitude and 108 degrees west-longitude, in Aoneus Sinus.

Gotch's recollections continued to follow each other in sequence:

Getting out of the Lander to look. Of course, everything televised for eight-minute distance-lag transmission to the billions of armchair adventurers on Earth. Hero and heroine, Gotch and Manning, standing there, in vacuum suits, with the dust-yellow sky, the laminated moraines of glacial sediments and, distantly, the edge of the south-polar surface cap, heavy with dry-ice deposits in the background in the early, southern

7

spring. Soon their President should be congratulating them.

They were historic first arrivals—like Columbus or Ericson to America; like Peary and Amundsen to the two terrestrial poles. But much more for their own fascination in being on this other planet.

In his helmet phones, Gotch heard Marie talking to their audience:

". . .We're here, folks. Hope you're getting the picture? Low, subantarctic sun, only about two-thirds its apparent diameter, as seen from back home. Atmospheric pressure very slight—just under eight millibars. Temperature, minus 80 degrees Celsius—112 degrees Fahrenheit below zero—mild, this far south . . . "

Yes, peak point in their lives. Success! Wild thrill, spiked, of course, with scare! They were supposed to stay 1,480 hours—sixty Martian sols—about sixty-one and a half Earth days.

They had landed at this fairly high latitude to begin their explorations by checking subantarctic conditions. The first thing they did after they had unlimbered their surface vehicle—their Mars Wanderer—was to use its power drill, extracting a meter-long core from the layered ground. The bottom end of the core was almost transparent. Thus they proved again what landed robot-probes had long ago proven—that the Martian polar regions, and a considerable fringe beyond them, had an only shallowly buried underlayer of fossil water-ice. Here was a little more to be added to their fulfillment, but the pinnacle of their triumph was only thirty minutes from an abrupt plunge to nadir.

There had been perhaps the ghost of a popping sound in the hyperthin atmosphere. Anyhow they had turned their heads, then dashed back to the Lander to staunch an outflow with their gloved hands. As useless as trying to stop the rush of blood from a terrible chest wound. In

8

a minute, all the oxidizer for the Lander's fuel had spewed through a jagged rent in its flank. The volatile liquid, quick boiling in the low air pressure, made a prismatic shimmering under the cold, muted sunlight.

Now Gotch relived that terrible realization, that they —Marie and himself—had had no chance at all of returning to the ship in orbit. Death sentence. They were marooned as nobody had ever been marooned before. Far out of reach of any reasonable hope of rescue, on Mars, which could not even give them breath!

The stunning effect of shock helped cushion their wits from complete grasp of their situation, and possible screaming hysteria. Besides, they had their intrinsic coolness and their training for emergency. To anyone who gambles realistically with disaster, there must be a backdrop of emotional bracing for the worst. So they continued to think and function calmly.

Had their Lander suffered an accident, a failure of some part? Evidence insisted on a cruder cause for catastrophe. A small element of the home world's populace still hated space programs that much, and for more than their price in tax money. Maybe, to the retarded and frightened view of some, planets and stars should retain only their original, primitive purpose, that of pretty sparks to adorn the flat-Earth sky after sundown? Yet, in their ignorant, phobic savagery, such persons could call on science from nobler brains to accomplish their trite abominations. It was a constant, tiresome threat, in spite of careful security.

"We're stranded—sabotaged," Gotch remembered saying quietly, into his helmet mike, and to the watchers back home. "A character got through, probably at the last hour, when our ship was being serviced in Earth orbit . . ."

A skilled, conscientious technician, it had to be, but

9

with an emotional quirk: a person bringing some dot-size electronic device, to time, and/or to trigger, by a certain condition, or lack of it, a minute, explosive charge in the oxidizer tanks. The outward curl of the rent edges in the Lander's metal side proved the kooky misdeed. By someone outwardly mild, able to pass security requirements, and also to blend into a crowd. One working alone, or hired by a group? The difference hardly mattered.

Yes—such a man had been hunted down, on Earth.

Remembering this much with an incongruously muddled vividness almost hurled Gotch's present through thready consciousness back to Then. In rage and fear, he opened his sticky eyes once more. His homely and wasted features twisted. Dimly he saw the small, arching, air-pressure-sustained interior and the few hospital-like furnishings.

Confused panic still drove him. He tried to raise himself on an elbow.

"Marie, Babe . . .?" His gravelly voice was only a painful, whispery croak.

The nurse's hands pushed him back.

"She's still right here in the next cot, Gotch. The same. At least, no worse. Relax. Rest. You shouldn't move much. You'll disturb the intravenous feeding."

His mental muddle quieted. His eyelids went shut again. He smelled—not the fantasized aroma of hot dogs from his youth in Dakota—but, faintly, the real, dusty-dry pungence of Mars. He was still here, then. His groping recovery of events continued.

There was something his mate and he had almost agreed on, after true grasp of their plight had seeped into their heads. Marie had voiced it cheerfully. "We're the mad kind, Frank. We *wanted* to come here. So maybe we can pack a whole lifetime of satisfying and *different* living into our two months! And whatever

10

more time we can squeeze out of our limited supplies. It'll all be entirely new!"

So they had followed AP-Q—Alternate Plan Q—not so very much of a change from their originally intended, normal schedule. Drive their wheeled vehicle 2,500 kilometers northward, toward the equator, and slightly less-cold conditions. Only, they wouldn't be testing the environment all along the way so much, and they wouldn't be coming the long distance back to their now useless Lander. Instead, they had to cannibalize it of everything helpful that could be loaded onto their Wanderer.

It hadn't been so bad for quite a while. In fact, some of it had been rather wonderful. AP-Q wasn't truly a survival method, but a means to create the illusion that it was, and to fill the time with still applicable Martian research activity, insteady of brooding in horror.

The first horror was mostly on Earth, among that horde of TV watchers. Unless the motive was pure, deranged mischief, what the saboteur—and his possible backers—must have envisioned was the morale-wrecking spectacle of slow, inevitable death to wear down the audience and to "prove" to it, once and for all, that space projects were an unnatural, immensely costly, and cruel foolishness. This intention certainly had its psychological validity. How could two people, with, at best, a three-month supply of oxygen and food, possibly last through the twenty-five-month interval, past the most favorable orbital positioning of two worlds—window time for a launching from Earth—until a rescue craft could reach Mars? Worst was the problem of unpreparedness. Very little at all was ready.

But at least the sabotage, and its dragging, anguished sequel, claimed world-wide attention of an intensity never equaled before in the history of matters made

11

public. And again, the uneven nature of Man was proven to be of sounder mettle than some had supposed. Most people were not frightened into feeble retreat. And hadn't they always responded favorably to tense, agonizing drama? Miners, sealed off by a collapsed tunnel; child alive at the bottom of a deep, dark well. The more terrible the place, the stronger the will and the outcries for rescue. This was on another— a deadly—world! Crash program, please, for God's sake! Call the senators, the President! Hang the costs! We see and hear Gotch and Manning! They're our friends—our bolder selves!

Here, the intention of the sabotage—if rightly assessed as a lesson in awful futility—had begun to backfire.

Gotch reviewed his thoughts of how *then* must have been on Earth: Sure that it was impossible for the marooned to survive, people had still watched them try. To some, it must have had the sadistic appeal of an ancient Roman holiday. To others, it was the just outcome of folly. Still, others hid their eyes in weak capitulation to the unendurable. Let others worlds be! But many more had reacted positively. At minimum, there must be an effort to help.

Gotch brought back to himself the memories of those first Martian days, after Marie and he had selected a site for their attempt to remain alive near Arsia Silva Mons, the great volcano, only ten degrees south of the equator. Just as at their landing place nearer the south-polar regions, there was permafrost and water-ice here, less than a meter below grond level. In the peculiar Martian surface soil there were peroxides, perhaps generated by strong solar ultraviolet rays, unscreened by any dense atmosphere. These exotic peroxides should assist minorly as an oxygen source.

Following AP-Q was back-breaking toil. But who

12

should complain about that? Spread two salvaged crowns of the Lander's descent parachutes made of thin, transparent plastic, such as was used to make high-altitude balloons on Earth on the ground, one on top of the other, and over the Wanderer. Stake the edges with magnesium rods. Pile rocks and dust around the rim to provide a reasonably effective gas seal. Dig a shallow tunnel, plugged in two places with wadded material from the third parachute, to contrive a crude airlock. Start the pumps taken from the Lander, thus beginning to inflate the whole construction with the much-rarefied but plentiful carbon dioxide of the Martian atmosphere.

Gradually, the crude bubble—double-walled for insulation against the cold—had arisen, to be further strengthened by an external net of nylon cordage, fashioned from 'chute shroud lines. For safety from rupture, the internal pressure shouldn't exceed 350 millibars, about a third of terrestrial atmospheric norm at sea level. Then, dig into the ground of the dome floor, mine the shallowly buried fossil-ice. Turn on the heaters, energized by the Wanderer's small, shielded, nuclear-fusion power supply. Outside, rig movable magnesium-foil reflectors, to add more of the weak sunshine's warmth to the dome's interior.

"See how it's done?" Gotch remembered saying often.

And Marie had added her portion to the running commentary:

" . . . So we put algae spores into the pool of water here under the dome, where there is enough pressure to keep it a liquid, instead of evaporating at once. Now we plant seeds in the moist ground—lettuce, onions, tomatoes. Like the algae spores, the seeds were intended only for research purposes. But now this is *for real*. We have a total planting area thirty-five meters across. The vegetables and algae should give us some food. More

13

importantly, oxygen to breathe, derived from the carbon dioxide, by the usual green-plant process of photosynthesis, under the action of sunlight. We'll see if it works, adding more to the little that seeps up from soil-peroxides.''

Perhaps remarkably, it *had* worked, in a month's time. The algae were a fast-growing, vigorous kind, specially developed at a Moon station for extraterrestrial use. And the Martian soil, like the virgin lunar dust, seemed to have a particular fecundity, under reasonably favorable conditions. Even the vegetables hadn't done too badly, at first. The air under the dome became more than three-quarters oxygen, breathable at last.

For a considerable time, it hadn't been too difficult to get along, Gotch remembered. But the constant struggle to keep vital balances somewhere near right within the dome: scraping away the hoarfrost that furred its inner surfaces in the profound nocturnal cold; trying to squeeze more warmth out of the heaters when the internal temperature at floor level almost reached the freezing point of water; detecting and patching leaks in the fragile, makeshift structure, when winds, tenuous but of 200-kilometer per hour velocity, made it quiver perilously, at last joined forces with the starvation-rations that were wearing Marie and him down. They had started out with food for a maximum of ninety days. How could they stretch it for so much longer? What they could raise helped, but it was far from enough.

''We mean to stay alive as long as we can,'' Marie had often asserted into the Earthward distance. ''Who knows? Maybe we'll even win till you come! Thanks for trying!''

Everett Holsten and Bessie Blythe would have stayed in Mars orbit for more than the sixty sols, had this been of any real use. But conversation between the two

14

couples soon began to seem like living friends trying to cheer the living dead. No help.

It was best that they leave for home sooner, parachuting down to Mars in a freight-canister, the additional supplies that they could spare from their own marginal survival capability because of their shortened time in space.

So it had been. The canister had landed within four kilometers of the dome. Still, its retrieval was strenuous, because the Wanderer, now almost necessarily confined inside the rude, pressurized habitation as its power-source for warmth, could no longer be gotten out for any field excursion. He, Gotch, and Marie had had to go forth on foot, and carry its forty-five kilograms, Mars weight—more shell and oxygen bottles than food —over rough ground, and in the 0.38-g gravity, to which their leg muscles were even yet not fully attuned.

The extra supplies would help. But again, far from enough.

Gotch recalled the falsely light banalities of the departure of their colleagues, spoken and responded to by radio:

"So long, you pair! Keep pitching! We'll be talking you up good all the way, and better still when we get there! Reports already sound good! There's super-activity . . ."

"Sure—you other screwballs! And don't drown in the ocean. Or some handy bar. Many thanks, though, Everett and Bessie . . ."

That much had been finished, with regret, yet also relief.

But Gotch remembered parts of Marie's and his own talks to Earth, begun much earlier, almost from the start of their tribulation—soft-sell stuff, mostly. For instance, Marie speaking in her quiet way:

" . . . See, folks. Five months here already—not just

15

two. And we're still fairly all right. All the basics for sustaining life are available on Mars. Water, sunlight, carbon dioxide for reduction to oxygen, and for the synthesis of nutrients. And isn't it odd that the Martian day—sol—is only forty minutes longer than the terrestrial? In fact, any good wristwatch can be slowed down enough to synchronize with the otherwise imperceptible difference! It's a comfortable thing—as if Mars has always been waiting, mystically, for folks to come, not just to explore, but to stay.

"Of course, the rough conditions need manipulation. But—where was it I read?—of five persons who migrated from Europe to the Americas in the sixteenth and seventeenth centuries, two were dead from disease, malnutrition, and violence within three years. Yet the migration was successful. Considering the enormous advances in technology since then, couldn't the record here be better—or at least no worse?"

And he, Gotch, would add his bits, wondering a little if he argued a thesis in which he truly believed, or did so merely, perhaps, to increase their own almost non-existent chances for survival.

"Solid resources are here, too. We've seen them. Copper, much of it in metallic form, in outcroppings—green with carbonates on the outside, but bright metal within—not just as sulfides or oxides. And nickel-iron from big meteorites that fell. Not iron ore, needing smelting—but, again, metal almost ready for use! Some rocks give strong radioactive reactions, so uranium is also available. Look ahead half a century. To cities and fields covered by their plastic domes. Factories, universities, cultural centers. A population growing toward millions. Orbiting reflectors of magnesium foil to warm the climate with stronger sunshine . . .

"Look, it's not Mars that is threatening us, here! It's what a mixed-up man did! Plus human stinginess! If three ships had been sent, as originally planned, we wouldn't be in this fix!"

Gotch had tried to mellow his occasional rough outbursts:

"Of course, it'll take time, money and patience to really open up Mars to immigration. To make settlements here self-supporting and then productive. But it'll be giving people a whole, natural world! Isn't that better than just some nice, neat, manufactured, habitable cylinders, floating in space?"

Frank Gotch had never before thought of himself as a salesman. He lacked the desire and the vocal enthusiasm. Still, he had tried. This, even though, during that interval of deepening desperation, he often wished that Marie and he had never wanted to cross space. But as time moved on, taking them closer to personal extinction, it was clearer and clearer, from communications that came to them, that instead of wrecking extraterrestrial ventures entirely, the fact of helplessly watching a slow horror develop from sabotage was having an intense and opposite effect on Earth.

For here was the right combination of compelling forces for the common soul of Man: drama, rage at a disgusting wrong, sympathy, admiration for courage, challenge of every capability; an old vision thrust forward, the inspiration of perhaps doing the impossible—fulfilling not folly, but a huge and logical dream that shouldn't be denied!

Yes, there was a crash program in progress for rescue, but going beyond that, to an actual pilot settlement project! Five small, hastily prepared robot craft, carrying provisions, had first been launched at high speed in spite of poor orbital positioning and distance, in a desperate effort to resupply the marooned pair. But then five ships had followed at proper window time, and

17

were on the way, carrying ten selected couples, each person highly competent in various fields but with a particular specialty.

At the launch time of the ships, there had been four months yet to go, before their arrival. Much earlier, stringent rationing of food, plus other straining circumstances, had already thinned and weakened Marie very much, and Gotch remembered that the effect on himself had been even worse. Both of their minds were getting fuzzy; every necessary effort took more out of them. Inside their crude bubble habitation, he crept about as if often half in a trance, though his starved gut had stopped aching.

Yet they talked on, now and then, to those ships gradually spiraling out toward Mars:

" . . . Gotch here. Hi! Everett Holsten? So you're truly headed back! Marie is right beside me . . . "

Minutes later, across the shrunken but still huge distance, the answers would come:

"Yeah—me, Frank. Everett. We'll be with you! Hello, Marie!"

"Me, too, Marie! And was that old Frogface Gotch? This is Bessie. Hey, those little supply craft have landed —two of them quite close to where you are, according to telemetry . . . "

"We know," Marie had replied. "One, nine kilometers northeast. The other about seven, west. We tried to get to it. We went a kilometer, and then blacked out. Silly, huh? We're sort of feeble. We had to crawl back to the dome . . . Just barely made it."

Sometimes he, Gotch, had wondered, inside his vague and rambling wits, how it really was for Bessie and Everett. Once in a while hearing Marie or himself talk— his own rough voice now like dry straw rustling. No television views, anymore. Trying to save power—and effort—and maybe pride. It was harder and harder to

18

do even the most necessary. A ghost at last, still trying to speak:

"I gotta. . . M-marie . . . We'll . . . "

His head had been full of dim murmurings. He could scarcely creep anymore. Marie was lying in a coma, one side of her face and body a crust of scabs. Some weird Martian allergy seemed to have sneaked up out of the ground while her resistance was all gone. Their own filth and stink was all around them . . .terrible squalor . . . but what the hell difference, now? The thin croak in his throat had found no force or thought to continue. Yet he remembered sprawling prone on his wasted belly with a filthy blanket over his mate and himself. All they had had to eat for seventy sols was algae strainings, often uncooked.

The microphone on a cord from the radio inside the Wanderer's cab had dropped from his unfeeling fingers. There had been frost on the curved ceiling above, but the deepening chill was also unfelt.

That had been the end—in a timeless blank.

Until somewhere—here—a few hours—or sols—ago? Had he tried to find that microphone again? Gone, though . . . . Then had come the muddled, urgency-resisting confusion.

But he had been finding out better ever since. Now it was all almost clear. Those ships hadn't come too late! He was alive! Unless he'd been fibbed to, so was his woman. Thankfulness, and thanks for everybody—for all of Earth—throbbed in his brain. Goddammit! Wonderful!

He opened his eyes again, and with an effort, turned his head to look around; he had all the strength of a pinch of dust. He saw Marie, terribly wasted, but very clean now, and visibly breathing, on the couch beside his own. Likely, she was still in coma, or maybe she only slept?

19

Overhead was a curve of roof, not of their own place, but of some other—contrived too of parachute plastic, put to double use. For efficiency? Amid the austere but wondrous cleanliness, a tawny girl in hospital white sat on a camp chair nearby.

And beyond the transparent double walls was a carmine scene of outdoor activity. Figures in blue Mars suits were moving about gingerly in the desolate bleakness of early morning. Some were mounted on busy machines. Work must have proceeded with swift efficiency. Two more domes were already being inflated.

Marie and he hadn't been returned to Earth, as sometimes, in his blurred state, he had foolishly imagined. There hadn't been anywhere near enough time! But, just then, he wished that they had!

The tawny girl came toward him.

"Things are pretty good, Mr. Gotch," she said. "I'm Ella Duross, Dr. Pharr's companion and assistant. You may remember him from your training, before you came out here. He's a Marspro physician. Want some good broth? You're about ready for it."

Gotch gave a breathy, achy chuckle, but there was good humor in it. He struggled to speak. "Sure, Nurse Duross. Another thank you! But tell me—how bad did our refuge stink when we were found?"

Before Ella Duross could return with the broth, he had slipped into almost normal slumber.

# 2

After two more sols, Gotch had graduated to scrambled eggs, made up from dehydrates, of course. Marie was improving, but still out. That worried him.

Before a TV camera bracketed on a lightweight bulkhead, he spoke out his earnest thanks. " . . . Except for all you good folks back home, Marie Manning and I wouldn't even be alive. I wish I could find better words . . . "

No matter what he said, it didn't reach, it wasn't anywhere near enough for his gratitude of just then. It might even sound phony. Well—let the simplicity of it stand. It would have to do. And did a speck of cynicism creep into him at last? At least Earth was getting a continuation of its Big Show. Like he—big adventurer! —had been given his risky chance to come to Mars! And the Fool Killer had almost got him! But his appreciation for people who came to visit him remained at absolute, unsullied tops. They, too, were actual participants in new and dangerous ventures. Strangers, mostly, except for a few.

"So here's the really important hero, Frogface!" Bessie Blythe greeted him aggressively, her broad, florid visage shining with pleasure.

"You too, Bessie," he responded in kind. "And, of course, you yourself are getting better looking all the time!"

21

Though Everett Holsten resembled his big mate physically, he was of a milder disposition.

"Whew! It's been a sweat, Frank, all around!" he said, almost diffidently. "Awfully close, for you and Marie! But we won! Now comes the real test, to see if Mars works as a place to live!"

Dr. Jess Pharr was speaking to Gotch a little later, his swarthy face grave. "A problem, Frank. There's a ship waiting in orbit, and a matching Lander on the ground. To take Marie Manning and you back to Earth."

"So, Doc? What problem? It sounds right—the way I feel now."

"Yes, I'll bet! There are complications, though, Frank. It's the only ship with a Lander and return capability. The others aren't much more than mere cargo-and-passenger shells; they grounded entire from orbit and can't climb up again. That was a simplification, to save time, when time was very short. It also saved on materials and expensive special features. Some ways, this was a good idea, but it also has aspects that are slightly dumb and dangerous. For instance, what if the whole expedition has to go home at the next favorable orbital positioning? Of course, with enthusiasm high everywhere, that risk was considered most unlikely. The big, more immediate difficulty is that the returning ship has to start out within the next thirty sols, for optimum trajectory advantage. Besides, if you two aren't on it, a major purpose of this expedition to rescue you—bring you home, that is—will not have been carried out, and some persons, including yourselves, might be annoyed! But our particular dilemma is that I don't think that Marie, or even you, Frank, will be sufficiently back in shape for such a journey in only a month."

"For the best medical attention, she's got to go!" Gotch burst out. "Though, for me, it doesn't make so

22

much difference."

There was a silent moment. Marie Manning lay, seemingly inert, on the other couch. Until now, she hadn't whispered more than a few words, even in these last days. Suddenly she spoke, faintly but clearly, "We wanted to come, Frank. Now our best friends are with us. The bad part is over. Can we quit while we're ahead?"

Gotch's mind did some flipflops. Rejection of Mars had never been complete in his strained emotions. Sure he was mad to have come here. They all were! A crazy but disciplined lot, restlessly eager for the unknown. On the crowded home world, he'd been a misfit. He had wanted the rough openness of a frontier. And even now, Marie was the same. Her spunk and interest had lasted.

He bent over her. "If you're sure, Babe?" he gruffed.

Even her slight nod was definite. He knew her decisive way.

"Give us a couple of sols more, Doc," he graveled. "But I think that's the answer. Our weight, and that of the supplies we would have used up enroute, can be replaced by more rocks and minerals for study, when the ship is remote-guided home . . ."

The allergy left some permanent bronchial damage after healing. So Marie Manning's recovery was limited. She was all right, but she could never be as furiously active as she had been. However, the application of her main skills in botany and food-crop management seemed undiminished.

Gotch turned out about as good as ever, and he now had a lot of experience in the local scene. He wanted to get back to exploring and resources survey work, but there was a good deal to help with first.

The twenty-two people now on Mars toiled furiously

23

to get the first habitable base set up there in the foothills of Arsia Mons, rival of Olympus Mons, mightiest of known volcanoes, farther north.

Doubled crowns of landing parachutes were used as dome skins in an efficient, secondary application, much as Gotch and Manning had done to put up their smaller survival refuge. Other procedures and means were similar, though much improved by better preplanning and preparation on Earth. Water was plentiful from the large deposit of underground ice discovered nearby. This was the reason for siting the Base five kilometers from Gotch's and Manning's original shelter. The water source was ampler. All initial objectives moved along swiftly. One dome was for living quarters and related functions. Another was for workshops and labs. The rest were for hydroponics, agriculture, algae culture, even animal husbandry.

It all seemed a straightforward set of basics to be accomplished, lunged at with enthusiasm, and gotten completed. Of course, some problems were to be expected. From hasty and faulty provisioning of the ships back in Earth orbit. From so much newness for everybody; they had to grope their way. Difficulties could seem minor at the beginning, but they could extend and multiply.

Climate control in the domes sometimes malfunctioned: crops were frost-bitten, or otherwise damaged. Terrestrial plantlife, itself seemed unsure in this alien environment. Chicken eggs hatched fairly well, but many of the rabbit, sheep, and goat embryos failed to develop and died.

A tall whirlwind—a "spinner"—part of a dust storm from the Tharsis desert, flattened two imperfectly reinforced domes. Though Martian atmosphere was very thin, a spinner's rotation rate could exceed a thousand kilometers per hour, enough to be hazardous to fragile,

24

inflated structures. The ripped and collapsed domes had to be patched and repressurized. The wheat sprouting on their floors had been killed at once by cold and swift evaporation.

The colonists made a lark of the repair job, but for some, the joking and laughter were a little forced. Most of them were face to face with the difference between what they had believed they wanted to do as a career, and the fact of it. This required some mental and physical readjustments, though they were a bunch carefully selected for toughness, dedication, and cooperative discipline. Homesickness came down out of the red hills and the unbreathable thinness. But everybody seemed to be winning through the various tensions well enough.

Everett Holsten and Bessie Blythe were cochiefs at Base. With a mixture of mild and rough kidding, they helped smooth flareups of overstrained nerves among younger colleagues. But various, more substantial misfortunes appeared or expanded. Food crops didn't yield as much as expected. Due to logistical errors, certain items from Earth were found to be in short supply; others dwindled more rapidly than estimates had indicated.

A man named Jeff Totten, a minerals expert, tunneling on his belly in the ice stratum twenty meters underground, suffocated and froze when the collar of his air hood became disengaged. His was the first burial on the hillside that became the Base cemetery. A few persons came down with exotic allergies.

Such conditions and events, audio-visually observed, or at least frankly reported, were not the best kind of news for sustaining substantive support from Earth. Enthusiasm for Marspro—the Mars project—once so high, was, of itself, having an inevitable decline as it became commonplace, less exciting. Now, also there was time to sourly examine the price tag. This against unreasonable impatience. The populace, counter to the lessons of history, had an expectation of quick and pleasing results, such was Man's way. Coldly then, some could ask: "So why does so much go wrong out there? Is this the foolishness we were suckered into? Twenty nuts way out there on a bubbleheaded experiment. Their own silly choice! Who would miss them if they die? There are still thousands starving on our own planet through no fault of their own!"

Human logic, reasonable sentiment—and yet fickleness.

The worst was that there was deeper trouble starting up again—talk and fear of war. It could absorb worried attention to the exclusion of other matters. And it was certain that the most primitive enemies of space activities and progress, encouraged by how poorly things seemed to be going at Arsia Base, were busy once more.

Aldo Carlye, their chief of communications, spoke out his patient explanations and arguments to Earth, since patience seemed best: "We've made a good beginning. As you can see, Arsia Base has been built, and is functioning where there was nothing before! This much in just a few months! Inevitably, for a while, there must be experiment—trial and error—in any effort as novel, far-reaching and *important* as this one! An outlet, a safety measure, a whole other world for our kind. We, who are here, know better than ever that it can be accomplished. In a decade or two, it will not only stand on its own, but will yield enormous benefits. Meanwhile, we, here, must be assisted with adequate supplies, a broader range of equipment, and small groups of new, willing, and trained immigrants at the regular, twenty-five-month intervals."

Others spoke to the home planet in a similar way,

26

Marie Manning among them: "When my man and I were stranded and alone, you responded so magnificently! Surely you know that what was started must be carried on to its good result! We at Arsia are the cutting edge of the tool and are doing our part. We need only to be sustained."

But there were others of the colonists who were less careful in their statements. And from the sidelines, scowls and angry epithets occasionally slipped into the audio-visual projections to Earth.

"Inconsistent, stingy bastards . . . We break our backs here, and what do they care anymore? . . . Television adventurers! What do they know? . . . I bet they won't even . . . "

These were usually just the remarks of busy, tired persons, grousing to relieve strain. Though it could seem otherwise, little real malice was intended. Perhaps it didn't matter. Perhaps no words, reasonable, subliminally pleading, or insulting, mattered anymore. They were only words, washing in from a great distance. They were repetitive and thus tiresome; the romantic shock appeal of tremendous rescue mission had faded. Earth, in its uneven history, was turning its attention back to its recurrent, local dangers which were profound.

Hints in the news continued to reach Arsia Base. The next supply shipment would be curtailed. There might be no more colonists sent. There might be two ships, not five—or just one.

Another possible adversity was already well advanced on Mars. It was a carefully planned but inane and sentimental scheme, unknown to anybody except one young couple. The idea for it had come to them when they were in training back in Florida.

They were Edwin Barlow, detail equipment technician, and Lani Davis, bioambience specialist.

27

They were orderly, industrious, soft-spoken, unobtrusive, not overly social. It hardly occurred to anybody that some of this might be a pose.

Lani Davis was blonde, tall, attractive, with a slightly exotic cast of features. Speaking to other women casually, she had once said that some of her ancestors had been missionaries in the South Pacific, and that others were theater folk—this much with a small show of pride that couldn't be called rebellious.

Edwin Barlow said almost nothing about himself. He was a big, slim, tawny man, and very mild. If anyone had time or inclination to speculate about his blended origins, they would have had to guess broadly: Irish, Scottish, French? Sioux or Apache American? Ashanti or Mandingo, from West Africa?

Both Barlow and Davis showed attentive interest in the photos and verbal reports that Gotch brought back from his survey excursions in a Wanderer. They asked questions about the surrounding country. But, in these matters, they were no different from the others. Ed Barlow worked in the shop dome, readjusting and repairing various equipments, and making whatever odd angle bracket, cover, or container that might be needed around Base, but was not among the standardized stocks. He was also good at guiding complicated ground-moving machines.

By her own choice, Lani Davis, after many hours toiling by hand and back in the hydroponic gardens and over the soil-planted crops, in addition to attending to temperatures, humidities, and air pressures carefully, would spend much of her sleep time keeping perishable stores neatly arranged and protected from possible damage. If she was no more conscientious than others about whatever must be done, she surely seemed no less.

Surprise was no doubt part of this couple's plan. Suddenly, without any pre-indication that anyone had noticed, they broke discipline and sneaked away from Base in a Wanderer, in the middle of the night, taking with them a husky load of provisions. Because such an act was almost inconceivable, full awareness of their departure wasn't realized until late the next morning.

A half dozen settlers looked down at the distinctive tiretracks of the stolen vehicle, impressed in the carmine dust and wavering northward, and out of sight in smallness in the sullen dessert.

"What are they trying to do—and why?" Sven Thorgersen, biologist and biological theorist, wondered in his accented voice.

"What kind of damn fool trick? It makes no sense at all!" Leon Bonard, machinist, growled furiously. "We'll go after them, Chief! Break their stupid necks, bring back the stuff they stole from us!"

Everett Holsten considered, his face like a pink squall cloud behind the transparent front of his air hood.

"I don't think so," he said. "It would cost us more than we would gain. They could be far away by now. I can't imagine what they're up to, either, but let them live or die with their choice. Likely, they'll come back. Meanwhile we'll just wait and see if they give us any explanation."

A radio message was picked up three sols later. It rounded the curve of the planet by being bounced off passing Phobos, the 5,000-kilometer-distant nearer moon.

It was in Lani Davis' rather theatrical voice, which now seemed to carry an element of disdain. "We've heard you callng us, Arsia. You're right. Following us wouldn't be productive. I apologize for any inconvenience we have caused. We want to try living on our own for a while. After all, the Wild West of North America was won largely by claim-staking families working alone. So—considering advances in method—

29

why not here? Ed and I are individualists."

Aldo Carlyle replayed this recorded message for everybody, that evening in the mess room.

"Trying to equate the relatively lush Wild West with Mars?" Marie Manning commented mildly in her whispery voice. "Now, that's *real* innocence."

Gotch was afield just then, in his Wanderer, as was frequently the case. So, though he was kept informed, he was rather out of events at Base. This time, his resources survey job had taken him westward. Steve Majorski, metallurgist, was with him. For the first time, it was suggested to him by radio, that when it was convenient he might sort of keep Davis and Barlow in mind, not to drag that worthless, ingrate pair back to Base, of course, but as a small, humanitarian gesture. If they got into trouble, and if this was known, and if giving help was not especially difficult . . .

It was Marie who had spoken. Gotch shrugged sourly.

"*Me*—a minor guardian angel? *Here?* And for *them* —now? Well—okay, babe," he growled tolerantly.

The hint had no application during that particular excursion. And he was back at Base often, afterward, without having gotten any improbable call to action about it.

But matters were moving in their mysterious ways.

Every ten sols or so, the runaways reported in by radio. Angles of the waves reflected by Phobos gave an easy check readout on their general location: close to Olympus Mons, 1,500 kilometers to the northwest.

# 3

Tentatively, Gotch ranged eastward, toward the Corprates Rift, accompanied by Steve Majorski, or the biologists, Sven and Ilga Thorgersen, the only pair at Base who used the same family name. But sometimes he drove north by himself. It was rightly considered a hazard to venture far, alone. Part of him preferred solitude. The country to the north was less rugged and dangerous. He was more experienced than anybody; besides, provisions for only one person offered greater range. So it was allowed. He stayed well away from where Barlow and Davis were; yet he was nearer, and was reminded of them.

There came a night of swift winds, streaming dust, and veiled stars. Gotch, asleep in the cab of his stationary vehicle, was awakened in the wee hours by a buzzer signaling an incoming message. He swung his lean legs, clad in longjohns, out of the recliner seat, and said, "Yeah? Gotch, here," into the mike.

All he got in response was a peculiar mewling. It was a sound that he should have placed at once from remote memory. Still, it was so misfitted here that it couldn't even identify itself to him just then.

The dish antenna on the roof of his Wanderer had lined up on the incoming waves automatically.

"Gotch, here—I repeat," he graveled. "Waiting for reply!"

He spoke thus several times. Still there was just that wail. No words, no explanation. Frank Gotch's hide prickled as suspicion of an incomprehensible fact fought with unbelief and tragic incongruity.

He had scanned his instruments: direction of the incoming waves, north-northwest. Their configuration and intensity, those of a Mars suit's transmitter from a distance of about 200 kilometers, and obviously from high ground. Yes, there was a pattern here. But how—what?

Phobos was not now even in the sky. Without it as a reflector, he couldn't communicate with Base, which, from here, was beyond the horizon. Rage surged up in him, mostly against the aggressive idiocy of a couple of naive malcontents who had somehow managed to pass the psychological tests—against intense competition too!—and had gotten themselves included among those sent to Mars! What stupid, irresponsible stunt had they pulled? Marspro was also at fault!

Let such considerations go. From far down in Frank Gotch's crusty self, softer instincts, seldom activated before, were aroused. He went into action. The fusion-powered motor of his Wanderer hummed to life. The gear system whined and grated in its stiffened lubricants that had stood inert since sundown. The outside temperature now was minus 84 degrees Celsius—119 degrees below zero Fahrenheit.

Gotch began to home in on the ululation. It was intermittent, but its carrier wave continued, so there was at least no problem in moving toward its source. The Wanderer bumped and rocked on through the remainder of the night. The ground rose into the Olympus Mons foothills, and finally up a steep ridge to a ledge.

Armored up, Gotch stepped out of his vehicle. Clad thus, he matched the scene even better than the tough,

32

experienced man inside his Mars suit. Under less pressing circumstances, he might have felt momentarily proud of his aspect, as, in the first golden blaze of the shrunken sun, he came forward, a bizarre, dim, and rather legendary figure emerging through the murk of the dying dust storm to stand triumphant and at ease amid all this lonely and deadly splendor.

Ground-clinging dust trains, aureoled in coppery luminescence by the sunrise, still streamed across the carmine dunes. Northward an abutment of Olympus Mons towered into the cold clarity above the setting, reddish, particulate clouds.

Gotch stood motionless, except for the movement of his eyes and craggy head inside the darkened transparency of his air hood, as, in perhaps five seconds, he searched out and interpreted evidence. Ring of stones, piled-up dust, and magnesium-alloy anchor stakes. Within this ring, suddenly blackened and dried stalks of common, terrestrial food garden plants, trembling in the wind. Also, some crude household appointments—a packing case that had served as a cabinet-and-table and a tiny electric stove. Outside the ring, and stretched away, past a dust-encrusted Wanderer, was a flattened expanse of crinkly polyethylene and nylon cording from two stolen parachutes, which, at Base, had been set aside as patching material. And two corpses.

This much of catastrophe was easy to read: explosive decompression and collapse of a fragile and perhaps insecurely erected dome. Doubtless a spinner had come down from Olympus Mons, part of it notorious as a brew pot for turbulence, had done this thing early in the past night of storm. Death had come to that foolish pair within two minutes, since they had been clad only in longjohns.

The man was sprawled on his belly just outside the ring of stones and stakes that had anchored the dome

33

edges. His face was pushed into the dust, as if to plug his mouth and nose against the escape—in the fairly high vacuum of the Martian atmosphere—of his last, viable breath. The woman lay on her side within the ring. Her mouth was wide open. Her central, upper incisor teeth, projecting from her blackened gums, already had the dry and ancient look of old ivory. All of her young good looks were changed to sad ugliness. Her cheeks showed the livid mottling of decompression hematoma, and there was crinkling of the skin, from rapid, sublimational drying in the low barometric pressure and extreme aridity, even in the deep cold. Like her mate's, her body was surely frozen through and through, to the rigidity of hardwood.

Frank Gotch was certainly no stranger to hideous realities in this environment. It wasn't a thing to disorient his thought and action very much. In him, pity and contempt contested briefly, and contempt was victorious. Lacking adequate obscenities to hurl at these dead, he merely grunted once in total disgust of such utter blockheads. They deserved what they had gotten. But the result of their abysmal stupidities remained a matter of concern.

Lani Davis' congealed hands still reached across the dust. Gotch's gaze jumped to the metal-box case beyond her fingertips. It answered much of mystery, though not all. It was less than a meter long, and half a meter high and wide, with a handle on top. At its back were a life-support pack and a two-way radio with antenna rod, both items obviously cannibalized from a Mars suit. This curious assembly had a whimsical aspect, yet its workmanship showed a care that could be the mark of love. Through the transparent plastic front of the case, hinged for opening, and gasketed against leakage of air within, was visible the crowning folly, the ultimate mis-placement: A live, human baby, not howling anymore,

34

but asleep. Diapered in a now very messy something which seemed to have been contrived from bed sheeting and surgical gauze.

So what Gotch had been sure of before, past unbelief, came together with its irrefutable proof. Saying nothing, only breathing hard through his blunt nose, Gotch checked the indicators on the case. Conditions within it—air pressure, oxygen content, warmth, and humidity—were all at optimum.

Now he read the legend, painted in bold, white letters across the olive-drab top of this ingenious, extra-terrestrial crib:

Timothy Davis Barlow, Firstborn here, Mars date July 43rd, Second Annual Cycle after Manned Landing. *He shall be great!*

Gotch wondered wearily if there was any bottom to the profound lunacy that he had found here. What could ever be the implication of such words other than some completely psychotic parental bombast and fantasy? This time, Gotch snorted. Yet nothing was changed in what he had to try to do. So his head began to function at levels outside of its usual fields, yet with quick and comprehensive care. He looked at the packing-case household-supply-cabinet within the circle of stones, stakes, and dust. Lani Davis and Ed Barlow would certainly have stolen and brought along articles needed for the care of their contraband offspring who must have been conceived before they reached Mars. With methodical haste, Gotch began rummaging. When he had finished gathering things, the kid was squawking again.

Gotch spoke at last, grumpily, "All right, Little Guy, yell if you must. But if you can't get used to dis-comforts, you might as well quit right now. Because

35

you're as far out of place on this world as a tropical orchid trying to survive unprotected in these hills. Especially considering the general provision problem we've all got. You might need magic to stay alive even a few months."

Gotch glanced back briefly. Take the corpses back to Base? Not now. The drifting dust had already begun their burial. Two lives ended, another begun—maybe with more futility. As for their Wanderer, he could probably start it, and slave its controls to his vehicle, so that it would follow him home along with the residue of pilfered supplies. But no, some other time. He had a long way to go, and he'd better hurry.

He lugged young Timothy and his habitat and the collected articles into his own Wanderer, climbed in, dogged the gasketed door shut, repressurized the cab, and started back along his tire tracks. As soon as he was on sufficiently level ground, he put the vehicle on auto guidance, and was free to attend the howling infant.

If he was out of his depth here, any immediate task of babycare daunted him little. He had been through infinitely more taxing emergencies. Wherever he had been inexperienced, he had trusted his common sense, thought coolly, and had done his best.

He removed his own air hood, and opened the front of Timothy's strange crib. He identified the things that seemed applicable to the job of getting the yelling kid cleaned up tentatively. There was dehydrated, vitaminized milk too. He shook it up with water from the Wanderer's cab tank. There was also a tiny food oven where the milk could be heated. Among the possessions of the Barlow-Davis pair, he had also located a new, plastic nursing bottle—fitted with a nipple!—more proof that those asinine characters had long pre-planned their caper. Else how would such ordinarily inappropriate articles have gotten to Mars?

36

Minor difficulty—the squawler seemed unacquainted with bottle feeding. But Gotch squirted some of the warmed fluid into the wide mouth, and sooner than was reasonable to expect, hungry and thirsty Timothy got the idea. He calmed, and sucked greedily.

Looking down at him, and holding the bottle, Gotch discovered an unfamiliar, achy warmth stirring in his lean gut and mellowing his steady rage. Here was this poor, ugly, cute, totally misplaced mite, softly, velvety tawny . . . . After awhile, the kid fell asleep.

The Wanderer bumped and hurried onward, on its long journey. Phobos was in the sky again. Gotch waited for its position to improve. The time arrived. He might as well spill the news as fast and bluntly as he could.

"Gotch talking," he graveled into the mike. "I answered a cry in the night. Barlow and Davis are both dead—from their spinner-wrecked dome. But they left a baby—I repeat—a baby, a live, twenty-sols-old son!— for us to sweat over. I'm bringing him in."

In his earphone, Gotch heard the distant message announcer buzz. Then, faintly, the automatic replay of his words from its recording. Then a medley of background shouts, calls, and imprecations from near and far in the vicinity of the communications equipment at Base. Then a silence so long that he almost thought he had lost contact.

He spoke again, "Look, consternation I expected. But not mouth-open dumbness from our kind of bunch! Please, somebody who can listen and grasp!"

Bessie Blythe's rough voice boomed placidly in his ear, "Will I do, Frank? I've heard what you said three times now from replay. I believe yuh. So tell us more."

Gotch tried. "Whatever their kooky motive, Barlow and Davis must have planned this from way back. They must have run away from Base to get their kid born—

37

expecting, probably, to return with it, not long after it was an accomplished fact. Only, the crazy scheme went partly wrong; the Fool Killer got them.''

"Listen, Frogface,'' Bessie cut in. "I'm not as startled that there's a baby as maybe you suppose. Way before they took off, there was a funny, pinched look around Lani's eyes, that any old mother could have recognized. I had half a hunch that didn't surface in my dense head—the idea was too nutty! But, of course, you can see some of the rest of it. They must have dug the contraceptive implants out from under their skins. Now, my first imperative questions: How's the kid? Need any instructive assistance about him?''

"I managed,'' Gotch gruffed defensively. "He's clean enough, and bottled. Burping wasn't necessary. He's asleep. And fine, as far as I can tell.''

"Okay, Frank, you rate A-plus. Now, how come the baby is alive when his folks are dead?''

"Damnedest answer, Bessie. Remember those carrying cases people use on Earth, to take their cats and small dogs with them on vacation trips? A thing sort of like that. And with a Mars-suit L-S unit and radio attached. I guess they wanted the radio so they could hear and talk back to their kid whenever they had to leave their bubble. Ed Barlow was always in the shop, making items we needed. I suppose that was how he built the case. They schemed their whole loony stunt pretty well! But they didn't even have the common sense to be wearing their Mars suits as a precaution during a dust squall!''

"That isn't as nutty as you suggest, Frogface,'' Bessie responded. "Ever try to eat, make love, or nurse a baby, while all gussied up in a vacuum armor? The big riddle is why would anybody want to bring an infant into a world like this? Against rules and reason, and now when critical stores are short, or running out, with

38

no certainty at all of sufficient replenishment? Those two must have had a truly terrible and frustrated craving to become mom and pop!"

"Huh!" Gotch grunted. "Bessie, you don't know how far those characters carried that! The television camera on this Wanderer isn't hooked up, so I can't show you, but let me read you what's printed on this baby carrier . . ."

Gotch intoned the words, particularly the brash final phrase: "'He shall be great!'"

Bessie Blythe gave a sharp snort. Then Gotch heard a background babble of expletives, imprecations, complaints, and arguments in various voices, masculine and feminine. "Why, those triple damned . . . Sure—and on Earth we'll all get called irresponsible and shiftless, too—by association, when it's just them! For certain, we'll be left to starve . . . The main difficulty—how are we gonna take care of a little baby here? Hey, Gotch should just lose the brat—it'll die anyhow! . . . Ah—fer God's sake, man—we can't! . . ."

"There's some local controversy, Frogface," said Bessie Blythe. "You just get young Tim to us, and we'll see. I didn't want to monopolize this mike. Here's your lady."

Marie's whispery voice sounded unruffled, and privately, wryly, amused. "I worry about you, Frank. But last night, while you were driving fast through a wilderness storm on a mission that nobody could imagine, I didn't know, and I slept soundly. How about that? Now I've got a thought. Maybe it'll come to you, too. While you're bringing the child in, we'll be looking for ideas, here. So relax a little."

"Hah, Babe, don't I always relax?" Gotch growled in wry doubt.

Phobos, in its hurried orbital passage, was moving out of best position as a communication-reflector.

39

Contact faded out swiftly.

The Wanderer rolled on, dust kicking up from its tires. When it seemed appropriate, Gotch tended Timothy Davis Barlow. Otherwise, he let him sleep or yell. The yelling was infrequent. Sometimes, in flat country, Gotch could doze, with the vehicle on full automatic. Haze-fringed noon came, with the outer temperature actually up past freezing. The carmine scene extended on, to the horizon: Low crater walls; empty, magnificent, colorful desolation; three-billion-year-old stream beds, eons dry. Funny how such things could grab the guts and hearts of folks like himself.

Sunset . . . . The long drive continued through a night of blazing stars, with Earth the blue queen among them before dawn. Wearily onward, through another sol. Twice, when Phobos was in the right place, Gotch reported his position, but didn't bother to say much more. Later, he laughed to himself. This whole thing was so ridiculous! But a thought, linking the present with his own chancy past, had finally reached him, bringing a crookedly whimsical peace.

Near sundown again. Shadows filling desert hollows, in the muted, slanting light. And off there ahead, visible at last, against the backdrop of Old Hunchy, the Arsia Silva Mons caldera, was Base—ten dusty, cord-netted domes—an extraneous intrusion that still matched the landscape. It looked lonely there beyond the fluted dunes that had piled up just inside the slotted dust-fences. Those fences slowed the drifting granules enough so that they did not encumber the areas around the structures. Yeah, lonely. Gotch half wished that he was an artist or poet, with free time enough too, to pin down a bit of his sudden pleasantly chilly mood. The last sunshine glinted on the solar reflectors for the domes, and on the metal capsules of the little nuclear-fusion plant, set apart on a low knoll. Now, several

Mars-suited figures came into view, to be at hand for a momentous arrival.

An hour later, Gotch was taking a short snooze. But still in rather wry good spirits, in spite of circumstances, he had had a brief conversation with his mate, here in their cramped quarters.

"Frank—I believe I know what Davis and Barlow had—at least partly—in their muddled heads . . ."

"Uh huh, Babe. So do I—now. I might have caught on right away. But I was too goddam disgusted with them. So let's keep our mouths shut this evening, and see how the bunch reacts."

# 4

Timothy Davis Barlow's ingeniously contrived shelter, with its hinged front open, and Tim inside, had been placed on a provision-carton table in the mess room. Bessie Blythe, who, appropriately and by nature, had taken charge, stood guard. Most of the Base personnel were already clustered around the slumbering infant.

Now a straggler, Tony Mancuso, meteorologist, who had been several kilometers afield to a narrow, always-shaded cleft in the hills where he had set up some atmospheric instrumentation, came into the room. In his specialty—definitely a sideline among all the other, rougher, more urgent jobs that everybody had to help doing—he was a bit worried. It would take a while to develop any firm basis for predicting Martian weather. Still, there had been that turbulence three nights back. And did the high wind-velocity in that funnel-like cleft, with temperature and pressure both up a whisker, presage a general storm? Time might have to be found for rechecking all the domes for stability and weak points.

Tony Mancuso's attitude was typical of most of the others. He entered, still in vacuum armor, but with his air hood under his arm. Some of the dry cold and burnt pungence of Mars came in with him. But he left his meteorological concerns behind. There was this different emergency, this what-in-hell thing. Very curious,

Mancuso crowded close, hunched his large shoulders, stared, puffed out his bristly cheeks. As with many hardy souls, he believed that rough humor could help anybody through any situation.

"So that's it, huh?" he boomed. "Sure Gotch didn't find it under a rock? Homely little devil, ain't he?"

"Sh-s-sh!" Lida Sturm, Tony's physicist mate, admonished. "I think he's real cute."

So the contesting talk among the small crowd, momentarily suppressed, started up again.

"This occasion calls for beers all around!" said John Tenaka, volcanologist.

"Oh, of course," quipped Ruth Parkins, chemist. "When have you last tasted beer? Or used real toilet paper? How are we going to keep this tyke from starving? With fried algae-meal cakes?"

"Don't knock the scratchy paper you chem bugs are trying to make out of ground-up straw, Ruthie," John Tenaka, who was her man, quipped back.

"Hey, Doc Pharr, do you know anything about neonatology and pediatrics?" Steve Majorski teased.

Pharr spread his slim brown hands, with the paler palms upward, in a humble gesture.

"Very little," he said. "From way back, during my internship in Philadelphia."

"Timmy can have dried-milk ration—such as it is," Ilga Thorgersen offered. "Poor little fellow! He didn't ask to come to Mars, like all the rest of us did. And he certainly didn't ask to be born here."

"I didn't ask to be born in Peoria, Illinois, either—but I was," Arelle Mather, industrial-processes technician, stated dryly. "Still, I'd like to hold him a second. Deep down, in spite of my contrary resolves, I'm a frustrated mother. Could I, Big Bessie?"

Bessie Blythe shrugged. "Guess so, Arelle. Here, let me show you. If it goes all right, pass him around."

43

"Aw, shimmering Tharsis!" Tony Mancuso moaned. "Do you have to slobber all over the little guy? Now you've waked him up, and made him bawl!"

"Hey, will somebody ever get serious around here?" Leon Bonard, machinist, grated. "We've got this forbidden infant! We were in bad trouble before! Earth, involved in its own messes, is turning its back on us! And its politicians want to blame as much as they can on us, so they've got an excuse to forget about us as far as possible—maybe entirely! There were errors in provisioning our ships—partly our fault; we might have watched closer. Crop failures and other schedule slippages can be made to look like part of our poor record, though they don't belong there. Now—topping it all!—is this Timothy, issue of two of our original number, and against the firmest regulation. By association, doesn't that make us all total slobs, engaged in an expensive idiot project and no longer worth a qualm or a thought? So we've got to think hard and decide what we're going to do!"

Helen Miller, an industrial-products chemist, spoke up diffidently, after a moment of silence, "So maybe we should keep Tim a secret. We haven't activated the television cameras very often here lately. Unless somebody on Earth managed to pick up faint messages not beamed there, they don't know about him. We needn't tell. We didn't advertise Davis' and Barlow's running away, either."

"Sure, suppose we tried that," Bonard retorted with seemingly heartless cynicism. "What have we got left to keep a baby marginally nourished for more than a few months, even if we, ourselves, gave up all of the few foods still around that it could tolerate? Many of our stores of terrestrial origin are used up; other important ones are way down. The kid's chances for survival and normal growth would be very poor. As things are, we

44

could be starving to death ourselves. Or suffocating and freezing when other things break down, and lack of critical spare parts prevents repair. So we'd better think further."

Eyes groped at other eyes, questioning.

"You're a bastard, Bonard," declared Steve Majorski, mineralogist.

"No, he ain't," denied Aldo Carlyle, chief of communications, and the others saw that he was grinning. Carlyle waited till he had their full attention before continuing, "This Tim Barlow is here; he exists—a perhaps unwise, unwanted fact. I doubt we've got the heart to destroy him! And there's no good in trying to hide him, either. We can't look after him without help for very long. Our own lives are on the line, anyhow. We all gambled by coming to Mars. So let's gamble big, again! Not only tell the home crowd everything, but build up the telling! We haven't been showing our activities on TV very effectively or very much for a long time because so many watchers on Earth are fed up with us. So maybe they need another shocker! This could be it! Almost as good as Manning and Gotch, hopelessly, fatally marooned. But somewhat more cheerful, eh? Firstborn on terrible, useless, distant Mars! Little, delicate, cuddly baby there! Contrast, drama, awful need for action!"

Among the assembled Base personnel, there were loud murmurings, nods of approval for what had seemed obvious, a scowl and growl or two of hesitation and doubt.

Carlyle's gaze went to Everett Holsten's face. "Chief?"

Holsten, like others, had stayed out of the discussion. In his shared leadership with his woman, Big Bessie Blythe, he was seldom anything like a serious autocrat. In this selected and supposedly always cool and steady

45

band of pioneers, he wasn't meant to be. Some might have thought he lacked guts. But he could be very tough, though he much preferred a reasoned consensus. He winked at Bessie, who had just put young Tim back into his exotic crib.

"So you're playing original, Aldo," he said. "When we've been talking this idea around, ever since we knew there was a kid. I vote 'aye.' Who else? It's time for a count."

There was a quick chorus of voices, and a flutter of upraised hands. Only a few lagged slightly.

"Nays?"

There was silence.

In the background, Gotch squeezed Marie Manning's shoulder, and chuckled. They had been the last to lift their arms. But they were satisfied that they understood the human race, here, and especially on Earth: inconstant, uneven, easily wearied. But responsive to whatever truly grabbed them. Soapy? Yet basically good.

"Your show, Aldo," said Everett Holsten briskly. "I suppose you have a notion of how it should be set up?"

"Oh, yes—I do."

Mona Schultz, Aldo Carlyle's mate, was already pulling the fabric cover from the TV camera, bracketed high on a bulkhead.

Aldo began moving around, speaking sharply in command, maybe getting a bit officious, "You, here, Bessie —uh uh—holding the kid right in the foreground. Better quiet him for the beginning, if you can . . . Frank and Marie over here—not too close . . . . The rest of you—Ilga, Sven, Doc and Ella, Steve, Tony, Helen— everybody!—moving around, discussing. But keep the voices down—please! I guess we should all look worried about Tim. Maybe even contrite, as if the fault was ours."

Aldo spent several more minutes rearranging and assessing his artistry, while the baby's stormy face threatened another loud protest, and others grumbled. At last Aldo touched a switch, and signaled with his hand. Begin!

He spoke as a nameless, faceless voice, "There is an emergency, in which we adults who are still alive here took no part, except to rescue. Yes—you see him—he's real. An orphaned baby boy—Timothy Davis Barlow—born on Mars! There had to be a first . . . "

The audio-visual impulses, beamed from the big dish antenna out in the deep-chilled desert night, started their light minutes of traveling toward the Blue Evening Star, like a sneak attack.

# 5

Even in a log hut, deep in Alaska—one of the few places left on Earth where an individualist might try to be himself—the live news was received. A woodsy old character, in a patched and soiled lumber jacket, bent closer to a battered and dusty television set, absorbing the pictures and voice sounds that were coming to him by way of Sitka.

"Well, I'll be . . . ! Those confounded . . . !" he roared in startled fury, causing his pet racoon to stare at him with questioning, burglar-masked gaze.

But in a moment, he repeated himself in a far-less outraged tone. "Well I'll be!" His own crinkle-lidded eyes had softened. He showed a crooked, snag-toothed grin, both benign and humorous, as if he had become privy to a vast, wonderful, and gentle joke on everybody.

In Washington, D.C., a fairly high official's similar though more controlled anger didn't abate. He turned to his aide, sitting behind him in his nicely appointed office.

"Ozzie," he said. "Watch this. Is it something to smother all space-oriented wastrels? Or will Simple Sentimental Simon and Family go charging the other way?"

"You know I'm a cynic, George," responded Ozzie blandly, after a moment.

And in rural Minnesota, a twelve-year-old girl—her name was Deva Corliss—shrilled from her room, "Ma! Ma, quick! On Channel 23! They have a baby boy way out somewhere—on Mars! His parents were killed! The people there have very little that he needs!"

These were just examples of small, intense reactions that were happening, millions of times, and in as many places, all around the terrestrial globe. The phenomenon expanded, fairly exploding. The Mars Project, which had been a dying topic, was instantly, irresistibly newsworthy again. Not even the one-time shout to save two sabotaged maroonees on another world could match the present demanding outcry. Newscasters apologized for recent public apathy. Little Tim Barlow was made the relighter of the light. He became a known and visible quantity, like one's baby brother, child, grandchild, or small nephew—lost out there! Maybe how it all functioned was sad in a way—a wry wedding of human sentimentality with what burgeoning communications technology could shove under its simple novelty-seeking nose, but it worked. Tim's dead parents were idealized too, made into far-seeing martyrs, leading the way to a great future—and maybe they had actually done that!

If a little child could be born on Mars, didn't that prove too that it was a livable place? So, to hell with the price tag on efforts that must be continued. Opposing factions were overwhelmed. All of the old arguments for Martian colonization were revived, and emphasized by new data which had been coming in from Arsia Base for months, particularly about untouched mineral resources found. Even if massive loads of metal couldn't be economically transported to Earth, it seemed clear that local good living and wealth could be developed and expanded on Mars itself. Adventure and greed stirred the blood and visions of many. Threats of

49

war were considerably blunted on their several sides by these massed diversions. Indeed, almost as if to join a common purpose, an opposing block of nations decided to send a small pilot group of pioneers to Solis Lacus, a region 2,000 kilometers southwest of Arsia Silva Mons.

And what might have been only one resupply ship— or none at all—dispatched to Arsia Base, immediately became five again. Soon, in heightened optimism, five more were added, to establish a second base near Olympus Mons. With standardized components just then available, along with construction facilities, the extra craft weren't too difficult to build quickly.

A deadline was met. The ships accelerated out of terrestrial orbit at window time. In terms of universe size, the goal was near; still it was very, very far. In due course, quadruple clusters of big landing parachutes, silvery diaphanous, blossomed in a dusty yellow sky. At 25-month intervals, more would appear. Another step in Man's erratic march into the Cosmos had begun. For quite a while, matters would go—imperfectly but not too badly—on Mars.

# 6

To many persons on Earth, Timothy Davis Barlow remained the most deprived of children. Had he known this, he wouldn't have agreed.

Tim didn't know he was famous, either. Most celebrities have to work long and hard to achieve even limited fame. But like some ancient emperor's heir, he was vested in it merely by coming into being. He was a marvel, a first in a startling birthplace. By luck or ill luck? And who could say for sure which was which?

Not wishing to spoil him, nobody hurried to inform him of his status. Anyhow, he wouldn't have cared, at least then. He had only a child's need for recognition and approval from those around him. He got sufficient of both, without asking. His first difficult months were masked to his memory by the fogs of infancy. When the relief ships arrived, his guardians on Mars didn't want to give him up; reluctantly, Earth folk conceded he was too young and undernourished to be taken the huge distance to his ancestral planet; it was better that he remain for now with those he knew.

Like any very young child any place, he began to be aware: of shapes, movment, light and dark; sounds that frightened and sounds that soothed; cold, warmth, tastes, smells; of brightnesses to grope at in wonder, wondering what they were; of other presences; and of course of his own self and being.

At four Earth-years old—a bit more than two, Martian—he had much more understanding. He was, by then, an alert, tawny little chap in a miniature of the blue coveralls that were the regulation within-shelter costume at Base. His sharp senses probed all things in the fascinating ambience immediately around him. He would scamper from dome to dome through the underground tunnels.

He was surrounded by sometimes gruff but usually friendly giants. He had scant time to consider that other children must exist, though he had seen some of them pictured in the television beamings from Earth that he was allowed into the communications compartment to watch, programs that wouldn't betray his importance to him, or perhaps disturb him with any painful contrast of Mars to the home world. Also, he had heard, with minimal concern, that there was another child, younger than himself, at a place called Olympus, but he was innocent of any direct contact with anybody of his own age. Yet, uniquely too, he lived much closer to sophisticated and dangerous technology that any small fry before him.

Often, his rapt interest made him lunge to touch, find out about, and maybe take active part in, important things.

"Get out of there, kid!" somebody would roar at him.

Leon Bonard, machinist, was one who had emphasized such an order with a fierce, ear-ringing slap. But then he had picked Tim up, laughed from his whiskery bigness, and had spoken grimly yet earnestly, "Look, fella, you're pretty young to start acting like a *man,* but you've got to. Poke at a plastic dome skin? Mess with any environmental control? You could be suddenly and very painfully smothered, frozen stiff—never to come back alive, or to see or know or have fun at anything, ever again! Worse, you might take us all to the same nothing-nowhere place! A *man* is forever careful not to hurt his friends, Timothy. He watches, listens, and learns before he acts. Then he asks permission from whomever is in charge. Here, I'll show you how this gauge works, then, maybe . . ."

From such early incidents, Tim Barlow began to be very conscientious and responsible. He had his heroes and heroines to be like, to imitate in pride for himself. And in this small society where caution and discipline were so necessary, he was molded to its pattern. He knew that unobtrusive TV cameras were watching activities at Base, but he wasn't told that they were particularly intent upon him. Nor was he told that the big folks here were specially concerned about him: first because they all had natural but blocked-off parental inclinations which his presence fulfilled; second because he was their talisman, their propaganda support on Earth, giving them the means to carry forward their purposes for being on Mars. This was his real profession, though he knew nothing of it then. And in their hard-bitten, rather undemonstrative way, they doted on him, and did what they could to make his existence agreeable and his education in local matters practical and competent.

They said that the Blue Star, sometimes of evening and sometimes of morning, was Earth, from which people, and almost every useful device came. He accepted this without any deep probing, though occasionally he wondered to himself how a thing so big as a bulldozer, or even a person, could ever originate from a tiny bright point in the sky? But he never got around to asking that question. While, for adults, it is hard to perceive by themselves the curious, inconsistent gaps of comprehension that occur in the very young; furthermore, children have been accepting Santa Claus and other charming, illogical myths for ages. The real truth was that Tim Barlow, being then much more interested in the immediate world around him, and in wanting to fit into it, had scant attention for such remote tales. In this, he was like many other active, extroverted small boys. Except that his actual world was Mars.

Even what was in the airlock-and-tunnel-connected arrangement of domes was vast and marvelous to him. In the Number One habitation bubble were the mess room and galley. Adults might grumble about the algae-and-maize-meal breakfast cakes as an eternal abomination, but having known little better, he *liked* them, even when Big Bessie had no honey from the bees kept for pollination purposes in the garden domes to daub them with delicious sweetness! In the galley, too, when he wasn't yet quite five Earth-years old, he had his first, useful, proudly satisfying job: washing dishes, thus becoming almost one among the always-busy others. Finishing this morning duty, he would hurry elsewhere, where there were much more interesting things to watch, learn about, try to do.

There were domes where clear plastic tubing doubled back and forth endlessly on itself, with water—loaded with living green algae—being pumped slowly through it, for exposure to sunlight. Soon he knew that from here came most of the air that everyone breathed, and much of what they ate. He absorbed his first knowledge of reading from notices printed in red on various equipments: *"Warning! . . . Important! . . . Keep gauge pressure within the green range! . . . Check at automatic shut down . . . "*

Hearing such words read, he learned their visible equivalents, and mouthed them out accurately and solemnly later. His doing this made big people laugh. He didn't know that this was for his improbable sound of mature knowledge. But he noticed that, though their

54

laughter was loud, it was also approving. So he must ask and find out more about what he was saying.

He insisted his way into many simple tasks: "Hey— lemme do that?" So he tended tomatoes, potatoes, and other vegetables in the hydroponic tanks. He dug into the irrigated red soil that floored the agriculture domes, readying it for maize, grain, and flax planting. At harvest, again with simple tools—scythes, machetes, threshing flails (since farm machinery would have been both difficult to transport from Earth and of excessive capability for a small-scale operation), Tim happily carried bundles of stalks and straw, much larger than himself.

Before he went to sleep at night, weary but happily proud, on a pallet in his tiny compartment in the Number One habitation, his mind would fill with many vivid impressions from the more-and-more that he remembered. The shower of sparks from a spinning abrasive-wheel, as Leon Bonard shaped metal in the machine shop. Tony Mancuso, meteorologist, singing songs that he called Italian. The smell of blossoms on young apple trees in the garden dome, while bees hummed and water trickled, and the sun shone through the transparent roof curve, though, low down, there were needles of hoarfrost. "Aunt" Marie Manning was often busy there. She of the rustly voice and kindly eyes, that could go scary hard when she was displeased. The time she had set a red thing on his open palm, saying: "The first strawberry, Tim, eat and enjoy!" Then she'd be telling him how to take care of the clover and the young chicks and rabbits, and the six goats. This while her gaze wandered out through the dusty clarity of the garden's sealing, plastic bubble, to the great Outside where he had never yet walked, himself, though the bootprints in the red dust were numerous, and the wheel tracks of vehicles rambled beyond the far horizon.

There was so much more. Gotch, so often gone from Base for several sols, locating and charting mineral deposits. Also bringing back visual recordings to show at night in the mess room. Scenes: of the inside of the Arsia Mons crater, where he often went with volcano ologist John Tenaka; of the monstrous gouge called the Coprates Rift. Bringing back samples, too. And for him, Timothy, gifts. Rock crystals as clear as pure water-ice. Once a great, blue-white lump with shifting shadows and lights in it. Steve Majorski, the mineralo gist who had been with Gotch then, called it "hydrated. amorphous silica—opal."

But there was also a clear, pale-yellow stuff which Steve named Memnonia-Gum, because it was first found in the Memnonia desert to the west, supposed to be resinous remains of tiny water creatures from very long ago. It had high tensile strength; rolled out thin, it should have made excellent dome plastic, so it had everybody excited for a while. Only, in the lab, it couldn't be flattened into patches larger than a few centimeters across; it stuck to the rollers, it crumbled.

Sven and Ilga Thorgersen were others who often rode out into the desert with Gotch, looking for layered rocks with microfossils in them. Sven, who, on rare party evenings, played tunes on his homemade violin, while other people danced and were happy, though Tony Mancuso and Steve Majorski usually got into a loud, make-believe argument about which was the stupidest for having come to Mars, or some other silly subject. It was all for everybody's amusement; but once, after the lab crew had produced some strong liquor out of corn, those two big men had gotten into a real fight that others had to break up. He, Tim, was scared. Yet, at the end, Steve had reached down to twist his ear, and, with his nose still leaking blood, had grinned and said puzzling things: "Don't worry—a scrap relieves pres-

56

sure, kid. So we older folks don't explode inside. We're still glad to be here. But a strain builds. We have to get rid of it some way. Guess you wouldn't know. Because Mars is *all* you know. You're lucky.''

More about the Thorgersens: The Time they came back from an excursion, looking very pleased indeed, showing a flattish, blackish-green lump no bigger than a man's hand. They displayed it in the mess room. He, Tim, had wriggled forward, close among everybody else, while Sven had explained, "Macro-botany! Macro, not micro—big—visible, not microscopic! Nobody thought it could exist anymore on Mars! But a little of it still does, and here is a proving specimen! See how it works? See all the little trapdoors among the spines on its top side? They're closed, now, but at night they are open, rather like flowers! At night, in some regions, a little waterfrost is sometimes squeezed out of the very dry atmosphere by the deep cold. It collects best on the tiny hairs within the open trapdoors. When the warming sun comes up, the trapdoors close, before the frost can evaporate. Sealed in, it creates vapor pressure as it warms, so that most of it can melt into liquid-water instead of becoming gaseous. In that form, it can be absorbed! So, even on Mars, there is macro-botany! Thus these plants have adapted through the ages, to get the life liquid they require, when perhaps they could not use the hard-frozen permafrost, or even reach it with their roots. Otherwise, they have also learned. Their hard shells seal in the water against escape, and their dark coloring converts the sun's rays better into warmth. Doubtless these plants freeze solid in winter, reviving in summer. Perhaps they can even revitalize, after many seasons of being almost completely dried out! Ilga and I have found an appropriate Latin name for them—*Gelucipulae*—Frost Trappers! They do not make any practical difference for us—without them, we

57

would still be trying to settle successfully on Mars. But are they not splendid?''

Tim, who was about six Earth-years old then, had not grasped all of what Sven Thorgersen had said. But he could remember how Sven's pale beard had wiggled happily with his hurrying mouth. When conversation had quieted enough, Tim had asked, "Why splendid, Uncle Sven?"

It was Ilga who had answered, "Tim, it is like seeing another face of—whatever it is that makes everything happen. It suggests better that what exists on one world can exist on many—out to as far as anything can go. It is like saying a prayer. It is worth lifetimes of trying to find out more. If you do not understand so much now, you will . . . .''

Maybe he had understood some of even this. There was a tweaky feeling. Of Bigness that made him feel smaller than he was—though comforted—when he wanted to feel big. Beyond this much, he didn't have the right words, or even the clear thoughts. So let all such fuzzy stuff go.

He liked best what he could touch and do. Beating out flax fibers for the little spinning machine, or feeding grain to the small, electric flour mill. He liked the sounds in the dome where the shops and manufacturing areas were. And the various smells from that of straw to hot metal. He liked to tend the livestock. Maybe most of all, he enjoyed climbing a stepped pole, which somebody held firm while he patched a small leak high in a dome. He was lightweight and nimble and on the way to becoming a man.

Yes, lying in presleep in his pallet, Tim Barlow would review and ponder many good things. The lumpy, ruddy moon, Phobos, crawling up swiftly out of the west. The noises of busy people and things all around. Even the noise of Mona Schultz and Helen Miller scolding each

58

other about who had left the shower in a mess. The comfort of being warm; the sting of cold. Awakening in the dark, when a big wind came down out of the Tharsis desert, making the whole habitation bubble quiver and rustle ominously. Scary. Lonesome, yet pleasant. Did the giants worry too much? And he liked deep silence, too.

Of course, there were the bad things. Ruth Parkins, all swollen and red from an allergy, which must have come from soil samples, brought from far Outside, which she had been studying in the lab. The scared look in her mate's—volcanologist John Tenaka's—face, when he saw. But Doc Pharr had pulled her though, hadn't he? Same with Mort Lovan, Helen Miller's engineer companion, when the fingertips of his left hand had turned blue-black, and had to be cut off at the first joints, because his glove had been punctured, and the cold, outside vacuum had gotten in. And out on the cemetery slope were the grave markers. From inside the dusty, transparent walls of the garden dome, Marie Manning had pointed out those of his "parents"— Gotch had sometime brought their bodies back from somewhere. Parents? The man and woman from whom he came. Still a puzzling unclarity to him, since he hadn't known anybody's parents. But chilly-pleasant to think about, once in a while.

Tim Barlow grew. He even got a little interested in that other kid that he heard about now and then.

"Yuh, just a girl," Steve Majorski told him. "Up at Olympus Base. Her name is Agnes Frost."

Nobody gave him the whole story then. Arsia Base had had a propaganda advantage over envious Olympus. The rumor was that couples up there had drawn lots to equalize this discrepancy by violating a rigid rule again. So, without the original foresight of Ed Barlow and Lani Davis, the Mars Project got another sentimental

59

boost, in the form of a second contraband birth: But a second is seldom as effective as a first. As for a third, it better not happen! Some folks might get truly annoyed. Life on Mars was still far too precarious to permit any more freedom in producing children. Young Barlow's very minor concern about this Agnes Frost was eclipsed by another matter.

"When do I get my Mars suit?" he kept pestering. "One not way too big? So I can go Outside?"

It arrived from Earth in time for his fourth Mars-date birthday—when he was seven and a half Earth-years old. It came out of the sky in one of five more parachuting ships, bringing in supplies, and ten more couples for Arsia Base.

Everybody made an event of presenting the suit to him after breakfast—he even got two fried eggs with his algae cakes, on that special morning.

Gotch was there to help him slide into the garment that represented the greatest thrill of his life. Then, alone, while all the others watched, hard-eyed, he proceeded carefully, self-consciously, to check it out; he knew how from observing how it was done from almost as far back as he could remember. But he hardly noticed that the suit, small, but with allowances for his growth, wrinkled badly around his ankles. At last, he sniffed the rubbery newness within the latched-on air hood, and heard the vaultlike ringing of Gotch's scratchy voice, as they tested the radio.

"Hello, Tim, how does everything go?"

"A-okay, Frank—all indications at optimum, ready for action."

The regulation patter came out of him like wistful make-believe turned real. But then he backslid into younger wheedling, "Please, Frank, can't we go someplace right now, instead of waiting till tomorrow? I can do my practicing on the way."

"All right, fella. One goof, though, and you won't wear that suit again till your next birthday . . . ."

Then they were barreling along a rutted track in Gotch's Wanderer. Timothy was all atingle. From the bumpy sense of speed, the ugly-beautiful old hills coming gradually nearer, and Arsia Base, in full view now, and getting smaller behind their kicked-up dust plume. The five kilometers to the ring of stones where the original survival dome of Manning and Gotch had been seemed wondrously much farther to Tim. From among some large boulders near it, Gotch retrieved a large, flat piece of plastic, and then led the way up a steep gorge where, three billions years ago, a stream must have gushed.

"What are we gonna do?" Tim demanded, his eyes huge with the novelty of climbing free, under a roofless sky.

"You don't know what going fishing is," Gotch answered, "and it's impossible on Mars. But I've figured out a substitute almost as good. You know how we winnow the chaff out of grain, after it's threshed, by pouring it down through a blast of air from an electric fan? So now we're going to winnow *gold*. Panning gold was once a common way of gathering it, but that calls for lots of water, which we don't have."

They proceeded farther up the gulch, to where crags from a shoulder of Arsia Mons made a kind of funnel that gathered and strengthened the swift, tenuous winds.

Here, Gotch scooped sediment from the dry stream bed with his gloved hands, held it high over the piece of plastic which he had spread on the ground, and let it dribble between his fingers. The wind blew the lighter dust away; the heavier granules fell straight down on the plastic. Some of them glinted yellowly.

"That's the gold," Gotch said. "Now, more handfuls. Then we picked out the useless rock chips, and repeat the winnowing serveral times.''

"Lemme do it!" Tim urged.

They were at this pleasure until near sundown.

Tim hefted the small pouch, which Gotch had brought along empty in his thigh pocket. "Now we've got a whole fistful inside!" he said.

"Uh huh, kid, small nuggets and dust. Of course, nobody ever worked this place before, except me, now and then. So there's quite a lot of gold."

"What's it good for, Frank?"

"I have fun collecting it, when I can steal a little time. There isn't much use for it on Mars right now. But if it got to Earth, it would be quite valuable for jewelry, and in electronic equipment. I save it in a plastic bag, down by those rocks where we left the Wanderer."

"Just to keep?"

"Um-m—maybe not." Here Gotch smirked up at the western sky, where the Blue Star was already faintly visible. "Tim, you know that, before so very long, you could be in school on Earth. The gold could be yours to take along for buying small needs. Meanwhile, we can come out here sometimes, and gather more."

Tim Barlow was still young and brash enough to accept bounty without embarrassment. "Thanks, Frank," he said simply.

They were silent a moment, until Gotch asked, "Do you *want* to go to Earth, Tim?"

Timothy Barlow made a small boy's scowl of serious cogitation. There were pros and cons, edged with worry about being hurled into *that much* strangeness and distance. He knew much more about the home world than he used to, but his knowledge remained blurred and slight.

"I dunno, Frank," he said at last. "Guess I want to go. Guess I've got to. But you know that, even before

62

Marie started teaching me, I had learned to read words and numbers pretty good right here. Guess I'll pick up lots more on Earth, though.''

''Yuh, Tim, we can't keep you here forever. Some folks back there wanted you sent in the return ship right now, along with Hank Karl and Lettie Harper, who got hurt when their bulldozer cab depressurized. But we at Arsia figure there's a better way—if you agree? So next window time, in about two terrestrial years, somebody who knows a lot about you and likes you, will come out here to be your teacher. That'll give you a good, long while to be prepared for the Earth jump at the following window time. Okay?''

The boy rolled all this new information around somewhere behind his dark eyes. Gotch's mildness warned him of more difficulties in his future than if he had been gruff. Still, he was relieved by the vast extent of time.

''Sure, Frank,'' he said.

# 7

Deva Corliss had been attracted to the orphaned first-born of Mars by the very idea of his improbable existence, from the moment that it had been so dramatically announced, back when she was still a child.

To be sent out with the new group of settlers she had companioned with, and duly married, in accordance with her family's Protestant faith, a physicist named Arnold Reese. She liked him, but all this was incidental.

The boy—and later, the girl, Agnes Frost—and her impending task assignment with these two, which she had struggled so hard to obtain—were the important considerations. Plus an enduring pioneer fascination with the desolate, carmine grandeur of that other planet.

About her job, she had wise cautions and some misgivings. Young minds could have fragile areas which were often not easy to find or deal with. The way to start was casually, naturally, and with no trace of aggressive approach.

So, seconds after she had first stepped onto the soil of Mars from the grounded ship, she only smiled at the easily identifiable person at the forefront of the little knot of greeting veteran Arsians. She had her own minor and momentary adjustments to make—to gravity, again, for instance, even though only 0.38g.

She felt slightly queasy.

"Hi, Deva Corliss! I'm Tim!"

This quick, uninhibited salutation fairly boomed in the phones inside her air hood. Though she knew from seeing and hearing him audio-visually so often across hundreds of millions of kilometers, that he was an outgoing child, still she was startled. And pleased.

"Hello, yourself, Timothy," she responded.

She meant, then, still to leave him alone a while. Only, he didn't let her.

"Carry that bag for you, Deva? Oh, I found out all about you! We want to get you to your quarters fast. Then I'll show you all around Base! Hey, you like it here? First, look—over there—a shoulder of Old Hunchy—Arsia Silva Mons—one of the biggest volcanoes there is, anyplace . . . ."

She'd been absorbing him with all her senses, adding the important differences of being side by side and talking with him to what she had known: Very tall and slender for not quite ten years old; weak gravity allowed such growth. His Mars suit was getting short for him. He was swarthy from his ancestry, and from the strong, solar ultraviolet that got through the tenuous Martian atmosphere, and through the minor shielding of dome and air-hood plastic. And he was brash, simple, loud and bright, like some intelligent, eager country kid, out of an old book, but without any bashfulness. Deva continued to be pleased, and somewhat reassured.

"I appreciate your help, Tim," she said. "Thank you very much!"

So a little later, he was guiding her through the interconnected domes of the Base. They were out of their vacuum armor now. Except for a word or two of greeting, everybody else remained aloof from them, as if by pre-arrangement. He chattered out his explanations in delight.

65

"An airlock in each tunnel, usually left open during daytime, unless there's a storm . . . . Here, let me show you how this one opens and closes . . . . Up ahead is the aerating system . . . ."

He showed her the workshops, the stands of maize and grain in the agriculture domes, the hydroponic tanks, the garden dome which included the orchard, the animal husbandry areas.

"We've got eighteen sheep and five lambs now. We butchered some of the goats, but there are ten left. The rabbits are down to a dozen, but we've got forty-eight hens, two roosters. No chicks again till after another thirty sols. But now that there are more landing parachutes, we'll be putting up more domes. There's plenty of fossil-ice for more irrigation water. And plenty of room Outside. Sometime, if we're lucky, there'll be domes and magnesium-foil reflectors to concentrate the sunlight everywhere, and no running short of stuff anymore. But you know what, Deva? It's all dead out there, but I kind of like it, too. I guess there'll be enough left."

They were looking through the curved, dusty transparency of two thin, plastic dome skins, with a 15-centimeter, heat-insulating space in between. There was the Outside, the Tharsis desert to the north—red, rolling, rocky and fluted—until it touched the dust-yellow sky. Deva's spine tingled coldly. The kid could not know as she, the novice, knew, nor could she knew as he, the first native, knew; yet the Outside had a special, superlative beauty that infringed on deadly ugliness. And she felt a sharpened kinship with her pupil.

"I like it a lot myself, Tim," she said.

In another moment, he got down to the really important topic. "Deva, I'm supposed to learn from you. I can read pretty good. Everybody helps me. But if I'm going to Earth, I'd better find out more about that to start with."

66

She smiled. "So tell me what you know about it, Tim."

His brows crinkled. "It's bigger than Mars, and has billions of inhabitants. It's warm, and there are oceans. I've seen on TV. They've been letting me watch most anything now, so I know for sure I'm different. Newscasts. Cartoon shows. And inside places, with lots of people, and somebody singing or making jokes. It's fun to listen to. And there are acted-out stories, with folks running around, getting into trouble . . . . Some of it is supposed to be here on Mars, but it isn't right. The outside scenes on Earth I like best. Though I like them here just as much."

"Do you want me to show you how Earth is, Tim? From recordings, giving perfect pictures and color and sound? Better than anything you've watched so far, I think. Besides, they're designed especially for you, by top psychologists. They might be different from what you might expect."

"Sure I want to see, Deva!" he enthused. "Right away, if you can rig it!"

She considered. He seemed perfectly ready to accept anything she could show him, without any bad effects. Still she hesitated.

"No, tomorrow morning would be easier, Tim. At oh-eight-hundred?"

"Okay."


What Deva Corliss was supposed to show young Barlow was called "A Free Hour for John Burgess." Something in this title irritated her slightly. Too pat and —well—sweet.

The screen of the audio-visual set lighted up in the muted daylighting of her workroom. She knew every detail of the thirty-minute presentation, so she only pretended to watch its crystal-clear and ever so naturally

67

colored flow of scenes. Instead, from the corner of her eye, she studied Tim's face, as it reflected the waxing and waning light from the screen. He was crouched on the floor. There were sounds, too: the twitter of bird songs, brook babble, wind in trees, occasional traffic noises.

And a sonorous masculine voice made appropriate and quiet comments, parallel to what was happening: "It's a summer day, Timothy. On a roadway with green woods all arouind it . . . . John Burgess is twelve years old. What he is riding is a bicycle. Of course, he wears just shorts, shirt, and sandals. No sealed garment. The natural atmosphere is right to breathe, and it is warm. Even in winter, when there is water-snow, he would need no such protection—only heavier clothing.

"Riding a bicycle is fun. Wouldn't you enjoy it, Tim? Swimming in that lake, too? With the soft feel of the water on your bare skin. The stronger gravity doesn't bother John; he is accustomed to it, as you will become. Look at the blue sky, and those great, white clouds. They are dark on their undersides, and may bring a rain shower . . . . "

Deva read young Barlow's reactions in his mobile features, and in the hunching, squirming movements of his slender body. Startlement. Then delight. Sudden chuckles. Then he would be happily rapt and silent once more. Usual TV reception here was often fuzzy; it could never have portrayed his ancestral planet with anything like this vivid clarity and beauty! Of course, the substance of the sequence was also contrived—slanted —for a favorable effect on the firstborn of Mars. And he was responding in a simple, natural manner. Nothing to worry about, then?

The masculine voice spoke on: "John has many friends his own age. But just now he only wanted to bike into the country alone, be by himself there. It is enough

—Oh, look, Timothy! Horses in a field. John stops, and they come to the fence to greet him. See how their hides shine? They are big, friendly beasts. John pats their noses, then he bikes on. The sky is darker. It starts to rain. John doesn't care. He is lightly clad. The rain feels cool and good on his body in warm weather. Don't worry about the bright flash of lightning; or especially, the very loud noise. It is only thunder.''

Tim's shoulders jerked visibly, as the crash came. But then he steadied and grinned.

The voice continued. "See, Timothy? John doesn't mind. See how the warm rain wets his hair, runs down his face, and makes his shirt cling to his shoulders? But he smiles. Hear the rustle of the raindrops on the forest leaves? I wish you could actually smell the freshness! But that would have been technically complicated to arrange.

"The shower stops. The sun comes out, big and bright. Oh—look!—look! Through a gap in the trees, you can see a rainbow! Isn't it a lovely thing!

"John's bicycle rolls fast down the curving slope of the road, into a town. There is the house where he lives. He leaves his bike in the areaway. He ambles to the swimming pool. His younger brother and older sister and another boy are in it. Hear them shout their questions about where he has been? Before answering, he dives into the pool, without troubling to remove his clothes.''

The sequence went on for several minutes more, through a casual—but surely by Arsia Base standards! —sumptuous family dinner. Deva turned off the set, and pushed aside a plastic shade to let full daylight into her workroom.

Tim was still grinning happily. But his eyes had a wondering, bemused, dreamy look.

"Do you want to see more, now, Tim? Winter?

69

School?"

"Yes, Deva! Oh, yes!"

But as she moved to comply, a turnabout came in his attitude. He was suddenly like a confused, pathetic savage.

"No!" he yelled. "It's not so! There's nothing like that!"

Here was the kind of adverse reaction that she had considered marginally possible. And, in spite of indications otherwise, it had happened. Its delay was odd, like a splitting of the boy's self. It was hard to imagine the contortions inside a young mind of so unique a background. But she could guess some of it. Some psychiatrists had worried, but, never having been on Mars, somebody had not thought thoroughly enough. Damn the characters who had sweetened and prettified the sequence too much! For Tim, it was that sudden, jolting contrast! The Martian environment he honored, and had been contented and proudly at home with, suddenly compared to this soft, saccharin richness, with its exaggerated appeal to unsophisticated senses. Like public-relations propaganda! Tim had been startled, and enchanted by it. But then he had seen cracks in his firm pride and belief in his birth world. Until he had this abrupt spasm of fierce and loyal clinging.

He still crouched there on the floor, his eyes wide and dry, his teeth gritted, and his shoulders trembling.

"In a way you're right, Tim," Deva said quietly. "Though everything you watched is real—true. But it's only a small part of truth. By no means everybody on Earth lives as well as John. And now and then, there's terrible danger, coming out of disagreements among groups and nations. And Mars is beautiful, too—in a harder, simpler, more challenging form. Its people— those here now, anyway—were drawn to strange newness and plenty of room, and, with hard work, to

70

the chance of living comfortably in it at last. That's one reason why I came, myself. As for Earth, I can show you sequences that point out its defects.''

"I don't need them! Keep them!" Timothy Barlow said in a choked voice; then he fled from the room.

Deva thought to follow him, try to soothe him further, explain. The errors of judgment had been partly her own. But no, she'd let him be, for the present. He was a smart, rugged kid; it was best that he sorted out matters for himself, if he could.

# 8

Next morning, Tim did his early chores among the hydroponic tanks as cheerfully as ever, as far as anybody else could tell. Discreetly, Deva Corliss didn't go looking for him. But he showed up at her workroom, which was also his classroom, promptly at 0-800.

"So how are you, Tim?" she asked.

"Uh—okay," he answered in an off-hand manner that still signaled his embarrassment about his actions of yesterday, before his lovely, blond teacher!

"I have to study math and chemistry, Deva," he declared, "so I'll understand better what's in the equipment instruction mannuals. Also, I've got to tone up my muscles, so I'll be ready for Earth."

Thus, he seemed to have gotten past his largest chunk of innocence and tension. He had found purpose. But maybe fresh and different tensions were already sprouting in him.

With Deva to guide him, he toiled over books and educational aids at regular hours. His other tasks became increasingly complex. Apprenticed to Leon Bonard in the machine shop, he helped lathe and tool out moving parts for simple devices: to advance the threshing of grain and the extraction of linen fibers from the stalks of flax a little beyond the primitive; to grind and pulp straw, and press it into rough paper, useful to wrap and contain food stores. And all the

72

hammering and lifting he did should help prepare his body for terrestrial gravity! Sometimes, when there was a chance, he went into the desert for an hour, or a sol, with Gotch.

At the end of an Earth year, Deva Corliss drove off toward Olympus Base with her man, Arnold Reese. Tim had enjoyed his allotted time; now Deva had to go instruct Agnes Frost, the second born. Tim hid his sorrow.

More time went by, and the usual ten ships were again on their way outward to Mars. But when they were past the midpoint of their long journey, the reports of dangerous trouble on Earth reached a climax. The emergency came from the old hazard, intrinsic to any sphere with advanced technology, and the inevitable differences of economic well-being, opinion and ideology, among its billions of inhabitants of various cultures. It was, perhaps in fact, the deepest—if rather arcane—reason why humanity should not inhabit only a single planet, if it is to survive.

At any rate, there was a Martian evening when audio-visual communications from Earth, showing clustered heads of state in acrimonious discussion, suddenly ended in total news blackout. Except for the natural whispers from endless, slow-churning space, there was nothing.

So this was it, the long-dreaded hours of ultimate danger. Sweating more than usual, but somehow primitively exalted—with mingled fright and thrill, as at a super contest, which this of course actually was—Tim Barlow, now a very mature almost-twelve-terrestrial-years old, listened for the tell-tale signs, the activating signals for such less-advanced missiles as might still be electromagnetically controlled from a distance, instead of being entirely self-contained. But again—nothing.

73

"This all feels like a bad and tired practical joke," remarked Aldo Carlyle, communications chief.

"Uh huh," responded Mona Schultz, his woman. "But real things are usually trite."

In the small, relatively new communications dome there was a stubby telescope for visual observation. Sven Thorgersen had set it to track the Blue Star, visible above a lagging trace of sunset.

"There are no city lights," Sven said quietly. "Otherwise, nothing is different, so far."

But a minute later, Dr. Pharr, at the eyepiece, cried out, "Ho—wait! A bright spark in the darkened portion . . . ."

Well down the line of opportunities, Tim had his turn at peering. With a wry smirk, Big Bessie Blythe pushed him forward, ahead of herself.

"You should be more concerned than anybody, kid," she said.

Earth was just a little blue-and-white-marbled crescent, with most of its Marsward hemisphere shadowed by night. It looked small, remote, pretty, and peaceful. He'd often seen it like this, before. Except that now, on its darkened face, there were dots of a fading, reddish glow, where specks of incandescence had flashed out, holocausts shrunken to triviality by millions of kilometers.

"I count five," he said.

As he yielded his place to Bessie, he was somehow on the verge of shameful tears, not just because his big trip probably would never be.

"We're far out from what's happening, but we're still in it," remarked Marie Manning, her whispery voice almost loud in the deep quiet. The ramifying implications of her statement were enormous.

Haggard of face, the Arsians watched further. Tim wished that Gotch was around, not out on another survey mission.

"There've been no more flashes, anyhow," Everett Holsten stated at last, optimistically.

Near midnight, in a sudden jangle of sound—there was still no parallel, visual communication—the good news came. The substance of what all those quaking, distant voices were trying to say was gradually made plain. Just over the line of demonstrated horror, minds still with some control had been frightened back to commonsense, which might not have happened.

There was ragged cheering among the rugged colonists, at their ample distance from immediate and personal extinction.

Yet it wasn't many sols before the future outlook of the Mars Project became entirely obvious: Not good.

On Earth, just from those few minutes of catastrophe, there were millions of dead, many more millions of maimed and sick, and colossal damage to essential industries.

So the terrestrial mentality turned inward on itself more emphatically than ever. Earth must lick its own wounds; beyond the huge and long efforts of restoration, there would be nothing to spare. Support for space projects, always subject to vacillations of opinion, dropped to nadir. Besides, hatred of technology was revived in its most bigoted form as many persons imagined, wistfully and unrealistically, that their single, habitable World ought to revert to the uncomplicated tranquility of—say—the eighteenth century, as they fancied it had been.

The last expedition of resupply and further immigration to Mars, en route when the trouble had come to a head, was expected to continue to its destination. But nothing further was even hinted at for the foreseeable future.

And there was another adverse sign: The small Mars station in Solis Lacus, which that other bloc of nations had long maintained—it had never been inhabited by more than three couples—was finally left abandoned, the last four persons leaving in a relaunchable ship that had been prudently provided.

In the middle of a general discussion in the Arsia Base mess room one evening, Everett Holsten summed up the state of things for those present.

"We don't have the escape means given to the Solis Lacus bunch. Oh, a few of us here and at Olympus can quit—go home. There will be facilities, as usual. But who needs to say it? Nothing like room enough for over one hundred and twenty persons. And in spite of some unreal beliefs that bases on Mars should be, by now, entirely self-sustaining, it isn't so. Food production is fairly well covered for the immediate present. But for complicated equipment necessary to maintain human life in an alien environment, we're still completely dependent on what has come from Earth; we just don't have the technological means, backed up by a huge network of manufacturing complexes. Imagine us trying to make, from scratch, even just the life-support pack for a Mars suit, with its hundreds of small parts and its involved chemistry! We can't even produce dome plastic in the required form and quantity. Memnonia-Gum hasn't been made to work as local raw material. So why am I saying what we all know? Only to totalize where we stand. Nor is a mass rescue mission, or any rescue mission from Earth, to be dreamed about. We're on our own. As for our survival, all we can do is tighten our belts and try."

"Bravo for the pep talk, Everett," said Gotch from the background. He had been afield with Steve Majorski, probing a deposit of sulphur, when those hours of terrible Earth watch had come and passed.

76

From around the room, there was wry laughter at his kidding remark. But nobody got sore, especially not Holsten.

"Sarcasm could get you a flatter nose, Frogface," he said.

Humor could still lighten grimness.

# 9

The final contingent of settlers could have bent the trajectory of their ships back toward a re-encounter with Earth. Even after they were orbiting Mars, they might have tried to drop the supplies they had brought onto its surface, thus eliminating the need to land and allowing them to return home. But their almost mass-produced equipment, built to a cost-cutting pattern, was not really designed for such complicated maneuvers. Most of the supplies would have been smashed, or so widely scattered as to be unretrievable by those on the ground who needed them. More importantly, those new immigrants were of as high an ethical quality as those who had come before them. They were pledged to Mars and to delivering the freight in the orderly manner specified. And they, too, had staked their lives on a venture. Further, troubled as Earth now was, they were unsure that they should even want to return. And they couldn't without shame. So, somewhat disgruntled, they came on and landed. More fools? Perhaps.

The question of who *should* go to Earth was still being argued, against a background of bleakly altered circumstances. This time, three, instead of only two, of the ships carried re-orbitable Landers. The others, as usual, descended complete. The third of the three had been designed as a special conveyance for Timothy Barlow and Agnes Frost; but now their going had be-

78

come a controversial matter.

Terrestrial insistence that these two famous personages come home, to be seen in the flesh, and properly educated, had dimmed to a few faint squeaks of "at least save the children from slow death by hardship!" But even this small outcry was lost in the general preoccupation of the Blue Star with its own large problems. Barlow and Frost might not even be very welcome there anymore.

Word came through to Arsia that Agnes Frost at Olympus Base would stay. Most Olympians agreed that, at not yet ten Earth-years old, she was too young to be hurled to the care of strangers on a radically different planet, still torn by sporadic civil violence, and where many were starving. Bad as prospects on Mars were, would she be much better off or safer there? No, Olympus would look after its own, as best it might.

With others around him, Timothy Barlow stood looking up at the Lander which could carry him up to the orbiting mother ship which then would take him on to the biggest of adventures. The craft brooded there in the desert, on its jointed, shock-cylindered legs, a kilometer from Base. Its details gleamed in the muted, morning sunlight. And Tim was truly torn inside. He'd have to choose within a few sols.

"A tossup, kid," Gotch said. "Who can foresee well enough?"

"Would you go, Frank?" Tim asked.

Gotch gave his gravelly chuckle. "Ha! I've been all through that one before. I'm rooted. I've been here too long."

Leon Bonard only shrugged, as did Majorski and Mancuso.

"Here's where the bad trail divides; even the markers have been removed, Tim," Marie Manning offered. "We'd like to keep you here, but it might be better for

79

you the other way. Your courage is high; your body is young and flexible."

Timothy Barlow looked at Big Bessie Blythe's florid face, behind the plastic curve of her air hood.

"Your own gut feeling, Lad," she said. "It should tell you that this or that is best. So sort it out."

Tim had already been sorting for a long time. He knew that most of the veteran adults here wouldn't seriously consider departure. Which by no means meant entirely that they all wanted to remain on Mars. Other factors were more intricate. Out of so many people, there was room for only a very few to leave. Who wanted to be ahead of friends who deserved the right as much? This situation fed back on itself. But perhaps their firmest trap was a physical thing. After so long in the lesser Martian gravity, their bones had lost calcium, their heart muscles had weakened. In the thinner, more highly oxygenated air of the domes, their lungs had adapted. Since they were older, they could have serious difficulties adjusting back to terrestrial conditions. Those few who had gone home in the past hadn't always done well. There had been Kara Ennis, widow of Jeff Toller, the first person killed on Mars. A few steps after her landing on Earth, her right hip had snapped. Later, one sick man had even died en route. And for the veteran settlers, too, doubts came from the home world's disturbed condition.

Timothy Barlow's thoughts and emotions wavered a moment more. Oh, the wonders of Earth pulled hard at him! Or did he fear the unknown so much? Still there were his companions. And all he knew . . . .

"I'm staying here," he said suddenly and clearly.

Everybody smiled, and right away he felt relieved—much better.

Then he wanted to be by himself for a bit. But, as he started a slow, loping run—the best means of moving

80

around on foot on Mars—back toward Base, he still heard voices in his helmet phones.

Gotch's voice: "Shoot! What in the name of bloody Phobos would I do back there, anyhow? Play golf? Lecture to fat-assed professors?"

"Oh, I dunno, Frogface," Bessie answered. "I might become madam of a fancy bawdy house in Chicago, and get rich . . . ."

Several sols later, the two Landers at Arsia, and the one at Olympus, flamed into the sky. From Arsia went a man named Othman, whose lungs were deteriorating. He was taking his chances on getting home, perhaps to die. With him went his mate. Another widow, brought in by Wanderer from Olympus, was crammed into the same Lander, the one intended for Barlow and Frost. The other Lander at Arsia—and the orbiting ship it served—took two couples, both novices. The single Lander at Olympus was easily filled there to its maximum of four persons.

# 10

Now had begun the long interval of tribulation for the Martian settlers. It was the time when Timothy Davis Barlow changed gradually from a cheerful, outgoing boy to a hard-bitten, introverted young man, able and quick before the physical challenges of his harsh and beleaguered environment. Earth had left him and his friends to shift for themselves, and perhaps to die. Therefore, let him be as much a proud and competent part of his birth world as he could manage: the frigid, thin, unbreathable winds; the carmine deserts; the lonely, splendid distances. Here was nothing more than his original aim, hardened to a conscious and determined bitterness. Better than to belong to the soft, beautiful, silly, unrealiable, and dangerously confused Earth! To make themselves entirely self-sustaining, *with no further help at all*, had to be the objective of the settlers now, though they were still far from ready. Likely, they would fail in the end. But they had to try!

The effort began with stringent economies. Save every scrap of metal or plastic, every worn-out part; you never knew when some idea would come, some need would have to be filled, from what now seemed junk! These rules were not totally Barlow's own, of course; but nobody sustained them more emphatically than he.

Time must be conserved, too, used in constructive, or at least hopeful, effort. He must learn all he could from every available text. Brains must search for ways through or around problems. His fingers—his whole body—must absorb every skill, learn to run every machine, perform every operation, the more difficult the better. Working in lab and shop; driving a bulldozer to push dust closer around the dome bases to reduce heat loss and lower power drain and strain on the little nuclear-fusion plant; climbing high and light across a dome top, knotting another cord into the covering network, to be surer that the structure would weather a threatened storm; lying on his belly, deep in the ground, digging along an ice stratum with a hand tool, to reopen a water channel that had frozen up. Such activities belonged more and more to Tim Barlow's life. Constructive ruggedness became truly his obsession. He would become the most Martian of those on Mars. He would be the best prepared when circumstances got really difficult. He would surpass even Gotch!

Of course, matters weren't bad at first. Minor "luxury imports," though rigidly rationed, began to be used up. But the bind would begin when essential spare parts and irreplaceable materials were giving out. However, such easy foresight wasn't the only cause for Timothy Barlow's bitter hardening. Man juices were now flowing through his body; their demands were getting stronger and stronger. He saw that he was alone. Every man at Arsia Base, except himself, had a woman, and every woman a man. He had never known a girl of his own age in all his life, nor did there seem to be any reasonable remedy for this. The frustration was twisting and souring him. Energy used savagely in work and duty was his defense. Others, being more experienced, guessed all this easily, and with sympathy. The antidote might be simple. So there was collusion.

Gotch hadn't been out on a survey mission recently. Most of the rock strata within a 500-kilometer radius of

83

Arsia Base, including the floor of the great Arsia Mons caldera itself, had been closely examined and assayed. There was no present, foreseeable need for more metal, mineral, or ice deposits. In fact, those already chartered constituted almost futile knowledge under existing circumstances; they far surpassed any minimal demand that a tiny settlement, without major processing facilities, could make, though it was starved for many more-sophisticated requirements.

Besides, though stores of imported nuclear-fusion fuel were still fairly plentiful, a Wanderer should not be subjected to unnecessary wear-and-tear by long jaunts into the wilds. Further, Gotch's hardy skills could be better employed around Base. But there could be other reasons for occasional trips. One evening, Gotch came to Tim Barlow, who was still bent over a workbench in the laboratory.

"I've got to go up to Olympus Base to swap some stores, mostly medical," Gotch graveled without preamble. "John Tenaka's heart has been showing uneven symptoms. Too bad he can't go along to check out the really big volcano. So you're elected as my safety companion. We start out at oh-six hundred tomorrow morning."

The already-existing task that Barlow had set for himself brought him regret and dismay.

"But, Frank, I think I've got a better means of rejuvenating air-restorer-canisters for life-support packs!" he protested. "A bath of sodium-hydroxide solution. With simultaneous electrolysis—that's the new trick. And slower baking. It was the engineer, Morty Lovan's, idea, mostly. We tried it once today, and it worked pretty good. I was just getting set up so we can have another go tomorrow."

"It'll keep, Tim," Gotch said. "Or Lovan can do it himself. You and I have got an appointment at six in the

84

morning."

To be thus commanded—relieved of responsibility for what might be considered a mere pleasure excursion in hard times, when there were more important things to get done—drained some of the tensions out of Barlow. And he wanted to go barreling into the desert again with Gotch. Farther than he had ever been. He wanted to see Olympus Mons, biggest of all volcanoes! For once in a long time, he smiled happily.

"Sure, Frank," he said.

They made the 1,500-kilometer drive in three sols. Olympus Base, smaller than Arsia, was sheltered from the turbulence that the mountain often brewed by being located between two buttresslike ridges of rock that angled down from the heights.

Barlow saw Deva Corliss again. The fine skin of her face was beginning to wither. That was an inner sorrow and disappointment to him.

"Timothy! You were pulled loose from whatever you were doing to come way up here! That's a marvelous surprise!"

As they met thus in the mess room—all-purpose place for anything social—her voice was as musical and her manner as cheerful and easy as ever. But he had changed. The easy flow had gone from his tongue. There were aches in his soul. His voice had a croak in it. "Nice to see you, Deva . . . ."

Now somebody else, clad, like Deva, in a neat, slightly frayed, blue coverall, was urged forward by a light touch. In a momentous and likely difficult occasion, Deva now tried for simplicity.

"Tim is here, Agnes!" she said. "Timothy, at last you two meet . . . ."

They had seen each other a few times before in television exchanges of poor quality, reflected between Arsia and Olympus Bases by the crater-pitted, quick-

85

passing bulk of Phobos, the nearer moon.

"Hello, Tim, glad to see you. We heard you were on the way," Agnes Frost greeted.

"Likewise glad," he responded stiffly, taking her proffered hand for a fraction of a second.

It was all a sorrowful disaster on both sides. Agnes' honest effort to be friendly, seemed to assume, by itself, a kind of disinterested truculence. And the similar hopes behind Tim's abbreviated answer were negated in the same way, or worse.

Here were two young people whose unique backgrounds matched perfectly; they had much in common to make them—each to the other—the special friend that both needed. But neither had been with any young person before; they lacked this social know-how. They didn't know how to act, or what to say. They were nervous and awed; they both felt their own painful and sensitive inadequacy.

Deva served them familiar drinks concocted of goat's milk and honey, and hoping, left them sitting alone for a while in the mess room. They struggled to converse.

"What's it like in Arsia?"

"More or less like here, I suppose . . . ."

Being unable to blame themselves too much for a failure, they began blaming and criticizing each other in silent bitterness. Agnes saw the vaunted Timothy Davis Barlow as a skinny, awkward, fumble-speaking oaf. What a ridiculous letdown! Tim saw Agnes as an utterly plain, graceless child, with pale, stringy hair. Of course, he'd had an idea before of what she looked like. But he'd kind of hoped for better things, otherwise, in the way she was! This forlorn optimism had sneaked into him desperately, even though he had guessed that Gotch's ordering him to come along with him on this trip was somebody's trick to maybe get Agnes and himself together. Well, here was the stupid ending of his last

86

and only chance. To hell with it all.

Deva Corliss came back to them. "Why don't you stay with us here at Olympus a while, Timothy?" she urged. "We could surely use your help. And I might still be able to help you lean a few things. Please think about it."

His refusal was blunt, cold and emphatic beyond argument. "No. There's too much work at Arsia. We only came here to make an exchange of medical stores. We've got to get back! I don't even know if we can spare a few hours so I can get a better look at the crater."

In a little while he was talking to Gotch in the sleeping cubicle that had been assigned to them:

"So I guess you saw Frost, eh, Timothy?"

"Yuh, Frank. And whose smart idea was that, I wonder?" Tim mourned wearily. "She's such a kid."

Gotch laughed to himself. Barlow was fifteen terrestrial years old, then. Agnes Frost was short of thirteen.

"Let's get out of here, Frank," Barlow urged.

Next morning they did. They spent all of that sol riding up one of the buttresslike ridges to the 25-kilometer-lofty lip of the colossal Olympus caldera. Anything like a thorough viewing of its details was out of the question; anyway, that was the business of the volcanologists at Olympus Base, who had already made a fairly complete exploration. Just now Barlow knew he had to be satisfied with much less. Still, it was good to look briefly down into that vast, tortured, terraced, splendid bowl, that it would have taken many sols to drive across—even if there was a fair Wanderer trail. Barlow stood at the brink, looking down, around and far ahead. His teeth gritted, and he grinned a coldly joyful grin. His pulses pounded and thrilled. Here he was back with things to which he belonged, that were his own. To hell with anything soft and easy!

"Guess we'll camp up here, Frank?" he said. "Tomorrow I'd like to go down to the place where I was born."

"If I can find it," Gotch answered.

They did locate the ledge. Still there was the ring of stones, half buried in a dune. Barlow bent his tall form to pick up a little fragment of magnesium foil that had been of some unknown use. In his head there were a couple of words for which he'd never found a use, either. Mom . . . Pop . . . He snorted with wry humor, as at a nameless myth. His parents' bodies had long ago been returned to Arsia Base.

"Enough, Frank," he said dryly. "Let's move on."

Barlow was driving now with careful skill, often ignoring the automatic guidance system entirely.

Bear a little more east of south, Tim," Gotch said. "On the way back to our own Base, I might as well show you something. In a couple of hours."

He didn't explain, and Barlow didn't ask what it was.

"Meanwhile, let's liven this empty Tharsis with noise," Gotch said further, smirking from the cab-seat beside his young friend. "There aren't any coyotes here, so I'll make some."

Thereupon, Gotch shaped his throat and large mouth to produce some sharp yaps, and then a long-drawn graveyard howl. It was an old fun trick of his, which Barlow knew about from way back, maybe the second time when they had gone winnowing gold.

Barlow had never, himself, heard a real coyote, but he had heard Gotch's fairly authentic imitation, and had learned long ago to imitate Gotch rather well. This, he now did, in a loud, protracted fashion. Next, pausing only to draw breath, he shifted to sounds he was personally familiar with in their fundamental forms: goat and sheep baaings, chicken cacklings.

Gotch offered the un-oiled, iron-on-iron sawing and screech of a donkey, lugubriously sorrowful. Since this

88

effort made him cough, he joined Barlow in a duet of barnyard sounds.

"Baa-aaa! Tch-tch-tch-tch-ter-raw-w-w!"

Often, then, they were laughing in such hilarity, that they could scarcely get their breath. It was all an idiotic thing to do; without any such excuse, they were acting like a pair of drunken fools! Yet it had something good in it. Timothy Barlow felt this. A release of strain, after his recent jolt of conviction that love between him and a girl was put permanently out of his reach by circumstances, that he must truly accept his hard course on a hard planet, alone. The baaing and cackling were a to-hell-with-it defiance even of embarrassment at doing something inane. It was a loony, comic, derisive declaration of freedom! It was part of the rough way of rough men, living joyfully in a rough land to which they belonged!

Barlow and Gotch's ludicrous noise ended at last in puffing satiation and a mellow mood of comradeship. Barlow drove on over more rugged ground, deftly avoiding rocks and boulders. A wispy whirlwind ahead stirred the dust momentarily into a faint pink column in the midday sunlight. It was a small phenomenon of no import; yet it reminded Barlow of the towering, carmine spinners of a planetwide duststorm, that came like a lofty wall of murk to darken the world. Awesome, frightening, dangerous! But just then he was particularly in a frame of mind to appreciate such grandeur.

Presently Gotch spoke in a musing tone, out of nowhere or from deep in himself, and as to a friend to whom he could yield insight. He began with a pebbly chuckle.

"Tim," he said. "I want to tell you something about me—and loneliness. I've been around here quite a while and through many events. I like people. I've worked toward making Mars inhabitable, inhabited, and civilized. I want that. And yet, do you know, I can still come out here into the desert and wait for nightfall. And then look all around the notched horizon. No light but the stars. Not a damned, artificial gleam or glimmer anywhere. And part of me is glad! That's how crazy-divided I am! That's one reason I got off Earth and came to Mars. Guess you wouldn't understand all of that. You haven't the background to make a comparison. You didn't come here. You weren't given the chance for such a choice. You weren't asked. You were born here. That's quite a difference. Might be damned unfair. But that's what happened. That's you, Tim. And what's the good of finding somebody to blame, even if we could?''

Timothy Barlow was feeling fine just then. In tune with his wilderness, and with his much older, but alike, companion.

"That's deep talk, Frank," he said. "What you say can be thought around and around. But where do you stop, and say this is the right view? Being born some-place can make a man closer to it—the way I've heard. Anyhow, I'm having fun! So why kick the mixed-up topic any further?''

Barlow chuckled happily at the end, and Gotch chuckled with him.

"We should sight what I'm looking for any second now," Gotch said. "Yup! I think that's it! Almost dead ahead. You aimed the Wanderer right-on . . . .''

The thing notched the horizon, like an isoscles triangle with the apex a little blunted. In a quarter hour, they were out of their vehicle and looking up at the strange phenomenon from close at hand: a three-sided pyramid.

It was nothing new. Way back in the nineteen seventies, clusters of such pyramids had been photo-graphed in Elysium from umanned, orbiting probes.

90

Barlow was well aware of this, but those were far to the west. Were they mere dust dunes, so symmetrically sculptured by chance, by freak winds? Or were they something much more?

Of this one, Barlow had seen pictures long ago, brought back by Gotch from one of his excursions. It was much smaller than those others—only about fifty meters on a side, and equally high, except that its peak was gone, or had never been formed.

Gotch led the way to the nearest of its sides. Just above ground level, there was a dark hole. Barlow peered into it. It was a rough tunnel, with a spot of daylight showing at the opposite end.

"The Thorgersens and I dug this, Tim," Gotch said. "All the way through. Just hard-packed desert dust. Naturally compacted like that? Or somehow artificially sintered? Even Sven and Ilga couldn't tell. We found nothing else—drew a blank."

Gotch picked up a lump of the stuff, and by squeezing it hard, crumbled it in his stout glove.

"Some insist that the three-sided Martian pyramids are natural," Gotch continued. "So—maybe. But that bothers me. Otherwise, though, what have we got? Indications are that the really active biological history of Mars was too brief and stunted to have produced anything like human capabilities, or even those of nest-building ants or termites. And, in this pyramid at least, there's nothing to point out what it could be, or have been, for. To protect or hide something for millions of years? Corpses or machines? Or as a place marker? Or monument of honor? But those are all human purposes. And just how much overlap, similarity, between human minds and—whatever else—can there be? How can we guess, when our wits are limited, and even our imaginations are bounded by what is familiar to us? Tim, you can see I've thought a lot about such matters. Even

91

Earth still has mysteries, thought it has been thoroughly studied for centuries. And Mars is big and different enough to be riddle-haunted for a very long time."

Barlow drew Gotch's words into his mind, where they matched his own musings: about the frosty pull of enigmas, a pleasant thrill in itself, and the ache to find out.

"I don't suppose it would help to dig anymore now, Frank."

"No. We don't have the best tools with us. Probably we wouldn't turn up a thing."

"Then let's move on."

"Yuh, Tim. There's another stop we're supposed to make. To collect Memnonia-Gum for more experimenting. If we move due south from here, and park and sleep tonight, we'll get a good outcropping of the stuff by midmorning tomorrow."—

These things were done.

At a place where underlying rock strata had been folded, broken and shoved to the surface by some ancient, seismic heaving of the planet's crust, Barlow picked up a fragment of the material. He didn't know that people on Earth might have said that it looked like amber. Otherwise, he was very well acquainted with, and informed, about it. Though first found in Memnonia, it existed more plentifully here in Tharsis. It was strictly a Martian substance. Long ago, the Thorgersens had traced out something of its history and origin.

About three billion Earth-years back, when Mars still had a relatively dense atmosphere and a warmer climate, certain minute and simple animals had swarmed in shallow lakes. Their bodies had a strong, flexible coating, composed of long-chain molecules, perhaps evolved to protect their vitals from ultraviolet rays, increasingly intense because of the progressive

92

thinning of the atmosphere. The fossilized residue of those coatings was the Memnonia-Gum.

This unique, Martian resource was a natural plastic; it didn't need to be converted from other materials by involved chemistry and massive equipment. It was tough and strong; it transmitted all useful, solar radiant energy; it even insulated rather well against heat loss. It should have been ideally suitable as a material for air domes, where the need would become critical.

Samples of the gum had been sent to terrestrial laboratories, too, years ago, for testing and development. But even there it had proven to have a large defect, related to its advantage of toughness. It had been very difficult to press out thin, except in very small sizes, particularly with machines light enough to be sent out to Mars, or with simple devices that could be contrived there. Some heating softened it; a little too much made it crumble and stick. The problem seemed a hopeless conundrum. Still, the effort at solution must continue.

Shards of Memnonia-Gum were here for the taking. Dig a little with a simple pick. The only difficulty was that the seam of the stuff was only about five centimeters through, which made hand collecting necessary. But in a couple of hours Barlow and Gotch had what, in Earth gravity, would have been about half a metric ton of the gum piled into the Wanderer's cargo box. More than enough for further attempts by Arsia's laboratory crew.

Finishing their simple, uninspired job, they continued their journey back to Arsia Base, Barlow still driving. Except to halt through the night hours for increased safety from trail accidents in rocky terrain, there need be no more stops. Now and then they talked.

"I like these trips, Frank," Barlow said. "I envy you; you've seen such a lot of Mars."

93

"Uh huh—some," Gotch answered. "But nothing like what I haven't seen of its one hundred and forty million square kilometers. I've never even been anywhere near back to where Marie and I first touched ground, not far from the edge of the south-polar cap. And there are puzzling details which showed up in photography from orbiting probes that I'd like to visit. Also, it kind of bugs me that Syrtis Major, the most prominent dark feature on Mars, is halfway around the planet from here, and I haven't a prayer of a chance of getting there! It happens, too, that one of the puzzles is close to it—in Moeris Lacus—three little markings, so faint in the photos that I'm not at all sure they're not an illusion. But they're radially arranged around a common center, and are exactly one hundred and twenty degrees apart."

Gotch paused for a pensive moment, then went on, "But the polar regions, north or south, are what I really think of. They're not so far away. Besides, there's an almost sentimental reason. Let's say I just want to look at all that dry ice—since we're not set up to make any practical use of it. Know what I mean?"

Half-secret glances passed between the older man and the younger.

"Yuh, Frank, a resource . . . Look, why *can't* we go, sometime? South—since it's a little closer."

"We've got a very hard row to hoe, otherwise, Tim. But maybe . . . ."

# *11*

At Arsia Base, the last of the hoarded Earth-chocolate was parceled out in tiny squares, on an evening of brief festivity for a good potato crop. Bless those hardy, tuberous plants! Caress the rough leaves of the newer planting, lovingly. Tend them, guard them from cold. There were some wry jokes, but continued high morale. Tony Mancuso sang his songs, Sven Thorgersen fiddled, people danced in celebration. They were still raising their own common grub!

Also bless the grain, corn, beans, cabbages, clover, turnips, algae; the few scrubby, but gratefully received, fruits. Bless the flax, and the bees, chickens, sheep, goats, and rabbits! Even more, bless the toiling machines and apparati, which continued to keep conditions within the domes approximately correct, holding back the deadly Outside. Guard this vital equipment with love, caution, and thought for its welfare, for it was under constant strain, and was not forever, and replacement could not be thought of.

Most of all, bless and care for the domes, those thin, dual bubbles, for they were the key to almost everything. They enveloped and contained moisture, warmth, breathable air; more than anything else, they meant continued life. And they were vulnerable. Their slight but tough material was subjected to wide temperature changes, to extreme dryness, to outer-atmospheric turbulence. It flexed and crinkled and developed cracks. And where was the means to replace it to come from? Nothing was really in sight. Petroleum, once the most common raw material for plastic on Earth, had not been found on Mars; animal life seemed never to have evolved here in sufficient quantity to produce it. And of anything like coal, nothing had been discovered except a few lignite-like fragments. Even if there was enough petroleum or other usable raw material, where, here, was the complicated means to process it in any bulk?

As foreseen, conditions at the two bases gradually deteriorated. There was nothing left with which to erect more domes. Then those that existed began to develop more leaks. These were repaired, first with hoarded scraps of plastic from Earth, then with small, pressed-out pieces of Memnonia-Gum or processed derivatives of straw cellulose. But it was a losing procedure; patches multiplied on patches. Meanwhile, the aging and weakening of the original material continued, and was cumulative in all the domes. Storms came. At Arsia, one dome was ripped, deflated, and flattened. During the next storm, it was three. Two of these three were repaired with tatters of the first. But already there were two less domes—out of fifty-one—in which to grow crops. In a similar interval, Olympus had lost one. The slow attrition had started.

Barlow was in the midst of efforts to hold back the inexorable decline. With others, he tried to piece together a complete dome from fragments. The Arsians almost believed that they would succeed in this. But their poor creation burst while it was being inflated.

When equipment broke down and there were no spare parts left, repairs or improvisations were made by whatever possible means. Still-usable items were cannibalized from junk. Some simpler parts were manufactured from salvaged or Martian metals. These even included small bearings. The diminished supply of lubricants was augmented with oil extracted from castor beans and processed for greater stability under operational conditions.

And there were the other normal—and abnormal—tasks and problems of the Base to be done and faced.

Maybe Barlow succeeded in working hardest of all. But everyone often labored to the limit of endurance.

Barlow had not remained as lighthearted as he had been way back when he was returning to Arsia from Olympus Base. Aloneness had its attractions, but it could become too much. In a society that was theoretically free, still there was a subliminal code of single loyalties. Yet younger women smiled at him, tried to hold him in conversation, sensing his need for an exchange of warmth—a little, or perhaps more. Yes, he might have loved with physical intimacy. Yet he pushed their attempts aside with a more-than-prim brusqueness: "I'm busy . . . I've got to go . . ."

His inside was a stabilized, grimed-in conflict of forces, with a proud image of how rugged and competent he wanted to be as the dominant factor. He could not stumble and blunder into that tender region where a portion of himself would be exposed as still that of a soft, fumbling, ignorant, inexperienced child! When he was the firstborn of Mars!

Yet sometimes, rarely, in the night, when he was not too exhausted, when there was no one about, he went to the communications dome and, in the deserted quiet, played through an audio-visual recording of terrestrial life that Deva Corliss had left him. It showed young people at play—sports, parties, easy, companionable talk. This was his one furtive and wistful indulgence. TV programs beamed directly from Earth had dwindled almost to nothing, and were of poorer and poorer quality. Later, back in his sleeping pallet, he might sob a

97

little for another world, and a way denied him.

Inevitably, with the harshening of conditions, there were accidents. Mona Schultz, Aldo Carlyle's mate, died when, with no warning and on a clear, quiet sol, a dome where clover grew blew out. Internal pressure had drifted a little too high for its patched and aging skins. Aldo seemed to take his loss well. Such fortitude was expected of everybody. Two sols later, he even joked and laughed, "Look what I found among Mona's stuff! A real antique! An ancient book of matches from her Grandpa! What did she want with that?"

But that same evening, Aldo walked Outside into the dark. From a distance of a kilometer, he called on his Mars-suit radio, "Hey, everybody, do you hear me? Watch! Isn't this funny?"

His call came in on the emergency announcer system. From where he spoke wasn't long in doubt. Through the blurred transparency of the Number One habitation dome's walls, a succession of tiny, orange flares were seen far off in the Martian night.

Aldo Carlyle's giggling, tragic-comic remarks continued: "Silly, useless old matches . . . Strike one, and it flames up for a second, even out here! Because its head contains a chemical that releases oxygen. But the matchstick can't burn. The air is too thin. Worse, it's completely dead! Mona's dead! Everything's dead! Ha ha, let's try another match . . . See—it won't stay lit! I'm dead! We're all dead! On useless, cold, dead old Mars!"

Aldo didn't seem to listen, as they called to him by radio to wait, while some rushed to suit up, and dashed out under the stars. Their flashlight beams showed him crumpled in the dust. He had removed his air hood. His livid, protruding tongue was already frozen.

A woman started screaming. A man uttered a string of curses. Everett Holsten was there, and he told them to shut up. Barlow moved forward to help pick up Carlyle's body, but too many others had crowded ahead of him, so he shrugged, and stepped back to where Gotch was standing.

"Sometimes there's no use hurrying, Tim," Gotch said quietly.

"Yuh, I know," Barlow replied in kind, showing a momentary wry smirk, mildly despising those who over-reacted.

What he didn't know was how coldly—almost casually—so habituated to horror he had become. At eighteen Earth-years old.

Some fifty sols later, when conditions at Arsia Base were fairly stable, Barlow came into the shop dome to see what job might next to done there. He found Gotch working over his long-unused Wanderer.

"It's now or never, kid," Gotch gruffed. "So I'm finally using the excuse I had in reserve: to bring back useful stuff Marie and I couldn't cart away when we stripped our disabled Lander."

Nine sols after Gotch and Barlow started south, they were beside the remains of the original Mars-ground-to-orbit vehicle, hardly changed after more than two terrestrial decades. Freed from the overload of disheartening toil at Base, they'd been having a fine man-to-man time, with no hint of sexual inversion.

Two sols more, and they were deep in the south-polar cap itself. Their Wanderer was ten kilometers behind them, because its spinning wheels couldn't bring it farther. Grotesque, scene-matching figures, arrogant of their aspect in their Mars suits, they plodded on afoot, through pervading whiteness: crunchy white under their boots; fluted, white slopes of the great, cleftlike valley leading toward the pole, looming on both sides. Mists from the substance of the cap coiled and swirled around them as it sublimated—evaporated—rapidly in the Martian springtime, almost as if they had entered some colossal, cryogenic cauldron in a laboratory of the gods.

"So, should we continue?" Gotch challenged. Both had the lighthearted attitude of men alive now, but with no future.

"Sure, why not?" Barlow answered.

"Okay. But if we keep daring each other, we could get in trouble."

"Or even to the pole, Frank. Hey, I guess I'm repeating myself. But just look at all that dry ice! Meters deep and piled high! Every summer it evaporates, becoming gaseous carbon dioxide again."

"Uh huh, kid, this I hadda see close up! A resource unique to Mars! Worth how many Niagaras? Man! But what's the use of empty visions? Except, they're beautiful!"

Gotch and Barlow tramped on for another hour. They were very tired. And their old boots were imperfectly insulated. Their feet had numbed with cold. With belated prudence, they reversed their course. Barlow felt dizzy. Gotch was almost staggering. On a long, steep slope, he slipped and fell.

"My left thighbone's busted, Tim," he graveled wryly.

# 12

Phobos, the nearer moon, because it orbited so close to Mars that it was always below the horizon in the antarctic and arctic, could not be used as a radio reflector in those regions. Therefore, the Arsians were not at first concerned about the long break of communications with their explorers.

But twenty sols passed without further contact. The two should be almost home by then. So, the way things looked, there was a double fatality for foolishness. Well, so be it. Bodily energies and other means for action were depleted. Faces went glum. Marie Manning's lips were compressed into a stoic line. But nobody seriously considered a search mission.

On the twenty-third sol since the two had first started south from Arsia, there was a brief, blurry message in Gotch's thinned-out, gravelly voice: "We're coming in . . . . In Icaria, now . . . . Babe, we're okay."

Phobos moved on, and the thready contact was lost.

Ten sols later, the battered Wanderer, loaded down with most of what had remained of the sabotaged original Lander, struggled into Base. No doubt the sheet metal, the shock cylinders, the extra, though empty, oxygen flasks, the insulated wiring, the electronic parts, the tubing, the pump details, and even the screws and washers, would be of some use.

Down there in the antarctic, Barlow, though

exhausted himself, had carried the injured Gotch ten kilometers back to their vehicle. And most of the other manual work had been his to do.

Gotch had to be taken out of the Wanderer on a litter. After Doc Pharr had reset his broken thighbone, using red Mars dust in the cement of the cast, he told Gotch he'd probably be all right, though laid up a while.

But before that, just as Gotch was being carried from the Wanderer, he had grinned slyly up at his mate, Marie, saying: "Sentimental object, Babe. Remember way back when we were loading up to leave our busted Lander? You were fussing about something mislaid, though we looked everywhere. Well, I found it in the pocket of an old blouse you left behind. Here . . ."

He dropped a University of South Dakota class ring into her gloved palm.

# *13*

Timothy Davis Barlow's life had been further marked by the grueling expedition into the Martian antarctic. Too much of a hardiness that he had tried to love? Still, now, a letdown, a loss of the relief of novel excitement in the constant struggle against slow, inexorable decay. Work, work, work, yet everything going down. Two more agriculture domes gone, rations poorer and less.

And his special, mateless loneliness had tightened around him. Nobody had time for him, nor had he time for anybody. Though maybe no one had much time for anyone? Many people had indrawn, cataleptic stares as they toiled at their tasks. Gotch was laid up; it was no use for Barlow to think of another, even short jaunt with him in the very near future; besides the means might be lacking.

Many things stirred darkly in Barlow as he labored tending crops. He did not review the audio-visual recording of terrestrial life anymore, but he remembered: the soft, easy, colorful imagery; the light-hearted friendships. His loyalty to harsh, deadly Mars was crumbling into hatred, especially before the contrast. His sentiments were pushed into reversal by hopeless hardship. Sometimes the thought of that strange crib that had been his as a baby. He'd seen it a few times long ago, hidden from him at the back of a storage compartment. With its mocking, painted legend: He shall be great! What a weary nonsense! But subliminally he may have noticed that television programs, beamed from Earth, were getting more frequent and a little better, as if Terrestrians were at last coming out of their long interval of strain.

Nobody could have said that Barlow pursued a plan with full consciousness. Mostly, rather, he just followed his nose—or his instincts—step by step, with a grim anger for escape driving him. He wondered vaguely, almost irrelevantly, if a trick similar to those used at least twice before, from Mars, could ever be effective again. Something very attention-grabbing. What . . .? The remainder of his activated motivation was almost subconscious.

He began by stealing hours from his sleep to see how well he could overhaul Gotch's old Wanderer. To keep equipment in the best reasonable condition was an established rule, so nobody would have been startled by the extra task he had quietly set for himself, even if most had not been too tired to notice. From remaining stock, he replaced a weakened bearing, and injected fresh lubricants into the others. Canisters of nuclear-fusion fuel were still available, and the Base laboratories were now managing to extract some deuterium-oxide from the water of fossil-ice to use as a supplement. The vehicle's fusion-power plant itself was a more difficult and critical factor to be assured of. He polished and minutely reset some tiny crystals of the pressure-heat-pulse-impactor system, and very carefully replaced some use-burnt thorium threads with similar threads salvaged from a bit of broken electronic equipment. The results were good. He rechecked the television camera, long demounted and unused, and bolted it to the swiveled bracket just outside the Wanderer's cab door. He, of course, remounted and tested all related audio-visual communication elements. He cleaned and patched the hollow algae-growing "saddle," which covered the top of the Wanderer. The saddle was a standard Mars-Wanderer detail. Sealed inside its transparent plastic skin was water containing minerals and algae; the latter would spring into rapid hydroponic proliferation whenever the Wanderer was oiut in open sunlight. Food substances would be synthesized, and breathable oxygen liberated.

Meanwhile, gradually, Barlow was provisioning the vehicle. He pumped the empty metal flasks full of oxygen from the surrounding dome air. He saved portions of his skimpy meals, wrapping the food in coarse straw paper, and let it freeze and dry in the Outside. And sometimes he stealthily pilfered from the mess-room larder, but not very much. A little freeze-dried meat and soup. Some algae meal.

As his activities moved closer to the fact of clear, conscious and inevitable fruition, his fear of many things increased. But against the surge of terrible need in him, he could never have stopped. He thought of the parents, of whom he had no memories of his own. But they had been inspired rebels, too. Now some Messianic mood, not too uncommon among lonely youths, came over him like a shelter. It was quite likely that he would soon be dead. But so what?

He wrote a note on rough paper, and left it on a shop bench where it wouldn't be found too quickly.

*Somebody has to try something. I'm going west, following the Blue Star. Maybe you should watch for me toward the east.*

*Tim*

Instead of waiting for nightfall, he started out boldly in late afternoon, pretending that he was only testing the refurbished Wanderer. He needed some daylight to get swiftly far from Base.

Just after sundown, he paused briefly to fix the dish antenna on the roof of the Wanderer on the silvery-blue spar of Earth, low in the west. The antenna would continue to track its position whenever it was above the horizon.

As he drove on, he activated voice communication briefly.

"Blue Star," he intoned into his microphone, "I'm Tim Barlow, and this time I'm coming."

At reduced speed, he barreled on through the night, and then accelerated once more. By midday he was deep into Memnonia, in roughened country just past Nodus Gordii. Here he stopped, got out of his vehicle, activated his audio-visual camera and transmitter, and made a speech that—in tone, fury and content, might have outdone some ancient holy man screaming in the wilderness. This performance was entirely unlike his usual manner, and it sprang up, unheralded and startling even to himself, from some hidden place of rage in his mind, where it must have been brewing for a long time.

"I am Timothy Davis Barlow!" he bellowed into his helmet mike. "Blue Star, do you remember who that is? Or have you conveniently forgotten? It is through your doing that I was born here on Mars! It is through your shameful neglect that my friends and I are suffering here! Yes, I accuse you! Because of honorable duty to my people, I could not leave before! But now, for their welfare and my own, I have no choice! Now I am coming home to you, Blue Star! You will help me to do this! You owe me much more, and I command it! If you don't help me, I will drive into the west until I am there! Damn you, I will claw and climb my way into the sky, to a place where I can spit into all of your billions of soft, cowardly, fickle faces! For I am stronger than the combined sum of your inhabitants! I am Timothy Davis Barlow, and I am on my way to my own!''

Barlow's furious, anger-propelled declamation ended at last. He was quivering, not only from the emotion behind his words, and from his physical tiredness, but from the awe and surprise at his own colossal and unexpected effrontery. He had been a mild person. Yet he was somehow pleased with himself.

That he might be a subject for laughter never occurred to him. He was deadly serious.

He shut off his transmitter, but did not activate for reception, telling himself that it was too soon to wait the many minutes for a reply. In order to hope for any attention, he might have to shout into the firmament at intervals for many sols. Besides, he was afraid to listen —afraid that there would never be any answer, yet, contrariwise, that there would! The latter fear came from the timidity of a creature of the lonesome wilderness, before the sophisticated, knowing, judging smoothness and mystery of terrestrial civilization.

He started up the Wanderer and continued westward, approximately along the Martian equator. After dark, he followed the white beams of his vehicle's headlights, until he had to pause to sleep. At first light, he ate an algae cake and a little thawed meat broth, and then jumped and jolted onward. By mid-afternoon he was well into Mesogaea.

While he passed into a narrow valley, he saw a small patch of the Thorgersen's rare *Gelucipulae*, root-anchored among the rocks and dust. The warmth he felt for living things touched him. Anyhow, it was time to declaim again. He stopped the Wanderer, unsealed its cab, moved a switch for audio-visual transmission, and stepped forth.

He could bellow up into the sky without nervousness,

for it was easy, here, to maintain the illusion of certainty that he was totally alone, with only his familiar wilderness around him—the carmine crags, the scattered boulders, and the flat, dark crusting of the *Gelucipulae*, brooding in the silence under the muted sunlight.

He threw his head back, and began his sonic projection with a prolonged and mournful coyote howl, which was like the keynote of the mad, Messianic shouting and bombast which followed:

"You know me, beautiful Blue Star! I am Timothy Davis Barlow, misborn on Mars! Damn you, it is your fault that I am here! From your cowardice, neglect and indifference! Come, take me home, Blue Star! Take me out of this empty world! I will lead you—show you the way! And, if you do not come, still I will climb the sky till I am with you! For I am strong! I am Timothy Davis Barlow."

As he continued to yell, his gaze wandered to the ground. He saw that, in spite of his care, in driving into this valley, a wheel of the Wanderer had grazed the edge of one of the *Gelucipulae*.

Now he crouched down quickly over the small, flattish, irregular mass. Yes, there was a broken spot in its hard, dark shell. Liquid juices, water-based, were bubbling through the bruise; unconfined, they were evaporating rapidly in the dehydrated thinness of the Martian atmosphere. From what the Thorgersens' had found out from observation of these plants, he knew what was happening inside this one. Tiny, threadlike creatures—perhaps the only remaining animal life on Mars—living within the plant tissues in a mutually beneficial, symbiotic relationship, were squirming to seal the wound with their glutinous exudation.

"Brave," Barlow gruffed. "Anything that has survived here for so many ages has to be brave. I'm sorry I hurt you. Maybe I can help.''

He had a very few medical supplies, among them a small can with a few drops of a wound-sealing fluid left inside. He fetched it from the cab, and sprayed the bruise, where it hardened at once to a thin film.

"All I can do," he said apologetically.

Minutes later, he drove onward, toward Zephyria.

# 14

The scopers were a little like the radio hams of decades ago. They were hobbyists with a strong, technological bent. They had sprung into being when the physical damage of a disaster what might have been total was largely repaired. They were among the first to turn their attention outward again toward space, away from Earth's preoccupation with its own woes. They worked and saved, and built small radio telescopes. They listened to the electromagnetic emanations of storms on mighty Jupiter, and the fainter, more distant ones on Saturn. More intently, they listened to the whispers from the stars, hoping always for hints of organized signals. They were an outward- and forward-leaning lot, bent on a general resurgence from a stultified attitude. Most were young.

Sometimes they even focused their antennas on Mars, to hear the dim, natural rustle of electron flow in its atmosphere, or perhaps a brief, infrequent, message from one of the two Bases, there: "Holding our own . . . . When?"

With the refinements of detection means, it was even possible, occasionally, to pick up the rhythmed static from the electric motor of some moving vehicle. An eerie thrill to accomplish that! Evidence of other, remote lives in action!

**Ronald and Penelope Lorenz were scopers. He, the**

elder, was a moderately successful public relations man. She was still a university student, aimed at a like profession. So, at 10:49 P.M. on a brisk October night, Ron was in the attic room of their big, old house on Long Island, routinely, almost idly, scanning—but with minutest adjustments of their equipment—the various regions of the Red Planet.

Suddenly there was a startling novelty—a long-drawn wail, followed by a voice, faint but clear, orating like a maniac.

"Pen!" Ron Lorenz said, with soft, tense emphasis. But she was already beside his chair.

The fierce voice yelled on: "I am Timothy Davis Barlow, misborn on Mars! . . . Damn you, it is your fault . . . ! From your cowardice . . . ! Come, take me home, Blue Star! . . . out of this empty world! . . . I will climb the sky . . . . For I am strong! . . ."

An indicator for video-reception was already winking red on the console, before Ron flipped a control. A wavery picture assembled itself on the phosphors of a cathode-ray tube on the table, and blended with the impassioned shouting. Desolation. Shadows on a pink, rock-strewn slope. And especially a fantastic form to match its own mad mouthings. Though the latter came quickly to an end, visual-reception continued. It wasn't very good, yet good enough for general aspect and for shock.

"How long since Barlow was last shown?" Penelope Lorenz asked the air around her, softly but very distinctly. "By gosh, look at him! Thin as a string, Ron, and—how tall do you think?—two hundred and twenty centimeters at least—over seven feet—to judge by the all-around extension inserts sewn into the waist, arms and legs, if that's a regular-sized Mars suit he's wearing! And, would he weigh as much as fifty-five kilos—one hundred and twenty-one pounds, even here? See, he's

111

swaying, tottering! Tired. Also malnutrition, of course. And shabby! Patched fabric . . . . Scratched air-hood plastic . . .''

"His boots," Ron added. "Cut apart, too. Rebuilt for greater length. Cemented back together, somehow . . . I didn't realize that those Mars colonists were so down . . . . Hey, he's squatting! What's that? One of those Martian plants . . .''

"Uh huh, Ron. *Gelucipulae,* somebody named them.''

The Lorenzes heard Barlow's voice again, gone gentle: " . . .Brave. I'm sorry I hurt you. Maybe I can help.''

They saw him administer to the thing, as if it were a friend.

"Hey, Pen, how about that!"

"Yuh, Ron, isn't he something useful, for what we want to happen? Sensible expansion into space—the cylinder worlds? A magnificent savage, if you look at him right! Legendary, like some mad teacher! And with that brown, gaunt, tormented face. If he lives. . . . What do you think, Ronnie? Hey, I don't hardly believe all this!''

"You stuck on him already, Pen? Oh, he's real enough! And he might be a help. Though, to many, he'll be a bad joke, an object of derision. Still, what is sick comedy to some is gospel to others. Still, again— he didn't seem very enthusiastic about Mars, which could mean space, generally. Oh oh, now he's getting back into his truck! He's out of sight. And now. . .''

The view of Mars faded from the tube; sound also went dead. Barlow had terminated his transmission.

"We didn't even try to answer him!" Pen Lorenz said.

"You know we're not supposed to attempt communication with Mars, Pen. 'Interfering with official channels,' is the way they put it. Hell, we've got enough to start stirring action up with, though! Our whole contact with Barlow is recorded. I'll phone a copy of it to George in California. Also, it's likely that Barlow will call again. We know his approximate location now, and can listen for whatever comes out of that spot. He can't move far very fast."

"Fair enough, Ron. But we do have a transmitter. Rules or not, I want to hook it up, and attempt to get through to him."

"As you choose, Penny. But you may find the frequency jammed with other impetuous tries. Meanwhile, maybe one of us should hasten down to Washington."

"Go ahead, Rod. I'll keep things alive here."

Before Ron Lorenz was on his way, she began talking into a microphone: "Calling Timothy Davis Barlow! This is Penelope Lorenz! I have heard you. I am your friend. You have many friends who will help you. Please speak further, Timothy Davis Barlow . . . ."

Except for numerous times when she had to answer the telephone, she kept this up through the night. Her call included a projection of her very charming smile, then of her troubled concern. There was no response.

## *15*

For five sols, Barlow drove on through Zephyria. As he approached Aethiopis, he turned his course somewhat north of west, to avoid the jagged orbital photographs. Dazed weariness dug into him. Still he slept and ate little. Shortened time meant better use made of his other stringently limited resources. He kept on.

However, since it was part of what he must do, he did not neglect to stop every afternoon at about 1400 to yell his challenges, praises, boasts, and unrestrained abuse up into the unresponsive firmament.

"Blue Star! I am Tim Barlow, and if you do not come to fetch me home, I will climb the sky! Help me, help my friends! You lazy, gutless bastards—you owe me! Take me out of this breathless hell world! Let me breathe free!"

More sols passed. In Amenthes he bent his westward course a little south again, and aimed for Moeris Lacus, at the eastern edge of Syrtis Major, great dark triangle of Mars. Moeris Lacus, an area where gray softened the ferric red of the desert. A minor destination was there. One of the mystery sites of the orbital photographs. A place that Gotch had particularly wished he might visit. The only one that was conveniently along Barlow's logical route.

Just within the uncertain boundaries of Moeris Lacus, Barlow halted, shook his fists at the sky, and made his usual exhortations. But then, torn between a terrible wish to know and a fear of knowing backed up by xenophobic dread, he dared to do something else at last. With one quick gesture, he opened audio-visual reception.

In his helmet phones, there was a roar of voices overlapping—who could tell how many? Hundreds, or thousands? Some spoke quietly, though who could ever distinguish what they said, through the blurred din of other shouting? He made out his name, "Barlow! Barlow! Skyclimber! Hero! Mars freak!" Enthusiasm seemed to predominate, yet there were curses, too. And the overall effect on Barlow, the loner of Mars, was terrifying. He loved and wanted that strange other world, yet it seemed to hurl itself at him in a flood of noise. There were even background threads of music.

Other names emerged dimly from the jangle: "I am Ross . . . George . . . Pen . . ."

Barlow willed himself to endure the contact a moment more, as he stared at the little cathode-ray tube set in the instrument panel of the Wanderer. As in the audio, there was a visual overload, as too many people in too many places on Earth, jammed the communication channels. There were faces on faces. Men. Girls. Elderly, scholarly faces, too. Did they make almost one face, with multiple, extended edge lines on both sides? A grotesque composite. The face of the Blue Star? Its smeared lips moving in dis-co-ordination.

When Barlow broke off communication, it was as if he escaped back into friendly silence. He found that he was trembling. His emotions were a mixture of elation and panic. One thing was certain—he *had* made an emphatic impression!

He started up his vehicle with a jolt, and a scattering of stones, and for some minutes, continued westward at dangerous speed, before slowing down. It was almost as

115

if he were fleeing something.

Next morning he was at that significant halting point in his long journey. He thought he might have trouble locating the place, but there was none. He found two small craters that looked like the landmarks he had pre-selected. He drove between them. Right in front of him, then, were the three markings, brooding and shadowed in the slanting sunlight. A trio of identical—trenches? Radially aligned at equal angles apart, and equidistant from a common center. Or so, at least, they seemed, to his flattened, ground-level view, which was not the best for accurate judgment. They reminded him of gigantic chisel marks.

He was out of his vehicle, now, pacing off and esti-mating. Yes, his first-glance guesses were right. Each trench was about ten meters long and two meters deep, with slanting sides. The angles between them seemed to come out exactly at 120 degrees, as nearly as his crude methods could reveal. Everything was just as in the dim, mapping photographs. The total diameter of the arrangement was about ninety meters. At last he stood looking at this curiously geometric phenomenon. Maybe it was not even as impressive as the three-sided pyramid Gotch had shown him. Yet it gave him much stronger feelings, perhaps because he was all alone, and had come so dangerously far—almost halfway around a planet!

Under his lumpy boot soles was the flat area of gray, natural basalt rock in which the trenches had been cut, impressed, or otherwise produced by some freak seismic folding of the Martian crust. According to all evidence, the epoch of extensive biological activity on Mars had been too short to have developed creatures that dug and built on this scale. Unless he thought of what he had only heard about in book recordings—*coral reefs?* But that was only his wild groping—to break the stereotypes

116

of narrow, human imagination.

The ancient geometry seemed to stare back at him with the passive, unrevealing silence of motion probably at least millions of years stilled. Yet he could not accept this sullen blankness! He had come so far, and he so much needed anything that might help him. He had to look closer, further. He had to try.

Staggering a little, he entered the nearest trench by its sloped end. Its bottom was covered with broken rubble and drifted dust. He shook his head to clear his suddenly hazed vision—that was how spent he was! He took the metal detector he had attached to his belt, and began to scan the trench. Nothing was revealed, except the almost inevitable iron-bearing compounds in underlying strata. He moved to the other trenches. Same negative result. Then he shifted to more careful visual inspection. But it would take many sols, and much more bodily energy than what remained to him, to examine all of the quite ordinary rock fragments, for those above buried many more beneath. No, he could not toss them away, one by one. Even if he did, the prospect had the look of futility. The chips he touched were nothing!

He stood at last near the central point where the axis lines of the three trenches would join. His legs were straddled wide apart to maintain his uncertain equilibrium. Perhaps his weary wits were too fogged for him to suffer true frustration; there was only a dull misery. It came to him that he did not know at all for what he searched—just something different.

Here, out of the trenches, he still studied the ground. There were scattered shards here, too. And one, off to the side, and almost covered with dust, was of a lighter color than the others. He swung toward it, picked it up. It, too, was a broken, irregular fragment. Meaningless! Porous, like vesicular lava . . . But looking closer, he saw that it had a layered structure. It was a little thing,

117

half the length of his gloved hand, and about as thick. Excitement began to uncloud his brain, as he lifted the object as hear as he could to the face window of his air hood. The unfractured side was curved, smooth, gray, almost glazed—perhaps silicous?

The broken edges and surfaces showed its interior form: tiered, with thin, separating flatness; fuzzed, full of tiny glints, and suggestions of intricate, overlapping repetitions. There were spherical hollows, from which something might have rotted or aged away.

Now excited further, Barlow hurried back to the Wanderer, and took a magnifying glass from his tool kit. With the glass, he studied the fragment for several minutes, knowing more and more that he had found something important, that ought to add another factor of interest and attention on Earth. He had been lucky. In his triumph, shyness vanished from him.

Without hesitation, he activated his audio-visual transmitter, and turned the camera lens toward the three trenches.

"I am Barlow!" he shouted. "See the place that I have come to, Blue Star?"

He waited a few seconds. Then he thrust the shard close to the camera eye, turning it over several times in his palm with his thumb.

"Now look carefully at what I have found, here!" he said in a quieter, but still intense, voice. "What is it? Yes, it is a broken piece of something. But what? See its fine structure? This is not the best way for you to examine it, Blue Star. But I can tell you truly that, magnified by this glass, the fineness still goes down and down, always orderly and intricate, till it is lost in smallness. Tetrahedral crystals fitted together. Precisely bundled but separating threads—what fraction of a micron in diameter? But still tough, to have lasted so long. I haven't the means to see or test further. But do your technicians of microcircuitry even have methods to make anything such as this? Was this thing made? Or is 'grown' maybe a better word? If extraterrestrial technology can have a different approach? If this is an artifact, for whatever purpose, do you want to guess where, by what, and how far away it was produced? Would you like to study it closely, and maybe find out? Then—damn you, Blue Star!—hurry! Help me get home!''

# 16

The next sol, Tim Barlow was in Syrtis Major. Its darker-tinted desolation was around him, meaning mostly just one thing to him, and that, dimly: he was at antipodes from Arsia Silva Base. He could get no farther away from it, while remaining on the Martian surface. It was 11,000 kilometers ahead, and an equal huge distance behind. A claustrophobic thought, considering how low all his resources now were. Temptation might have been strong to retrace his way over a known course, rather than to continue on into the unknown; but his hazy mind was fixed in a kind of rigid, almost unthinking doggedness, to do what he must have set out to do. At the outset, he had been desperately almost uncaring of his life. Now he merely wondered, with a numb and detached curiosity, whether he would ever see Arsia again. The chances seemed against it.

Westward of Syrtis was Aeria. There he began to lose track of the passing sols. The country was full of shallow impact craters; the going was slow and treacherous. His alertness had deteriorated. The Wanderer's wheels got stuck in a soft dune. Hours he had to shovel . . . . An hour later he was stuck again. He shook the gloved bones of his fists at the Blue Star, and in thinned-out shouts, gave forth with his usual bombast and vituperations: "Bastards! Lazy, soft-gutted bastards!"

But he never used his receiver again. He still half feared to. And he knew he must still be entirely on his own.

That second time his vehicle was caught in the dust,

he had no strength left for shoveling. But some dregs of prudence made him warm up a little broth, from his almost-ended store, and swallow it down, before he collapsed in sleep. When he awoke, his stringy body had recovered enough so that he was able to free the Wanderer and continue on westward toward Moab.

His progress was much slower now than during his relatively swift dash, halfway around Mars to Syrtis Major. His difficulties had multiplied. The country continued rugged and dangerous. There were threatening rattles in his vehicle, audible in the pressurized cab. Worst was his mounting weakness, especially the blurring of his brain, which diminished his capacity for attention and caution. Often, he functioned as in an agonized trance, full of mind phantoms that intruded on reality: the faces of friends at Arsia Base, the smell of food in the mess room; audio-visual images of Earth, its woods, its summer rain. Were these gentler things the truth, instead of the fuzzy, miserable, compulsive struggle? Digging at dust so he could go on; eating a little boiled algae, because he had nothing else left? He did not know that even in his intervals of stunned slumber, his feet and hands often made somnambulistic motions of compelled toil, as if this drive was grimed into his very nerves.

He fought onward, through Moab, into Gehon; then the rough extent of Chryse, where, sometimes blocked by chasms, he had to double back to take a different route; then on, skirting Xanthe, to Candor. Often, he hardly knew where he was. But he had lucid hours when he checked his position roughly by chronometer and star position.

There came the afternoon of his last shouting at the Blue Star; his shouts were only thin, tortured croaks now, but they had lost little of their fire. "I am Timothy Davis Barlow! Ahead of me lies Tharsis, the great desert that is mine! Watch from your comfortable chairs, Blue

Star, while I finish what has never been done! Only two thousand kilometers more, and I will have circled Mars! Have I entertained you enough so that you will help me come home?''

His boastful words were now only a bluff, embedded by habit in his misery and desperation. He was not sure at all that he would accomplish what he insisted that he would. And, as he entered Tharsis at a point well north of Tithonius Lacus and the Coprates Rift, his numbed brain made a deadly oversight. At sundown, he forgot to activate the heaters in algae saddle on the roof of the Wanderer. The water and algae sealed in the saddle froze solid in the nocturnal cold; no more oxygen could be produced for many sols.

Barlow kept on as best he could; there was the air in the cab, and one remaining flask of oxygen. But his wits and his consciousness hazed over, more and more. He could scarcely feel his numbed toes and fingers, yet his ears could still hear the grind and scrape of a bearing that was about to go. Belatedly—because it seemed unreal after having been so long out of range—it came to him that he could now radio Arsia Base. If he could determine the time when Phobos was in the proper place to act as a reflector. But doing even so simple a thing had drifted beyond his present powers, though he did turn on his transmitter—its carrier wave could be a guide.

His vehicle was aimed straight toward the declining sun, and he let it grind on. It was too early yet for his dimming vision to make out the Blue Star. His awareness was fading fast, but he did hear and feel the Wanderer grind into a dune, and slew around as that bearing broke. Emergency sensors shut off the motor.

As Barlow slipped into unknowingness, he felt no panic. There was no reason or good in crying out. It was logical that those who would help if they could, already knew.

# 17

Timothy Barlow suffered some disorientation when he again had a sense of being. But his head was soon fairly clear. He was between much-patched sheets in the little Arsia Base hospital. An IV needle fed nourishment into a vein in his arm.

And a gravelly voice was speaking to him rather glee-fully, "Earth kept us informed where you were, Tim. They even ran recordings of what you said for us. Doc Pharr, Ella Duross, and I started out in the one Wanderer able to move as soon as we had a chance. We brought you in."

"Like I half figured, Frank," Barlow managed to comment. "And I wasn't as crazy as I may have seemed."

"Yuh, we knew, kid. You sounded wilder than anybody I ever heard of. But you got us back some beneficial attention!"

Frank Gotch could be very critical of foolhardy action that made no sense. But a calculated risk that had come out with good results was something else. If he hadn't always fully believed this, he had learned since. When, in a desperate situation, somebody tried a dangerous stunt that had a chance to win, you didn't moan and worry over him while he was busy at it; nor did you curse him for a fool if he lost. Gotch, who had gambled his skin for high and fantastic stakes through most of his life, couldn't help but have such attitudes. And most of the others who had come to Mars were much the same.

"Your trick came out right, Tim," Gotch continued. "Some small, unmanned rockets, loaded with stuff we most need, are already on the way to us by a difficult trajectory. If they land within twenty kilometers of either Base, we aren't so incapacitated now that we won't be able to pick them up. And, at optimum, orbital window time, we're promised as much supplies as means constructed on short notice can carry. That won't be a great deal; Earth hasn't built any spacecraft for years; not much is ready. All but one ship will be simple, robot cargo carriers without crews. That single ship, designed for two persons, will be for fulfilling your emphatic wish, Tim, you can't back out on this occasion! It will take you and Agnes Frost to Earth— she now very definitely wants to go. So that's most of the news, Tim. Something worked again."

Barlow didn't respond right away. He was still too weary to be elated. But a vast, pleasant relaxation oozed through him. Any worries he might have felt were too remote to reach him.

"Should I talk some more?" Gotch graveled genially. "Or should I scram and let you sleep?"

"You don't usually talk a lot, Frank," Barlow answered. "So anytime you want to, I'd rather listen."

"Yuh," Gotch grunted musingly. "Once in a while I start thinking—*how it works*. I've survived these last twenty-some Earth-years because it *does work*. Still, I get cynical. A person calls for help because he must, to keep living. People respond from their good feelings. But somewhere, when it gets really big, it becomes a show—a spectacle. Did I ever want to be a showman? No. Once, the idea couldn't even have entered my head. So should I have been shocked and embarrassed when I

124

realized I was part showman? Maybe you don't know it, Barlow, but you're kind of a master showman yourself! I don't criticize; I honor you for it. You yelled, cursed, and challenged; you hammed it up; you risked your neck in a damn fool stunt that nobody else would have dared to think of, or do. You were more than anybody just fighting for his life in an arena. So where is the corruption in it all? In that some of those Terrestrians gloated while others wept? Or more in that you must have been *consciously* trying to manipulate them—the simple, innocent ones—barbarians, perhaps?—for *your* purpose? Leading them on, grabbing at their guts, and at their tame, routinized lives with dramatics? Oh, hell, Timothy, I'm leading myself in an empty circle that goes nowhere. There's something elusive here that makes me blink; it seems wrong, yet it's right. There are many good folks on Earth; they can make sound judgments; they have a good moral sense—and a wholesome selfishness; they're pretty much like us, here. Nobody fools them much. But they look for new things to grip their attention. Many of them want heroes to follow or emulate. I suppose I shouldn't be puzzled; it's all the complicated way that human life functions, and big jobs get done.''

Barlow had listened sleepily. He hadn't known that Gotch could be this philosophical, or idealistic. But now he remembered something made him fully aware.

"Hey, Frank!" he said with a sharpness that made a painful rasp in his throat. "There was a thing from Moeris Lacus! I had it wrapped in a piece of paper!"

"Uh huh," Gotch replied. "I wondered when you'd mention that. We heard about it first by way of Earth. They're calling it *'The Exofact,'* now, presumably meaning something made way outside of what is known. Yes, we found it in the Wanderer that you swiped and broke. Though that was better than a good

125

trade, worth for worth. Leda Sturm and the Thorgersens have been trying to check out this *Exofact*. With a microscope, its internal complexity goes down below the level of a quarter micron. There are countless little, cilialike hairs which seem, for one thing, to act as electronic terminals. Apply a charge of—say—one nanovolt to one, and it comes out differently on others —halved, doubled, tripled, or in a whole series of perhaps logarithmic relationships. Also, if there's a sound —if somebody speaks suddenly—or if the surrounding illumination changes, there are corresponding changes in some of our instrument readings. Can we say, then, from this evident light and sound sensitivity, that, in a way, the thing can see and hear? So just what *is* this *Exofact*? The best guess is that it is a chip off of some sort of analog device, which certainly was much larger. A kind of robot brain? Anyhow, the technology involved in producing it is way beyond anything we know about. As to its age, specialists on Earth will have far better means to determine that than we have here, but it is certainly very old. And where did it come from? Well, where *could* it come from, Tim? So, have I covered everything that you want to know right now?''

Gotch's raspy voice—speaking quietly—reached an end.

But Barlow was excited. With sudden force, he raised himself on his elbow, and croaked out a string of words, ''Frank, those wise Terrestrians must be itching to get the thing under their instruments! That's more assurance that the ship will come—to get *it*—and me— and Frost! That they'll send what is needed here! It was damn lucky that you got me to think of those three markings in Moeris Lacus, and that I went to look!''

Gotch grinned his frog grin.

''Sure it's lucky, Tim,'' he said. ''It's giving the suddenly renewed enthusiasm for space projects a further boost—with you as a guiding symbol. So far—

126

fine! Only, is there maybe a bit of an overplay, as far as we, on Mars, are concerned? First, there is freshened interest in cylinder worlds, to be made of lunar materials, easily catapulted into space against the low g. Axial rotation will give an approximation of terrestrial gravity on their inner curves. There'll be fields, towns, woods, lakes there. A really utopian environment, according to some viewpoints, and just what people like. Sunlight will be chaneled inside. It was all checked out for viability years ago, until the two very small prototypes got shot down in the Nuclear Emergency that stopped all forward movement. The way one story goes, settling Mars shouldn't have been attempted at all; that those cylinders are the best answer to terrestrial overpopulation relief, to safe, human dispersal, to progress in living conditions in orderly, parklike surroundings—all very attractive.

"Yuh—then there's this *Exofact,* which seems to say two things very definitely: One, affirmation of an old hope. *We are not alone;* and—two, *Interstellar travel has happened and is possible.* Both points are beautiful to know—better than a hint or two of organized messages picked up by radio-telescopes. But creating a disproportionate furor right now, considering that, at the human level of know-how at least, travel between star-systems can't be easy. So, for us on Mars, the *Exofact* could be another unfavorable diversion. The cylinder-worlds were already enough; there could be hundreds or thousands of them circling the sun in an orbital ring as tiny planets. And developing Mars into a fully habitable world could become an unattractive and forgotten obsolescence."

Tim Barlow did hear most of this; but in his exhaustion, it went beyond his radius of attention and immediate concern. He began to snore.

Chuckling in wry good humor, Gotch went away.

127

# 18

Important conditions seemed immediately much improved at the Martian Bases, well before even the small supply rockets could arrive and be gathered in from the surrounding desert. The struggle to live, under ever-tightening circumstances, continued; but optimism and promise had been injected into half-starved and overworked bodies. Survivors brightened, though there were recent dead from various causes buried in the cemeteries. At Arsia, there was John Tenaka, whose heart had given out, and Arelle Mather, Leon Bonard's woman, who had simply sickened and wasted away— these, from among the old timers. And there were several more from among the later arrivals.

Tim Barlow regained his strength after his ordeal of circling Mars. Maybe, being native, he was better attuned to Martian rigors. Certainly, Big Bessie Blythe put more algae cakes, sometimes dabbed with a few drops of honey, under his nose than she did for others, or more often fed him broths and bits of chicken and meat, which helped; but who could begrudge him, considering what he had accomplished?

From Earth, he remained in intense demand for attention. At first he sat patiently before camera and microphone in the communications dome, and tried to answer the questions from the innumerable faces of interviewers, regulated in orderly sequence now, instead

128

of being jammed into a discordant, overlapping mass. There were two—a girl and a man—of whom, for future reference, he should have taken particular note; but he didn't know this, then; and, like others, they were lost in the numbers and the brevity of contact. Much of his timidity before Earthlings had faded in his growth of experience, and the difference of present circumstances; from Arsia Base, while sitting quietly in a frayed blue coverall, it was inappropriate for him to shout like an inspired hermit of the wilderness; there had to be a calmer, saner way. Yet, soon, something of a wild loner's wariness, reticence, and suspicion reasserted himself in him. He remained polite; he even smiled as an especially insistent questioner wore out his patience.

"Look, mister," he said. "We have to work here constantly to stay alive. Right now it looks as though there's a dust squall coming up. We don't dare lose any more domes. I have to help doing the best we can to see that all are secure. If you haven't already heard everything about how I found the "intersteller object," you'll have to wait until I'm brought home and can show it to you."

The face just then in the receiver screen still grinned at Barlow ingratiatingly, as it must, considering the many minutes of communication lag. Barlow wondered if that expression would sour up when the man finally heard what he had just said.

From this incident onward, Barlow retained his policy of reticence. He smiled sometimes at audio-visual cameras that still functioned. He might wave and say "Hi," but no more. Maybe he did harm by this attitude. On the other hand, he may have strengthened his own legend with an extra touch of toughness.

Shortly after the small, preliminary supply rockets reached Mars, Agnes Frost journied from Olympus

129

Base to Arsia, beside which the Lander of ship that would take the Marsborn to their ancestral world was scheduled to touchdown. With the girl, in an old but lovingly refurbished Wanderer, came her parents, Mabel Larkin and Charles Frost, and the teacher, Deva Corliss.

Between Timothy and Agnes something was much better than it used to be. He was now all of nineteen terrestrial years old; she was approaching seventeen. They had grown, and grown confident; they were no longer rawly sensitive and self-centered children. Harsh experience had tempered them. They were both ready to put themselves forward toward each other, in the big— the colossal!—adventure that they were going to have to share.

Oh, Barlow was a bit awkward and stiff while meeting her folks, and especially at greeting his teacher after so long.

"So this is you, as you are now, Timothy," she said with bright interest, as she got out of the Wanderer, and looked him over.

"Uh huh—me, Deva," he responded. "Good to see you."

She looked sick and old, when once, long ago, she had seemed so beautiful to him. Their gauntleted hands met, and he tried to put warmth and affection into his light grip; more sympathy might have been an unkindness to show, before a proud and kindly spirit. He was glad to yield her to the attention of others, as his own eyes swung to a more significant interest.

"Agnes . . . Hey!"

His spontaneous exclamation was most admiring. She was almost as tall and slim for a woman as he was tall and slim for aman. Now he felt the matching likeness happily. And the face, behind that abraded air-hood window, was no longer plain and sullen. A wisp of

130

blond hair curved down past a nicely rounded and dimpled cheek to the right-hand end of grin that fairly sparkled with aliveness and adventure. Her blue eyes roved over him in quick appraisal. Then she chuckled, pleased. The tone was like rough music.

"Sure—me," she said. "And you—Tim. Dammit, you're so big and ugly, you're lovely! So, touch gloves, Timothy!"

As they gripped hands, he might have been a bit taken aback by her description of him—except that it matched his own proudly masculine image of himself. She was much more brash in her speech than he; he didn't quite realize how different it was for a girl, growing up among crusty, outspoken men—and women. Yet her open frankness and humor encouraged him to be the same, without strain.

"Yuh, big time coming up for us, Agnes," he said. "Going to Earth! I want to go—I've got to go! But I'm scared—almost more!"

Her face sobered. "Uh huh—I know. Me, too, Tim . . . Still—Red Tharsis—just the idea of going spins and shines in my head, and makes me all new! It's wonderful! I guess you're getting ready? Eating good from the new supplies? Exercising, like we're supposed to? I guess your doc gave you a lot of shots from the medical stuff that came in on the little rockets. Against terrestrial diseases. Damn—I wonder what a Common Cold is like? I almost want to contract it, just to find out, though I hear it's a rotten experience. Kind of glamorous, though . . ."

"I'm into all of those things, Agnes. About exercise —Leon Bonard—his woman died—even throws me around in unarmed combat; when he was young, on Earth, it was his school sport. Aghh—what are we standing out here for? Let's get to your quarters, right next to mine. And out of these Outside clothes. Then we

131

can talk for an hour before I have to go help rig a new skin from the rocket-parachute stuff—over at the Number Five dome.''

Minutes later, in her austere cubbyhole-habitation, Barlow was saying further, "Here, Ag, I made this for you. Marie Manning and Big Bessie Blythe—you've heard who they are—coaxed me to do it, but I felt silly not having thought of it myself! Gotch and I used to go winnowing gold. So it's from nuggets. Nice and feminine, they tell me—good for on Earth. A necklace . . .''

Balled in his fist, he thrust it awkwardly, and rather diffidently now, into her hand.

She held it up between the clusters of her fingertips, and gasped in spontaneous delight, "Timmy, this is elegant, and you are a marvel! Damn! The folks at Olympus used to make me silly dolls and toys, but nobody had any time, lately, for gifts. Help me hook it on, please!''

With some fumbling, he obeyed. And from somewhere, she extracted a small mirror, studied the reflection, and patted her hair. The polished gold lumps gleamed at her throat. Knowing persons on Earth would have called Barlow's creation a marvelous piece of primitive art, worth a fortune. But these two young folks of Mars weren't aware of this aspect; they just liked what they saw and what it meant.

"So now—well—I contrived something for you, Timothy," Agnes stated. "I even wrapped it up, nice. Here, open it." And she handed him a small package, done up in crude, Martian straw paper.

It was a linen shirt, hand-loomed in a brown-and-tan geometric pattern from Mars-grown flax. Another piece of charming, rustic artistry. Barlow flushed in happy startlement and other feelings, as Agnes held it against his shoulders to check the fit.

132

"Hey, it's real great, and many thanks, Agnes," he almost stammered. "I'll save it for Earth. Here I've got no separate pants—only these old coveralls."

"Sure, Tim, like I've got no dress, yet, to go with this necklace. But that condition will end for us both."

They looked at each other silently for a moment, and it was as if there was a big glow between them. Easy, then, to be entirely frank with each other? She seemed to think so.

"Tim," she began earnestly. "I was sent—and I wanted to come—here to Arsia, early. Mostly so that you and I could get acquainted, since we'll be traveling together. Nobody insists—and maybe neither of us should say yes or no yet—but they kind of expect us to mate, and would be pleased. Up to now, it doesn't seem like such a bad idea, considering that we're the only two real Martians. I've had to brush off men, mostly companioned, one widowed. That's the extent of my experience; maybe you've had more, if it matters. Anyhow, I've got the capsule under my skin—poor old Deva insisted—and one thing that Marspro made sure that there would always be plenty of around were those capsules."

Here, Agnes Frost patted her left biceps indicatively. Barlow made a corresponding gesture.

"Me—likewise," he said soberly. "Doc Pharr finally got around to that."

There was something incongruous in the way they were talking, bold in conformity with the ways of human culture in their time, but with a kind of subliminal diffidence—almost a delicacy—perhaps because they had never really known any of their own age group. They were like two country kids of a strict, bygone era. This was sad, yet maybe it was sort of good, too.

"I don't always like to hurry, Timothy," she said, and there was something apologetic and gentle in her

133

tone.

"Nor do I," he answered with sympathy, and the joy of tenderness. "So we'll let things float wherever they want. I'd better go to work, now. See you in a little while."

Of course, they were caught in an inevitable rightness. A couple of evenings laters, he would have gone into her quarters, as they had agreed he should. Only, a wind squall came down out of Tharsis, and they both had to keep dome-security watch until dawn. So it was another two nights before he awaited his chance, and slipped into her room. He could have just walked in, boldly, but they were both a little embarrassed by the watching, amused, benign, sidelong glances of others; besides, they wanted a bit of secrecy.

The rich fire that pulled at them so irresistibly, reached fulfillment. Flesh came to flesh and juices to juices in the manner of which many claim there is nothing better. They rode high together, and dropped, and rose high again, many times. Another kind of starvation ended. Now they knew and had grown, and they were changed. Having slept little, they still came to breakfast with smiling vigor, and a silent wish to announce to everybody who they were—this while the other people in the mess room struggled ridiculously to keep from smiling so as not to make them uncomfortable.

# *19*

The ships arrived; five and five for the two Bases carried only cargo; the eleventh, that stayed in orbit, dropped its Lander at Arsia, with a medical couple aboard; these would stay to help with the sick, while Barlow and Frost departed from Mars in the ascent vehicle.

Things were stowed to be taken along. Mineral and ore samples. A considerable quantity of Memnonia-Gum. Quite a sackful of gold dust and nuggets. Sealed in a box was a dried but revivable specimen of the *Gelucipulae*. The lab crew made a protective case, out of two small blocks of Styrofoam, its interior excavated precisely to fit and contain the *Exofact*.

The Marsborn pair went over the manual controls of the ascent vehicle. Of course, there wasn't much time for them to become effective pilots; nor was there much point; everything was automated, or remote-controlled. But they were curious, wanting to acclimate themselves to what would be around them on the long journey across space.

The farewell dinner featured real Earth steak and beer for everybody. It was fun and crazy and sad and musical, and at last a drag to be gotten over with.

"Don't forget us, Tim. Or you, Agnes . . . Keep talking us up on Earth . . . We still need . . ."

Most of these people couldn't safely go back to Earth anymore, even if they had the chance. Barlow and Frost knew that they had the advantage of youth. But they might have trouble, too. Possibly greater trouble, since they had never been on Earth. Prognosis for them was good. Still, nothing was proven, yet.

There were handshakes and good wishes all around. So long, Everett, Bessie, Marie, Steve, Tony, Deva, Mort, Sven, Ilga, Helen, Lida, Doc, Ella . . . . And widowed Leon Bonard and Ruth Parkins, who might be mated soon. So long, all of you others . . . . Agnes wept a little, saying goodbye to Charles Frost and Mabel Larkin, her parents. The end of it, then—party over. So sleep a little, if possible.

The two had chosen Gotch to walk all the way out to the Lander with them, in the far-subzero time of dawn light. He would make the final, visual checkout of the vehicle. The control systems had been counting down since midnight. The other people watched from afar.

Up the ladder, into the nest of dark, smooth padding, of metallic glints, of small, green numerals flashing out rhythmically in descending order. Strap to the couches. Gotch opening a little locker, placed high on a bulkhead.

His pebbly voice saying, "Just to show you again, Tim. Your *Exofact* is safe in Number One."

Then his big, gauntleted mitt shoved forward for final grips. But no more words. He was gone. The door closed itself and sealed. The green numerals counted: 07—06—05 . . . There was no time to think much. Except, is this like death? Like waiting for some ancient axe to fall? So much to be changed . . . . End of one life . . . . but beginning of another . . . .

The roar was sudden; the thrust seemed huge.

136

# 20

Events followed each other in flawless, programmed sequence in which the Marsborn took only passive part: the docking of the ascent vehicle with the mother ship in orbit; the former would remain attached and point forward. The slow and precise turnaround and alignment, while the yaw, roll, and pitch jets were activated in small, groping bursts. Then the numeral-measured pause, in the still strange and queasy state of weightlessness. Then the many minutes of furious, roaring thrust. To silence again, and the scary sensation of falling forever. They were now on the 120-day curve of trans-terrestrial trajectory.

They kicked off their rough, mended boots, and their much-patched Mars suits; there had been no reason to replace such gear for them. Now, unstrapped from their couches, they floated free, in cautious solemnity, and then laughed happily. In their longjohns, they glided about, experimenting. They propelled themselves through a tubular passage to a larger chamber behind the ascent vehicle. It was an amazement to them that this ship seemed so nicely designed, when they had been told that everything was prepared in haste.

They peered through a back window. The huge bulk of their native world was shrinking. It looked awesome, ugly, beautiful. A coil of mist curve away from the south-polar vapor hood. The dark markings were like the swirled dregs left at the bottom of a cup of make-believe coffee made from grain.

"Mars didn't hurt us, Tim," Agnes mused. "It kept us alive as best it could for all the time we know. Any wrong was elsewhere."

Barlow smirked. "Sure, Ag, maybe . . . Me, all I want is to think ahead."

"You're right—so do I," she answered. "And, do you know what? I'm hungry! I didn't take much breakfast."

She was already opening a small locker. Then she was sucking at the stem of a little plastic container.

"I've saved half for you, Tim," she declared honorably, regretfully, after a few seconds. "Honest orange juice! Yum! Aren't we exotic-luxurious!"

"Aghh! Red Tharsis, Ag!" he burst out. "Drink it all! Have another can! Or two! Or three! I'll take whatever I want! Get out of the old habits! We're not on rations anymore! We're supposed to get nourished, build ourselves up! There's more than five hundred kilograms mass of packaged Earth foods behind that main-locker door! Steak, eggs, milk, vegetables, fruit, bread, cake, ice cream!"

She looked a bit startled and blank, as if she felt stupid. But then she smirked back at him.

"Okay, Tim, don't scold. And, be careful, yourself. You could get sick from too much unfamiliar victuals."

They settled, then, for some egg paste and buttered toast, warmed in the food heater. They weren't sure, yet, that they liked the cow's milk.

When they were chucking the minor refuse in the disposal unit, she spoke primly, "We have to vacuum up every drifting crumb. Also I'd better go stow our old boots, suits and air hoods someplace."

But just then a buzzer sounded loudly. From their brief instructions, they knew that they were supposed to

138

return forward to their couches. Just as they got there, a face appeared in the videotube before them, and a slow voice began to talk.

"Hello, Agnes and Timothy. I'm Al Kensing—most people call me Ken. I'm here at the new Mid-America Radio-Scope—or MARS—near Chicago. It is small, but effective for communicating with you, and was hurried to completion in your honor. I hope you hear and see me well enough? Because of the transit-time gap between anything said and its response over great distance, I must speak largely in extended monologue. But you know this, of course . . . ."

The face in the screen was no older than middle twenties: Dark beard, benign, good-humored eyes. The voice continued briskly, maybe a bit nervously.

"I'm a physician. But I like boats and flying. I want to get into space. With the resurgence of interest that you helped start, I expect I shall. Right now I'm to guide and instruct you in various ways. To me, at this moment, you are visibly eating. But when you hear me say so, you will probably be finished with cleaning up any refuse. Next you should put on the vital-indications monitoring harnesses, which are in Number Eight locker, with simple instructions attached. You should rest then for thirty minutes, until we have done a checkout of how fit you are. But since your Dr. Pharr, and his new associates on Mars, have pronounced you vigorous enough, I don't think there will be any delay in starting your exercise program, which is very important. The devices you will use are folded down at the sides of your couches."

Barlow and Frost were both used to discipline, learned in an environment where it was particularly necessary. In their still-bizarre situation and surroundings now, it gave them comfort to be obedient. With word and gesture, they signaled accomplishment of

139

what the pleasant, but slightly pompous voice suggested.

"Harnesses in place, Dr. Kensing." This from Barlow.

And from Frost, in her less-formal way, "Right, Doc Ken . . ."

The exercise devices were like rowing machines, which could be swung up into active position, while the user was lightly strapped to the couch at waist and ankles, to restrain weightless drifting. Though Frost and Barlow had never been anywhere near an actual boat, much less rowed one, it seemed that they did the latter, now.

Forward—pause—pull! This to the quickening beat of various lively music from the sound system. Strengthen-those-sore-aching-arms-and-backs! Sweat—strain—puff! Until, as time passed, it seemed that they must row, in the colossal, quiet ocean of space, all the way to the Blue Star!

No casual outsiders intruded on Al Kensing's program. Evidently the channel of communication was now closely and reasonably restricted to keep out a jamming avalanche of interruptions.

"You-are-doing-very-well-Tim-and-Agnes," Kensing would say in cadenced rhythm toward the end of many hours of exercise. "So stop. Thirty minutes of rest. Then a good dinner, and your housekeeping duties . . . Meanwhile, another audio-visual cultural presentation. So many things you should become better acquainted with in order to be comfortable on Earth! Gradually, we are introducing more nitrogen into the atmosphere you are breathing, and increasing its pressure, so you will become adjusted to terrestrial norm. Soon you should sleep. I must sleep some, too. This hemisphere will be turned away from you, but you can always call me, as I can always reach you through our Australian antenna."

Barlow and Frost had plenty of boredom-fighting activity. They found the vivid presentations of terrestrial scenes and life fascinating. During the relaxed sleep periods, with the continuous sunlight darkened or subdued by window shutters, they experimented with lovemaking at zero-g. Yet confinement, routine, and the long extent of time still caused boredom to creep in. For a while, feeling that they had had too much of each other's company, they became withdrawn and rather sullen. But toward the end of their journey, with the strange, scarred Moon already behind them, and the blue, cloud-flecked Earth bulking huge ahead, they were driven close together again by their nearing moment of truth.

"It looks so beautiful, Tim. But all those smart, so-knowing Earth people . . . . They scare me the most most . . . . Hold my hand . . . ."

"It's all right, Ag. We'll just stick close . . . ."

"Of course, it's all right!" Doc Ken laughed indulgently; he could converse with them now as if he were actually within the ship. "Check your couch straps for security. There'll be retrofiring for capture in Earth orbit in just under forty minutes. Then you'll have forty minutes more to move around, and maybe freshen up if you want to before the shuttle tender attaches to your exit port, and takes you down."

The thrust of the retros was long, but not too straining. Afterward, the two changed into fresh, blue coveralls. Barlow put the Styrofoam-encased *Exofact* in an inside pocket. Let somebody else take care of the other baggage.

With Kensing's voice still guiding them, Frost and Barlow followed their noses. Into the tender to another couch with straps. Somebody encased in a white anti-contamination costume, entered the spaceship and returned with their gear, but there was no time for

141

verbal exchanges. There was another long burst of smaller retros from the tender, and soon, the hissing, streaming glow of atmospheric entry, until the craft was flying like a plane, and Barlow and Frost felt, at last, the true, stable tug of terrestrial gravity.

The shuttle landed at an airfield. Another accordion-like passage was attached. More people in white came through, and hands in soft, tight-fitting gloves were efficiently, gently busy, unstrapping, guiding, supporting, mastering. Light banter was slightly muffled behind plastic-windowed anti-infection masks.

"Ah—the girl from Olympus Mons . . . . This way, Agnes Frost . . . ."

"And you're the notorious Timothy Davis Barlow! Hello, Skyclimber from Mars! I suppose your next place to go will be up into the prototype dwelling cylinder, when it's ready. Never mind any arrival speeches to us medicos. We know—save 'em for later. But we get first crack at you, in person, even ahead of the media, and the politicians."

"Easy! Don't fall! Legs not too rubbery? Good! Well —this is a very historic moment! The two people whose names top the all-time list of household words! Welcome, Marsborn!"

"Ah, stop patronizing them, Nick, you crud! They *are* great!"

"Who's patronizing? I mean every word!"

"Here to the right, please, Agnes. And you to the left, Tim."

Up to this point, Barlow felt reassured. The one-g strain on his legs wasn't bad. And all the talk and attention was fun. Somewhere he'd been terrified by nothing! He had been getting the odd impression that he was walking in a pleasant dream. He'd even winked up at an unobtrusive and ubiquitous TV camera bracketed high on a white wall of the building they had entered.

142

He didn't much mind being given no chance to answer anybody back.

But now was different; he didn't want Ag separated from him!

"Hey!" he gruffed.

Agnes half turned, and smiled toward him. "It's okay, Tim," she said. "I think I'm enjoying this. Go along—I'll see you later."

Barlow was helped into another white room, utterly clean.

"We have to get the clothes off you," a girl medic told him, as she began unfastening his coverall. She wanted to take the Styrofoam case from his inner pocket. But there he balked.

"No—that's mine!—it stays with me for now!" he growled.

"Okay—okay! Sorry!" she answered. "You can set it down on that stand over there, in plain sight."

They stripped him down, gently but firmly.

"Where is Doctor Al Kensing?" he demanded worriedly.

"Al Kensing? Who's that?" somebody wondered. "Oh, maybe you mean the guy who was your in-transit orientation man? Was that his name? Still back at some central installation, I suppose. What do you want with him now?"

"He's my friend!" Barlow declared plaintively.

Everybody paused, and looked very hurt.

So the young physician who had just answered him about Doc Ken, explained with humble and injured patience:

"Please, Tim Barlow . . . Skyclimber. Big Voice. Loner who drove a broken-down car all the way around a world that doesn't even have a natural atmosphere that anybody can breathe. *All* of us here are your friends and admirers! Who else would be allowed close

143

to you? If it makes any difference, I'm Toby Klein, and I have a buddy who is a radioscoper. Even when you were still exhorting from those uninhabited red dunes, we tried to call you! That you never answered anybody didn't make us like you any less. You surely had enough to do! But now, please don't be a pain in the backside! Let's get on with your examination. It's important . . . ."

The procedure continued, with vocal callouts of data, almost as if Barlow weren't present:

"Height, two twenty-two centimeters—over seven feet . . . . Weight, still only sixty-five point five kilograms—just over 144 pounds, even with heavy transit feeding . . . ."

"There was that woman who came back from Mars, and broke her hip right away."

"Come on—this is Barlow! He ain't *that* fragile! We'll get a bone-strength rating when we check the marrow. Yeah—Rosie—take a skin scraping to see what kind of microorganisms are on it. Then the blood sample . . . . Wonder how much malnutrition still shows? God, did you ever see a chest expansion like that? A good three liters above anything I know about! Peculiar kind of encephalogram . . . But this guy has a right to different brain waves, and psychology . . . . Hope it doesn't worry the shrinks . . . . Temp a little low . . . . Good heart rhythm. But beat way fast . . . Tim, are you still nervous, or is it just that you still feel pretty heavy in this gravity? So lie down over here. Relax—rest . . . ."

Klein was evidently in charge, and he was doing most of the talking. Barlow was calmer again, and he obeyed.

Somebody sneezed, and got some sharp glances for so doing. The man withdrew from the room at once. Barlow wondered how much this was for his protection and how much it was for that of the man himself and of

144

the other Terrestrians present. It would work both ways. The medical team wore anticontamination gear for a double purpose. Though guarded by shots, he had never been exposed to Earthly infections. And they had never been on Mars, the complex soil of which could incite some virulent allergies.

Barlow turned his head from the examination couch on which he lay to watch the sneezer leave. That was how he noticed something else. Rebellion and xenophobic suspicion and anger awoke in him.

"The Styrofoam box I had!" he burst out. "I was told to leave it on that stand! Now it's gone!"

"I took it to the lab with his clothes," a rubicund youth admitted with puzzled contrition.

"Then we stop everything till you bring it back, Will," Klein said firmly. "Tim, it's just that everything that comes from Mars still has to be checked for contaminants. A little silly, but it's the law. I can't say for absolute certainty, but I don't expect that anyone around here would steal anything from you."

In another minute, the box was in Barlow's hands. He took the fragment out, and still suspicious, examined it very carefully, and then grunted with relief. No question. Nothing had changed.

"The famous *Exofact*—isn't it?—from Moeris Lacus," Klein said.

Barlow nodded. "I guess I shouldn't have it with me. Marspro scientists should be studying it closer than we could."

"We can seal the box in your presence, right now, Barlow," Klein said. "Doctor Henry Thorne, top man at their lab in Texas, will have it in his hands by armed courier within two hours."

Tim, still sitting up tensely, scowled.

"All right," he gruffed at last. "I guess that's about as safe as anything can be done. So do it! I'll watch."

There was considerable delay, while someone fetched necessary means. Barlow saw red seals affixed along the lid crevice of the Styrofoam case. Then the whole was placed in a metal box, which was then locked and sealed again. Solemnly, a signed receipt was even taped to his bare shoulder, since, being naked, he had no pocket in which to put it. Barlow experienced an unfamiliar thrill of power.

"Now, may we proceed with your examination?" Klein asked.

"Go ahead," Barlow answered.

Another needle was jabbed lightly into his arm.

"You should quiet down," Klein explained. "Some things we have to do might be a bit painful."

As Barlow sank backward on the couch, and began to drift toward unconsciousness, another young medic spoke up, "Hey, Skyclimber! Are you gonna lead us to the far stars, too?"

Barlow chortled in amused disgust. "Aghh, Red Tharsis! What the hell—are—you—talking—about?" he commented vaguely.

## 21

Tim Barlow had only a few fuzzy impressions of the next twenty hours: a lifting, and a clatter which might have been from the rotor of a helicopter. Beyond that, after more soft unawareness, nothing but some moments of jerky movement. Then, once more, the deep, all-enveloping blank.

When he finally began to emerge toward stable wakefulness, it was to a moist touch on his cheek.

He was still too weary to life his eyelids. But what was being said soaked into his mind without any effort. The first voice was masculine: "Bussing the guy when he's still out, Pen? But you have your own, rather professional approaches. Wups—I didn't mean to make the compliment left-handed! Doesn't an almost three-year age-difference make him sort of young for you?"

Another quick, husky voice, feminine and pleasant, responded to this playful tease in kind, and without the least annoyance: "Ronnie dear, when you philosophize, you only contradict yourself, canceling out everything you've said before. If I'm professional anything, at least I'm not very medical—he's had enough of that! And didn't it take some real, earnest effort on my part to get us declared his personal advisors? So why shouldn't I claim a minor fringe benefit, when he's the current big symbol, and popular driving force behind the revived thrust into space? Especially when audio-visual projection is momentarily shut off! Wowie, though! Didn't I say this before? What a splendid, alien being he is! If he's a little freakish and funny-looking, that's evidently no detriment after all—instead, it's mostly a help! Glory! He's like a big, dry-stalk-tall bird of that bizarre desert, from which he first yelled out his courage and insults and exhortations! Savage, brown, spindly, and magnificent! Yes, Homo sapiens martis! As far as I'm concerned, they can turn on A-V projection anytime now, though somebody may want to edit!"

Tim felt warm, moist pressure again, now on his lips, and more emphatic than before.

"Um-hm," the same voice continued. "Rise up, Timothy! Oh, oh! I suppose you heard some of what I just said? Well, accept it as honest approval. And you should be examining your new scene in detail."

Barlow had opened his eyes. For an instant, he had an almost explosive impulse to flee somewhere, but decided at once that it was ridiculous. He blinked to clear his vision. There was brightness and whiteness, contrasted with objects and fabrics of various vivid colors. He had to remember again, that walls were flat and firm here, not curved and pressurized, as on Mars. There was a row of windows, and a glass door, open to a garden terrace. He felt a warm breeze, and saw lush greenery under that brilliant, outer sunlight. He didn't even know the words for everything.

Only after a quick, intense scrutiny of this much, did his gaze return to the two human presences. The man, standing near, the girl, with pale, amber eyes, sitting on the edge of the bed. His memory groped back at some brief, fleeting images.

"I think I've seen you people before," he stated rather coldly, and in a dry, whispery rasp, which wasn't quite his normal tone; he hadn't spoken for many hours, and in the unfamiliar atmosphere his vocal cords

148

had roughened somewhat.

"Once, anyway," the man responded. "For about a minute. When you came back to Arsia Base, after rounding Mars. We both spoke a few words to you on video."

"I'm sorry if I didn't answer with much," Barlow said. "Your names are?"

"Lorenz," the girl told him. "Ron. And I'm his sister, Pen—or Penny." She was standing, now.

The Lorenzes had momentarily lost a lot of their easy ebullience, as if, somehow, by the way he had spoken, Barlow had awed them a little. He studied Ron: Not nearly as tall as himself, of course, yet fair-sized, muscular, lightly and casually clad, his russet beard neat, his smile waiting as if to find out what best his lips should say next—from a mind that was older, and far wiser than his own, Barlow was sure.

Barlow's attention shifted back to the girl, and lingered: smooth skin, fresh and lovely beyond his experience. Auburn hair, and those matching amber eyes, in which amusement was returning, plus—it seemed to him—depth after depth of enigma, that mocked him and yet led him on, almost more so than all the exotic things now around him. She wore a simple blouse, slacks and sandals, in which the colors of terrestrial trees, sky, and sunlight were mingled, as if she was a personification of the Earth. To Barlow, she could seem small, though she was taller than most of the women on Mars.

He retained his cool wariness, and formality.

"Lorenz," he pronounced. "I think I remember that too. A nice name, particularly as a clearer sound in this denser air. I'm glad to know you, Ron and Penny."

He shook their hands.

"I suppose you are here to tell me what next to do," he said further. "A kindness to a stranger who isn't

149

quite sure. Though I'd like to keep some choice."

Barlow swung his large feet to the floor.

"Is there anything for me to wear, besides my skin and this receipt-paper?" he demanded. "I'd like to get up."

Ron Lorenz hastened to assist, as Barlow left the bed, and walked about unsteadily, and naked.

"Here in the closet, Tim," Ron said. "Everything we got for you should fit. Hah—wait. Some of these goddam fastenings can bug me, too."

Barlow suffered valeting with controlled patience, though he had gotten over much of his scared and humble diffidence, deciding that he was going to be somewhat his own man, and not led around too much anymore, even in all this wondrous newness.

He rejected the flowered shirt that Ron proffered, choosing, instead, the homespun linen one that Agnes had made for him; it, too, had been hung in the closet, along with two of his Mars coveralls. Anyhow, just then, he felt like asserting his loyalty, both to Mars and to Agnes Frost. Where was she, and what had happened to her?

Sandaled, and in slacks, and wearing Agnes' gift proudly, he loomed above his not too dissimilarly clad companions.

"What is this place, all around here?" he asked, still almost brusquely.

"It was a small, private rest home," Ron Lorenz answered. "Taken over for you, now. Here in New York State."

"It has nice grounds," Penny put in. "Maybe we should apologize for the high, enclosing wall. But everybody figures you'll need a quiet retreat, sometimes."

"All right—can I try walking out there?"

"Of course, Tim."

She moved to take his arm, but he clumped heavily,

150

cautiously, determinedly past her, toward the open door and the outer sunblaze. His way to approach difficulties was alone.

Though everything seemed miraculously marvelous to him, he remained half phobic about going out into the free atmosphere, under the dazzling open sky, without even wearing an air hood. He glanced apprehensively up and around, trying to get rid of an ingrained, automatic, and once necessary habit of self-protection.

So there he stood, his long, thin legs spraddled wide for stability, his shadow stretching, like that of a sundial pointer, across the cemented, bluestone flagging. He made a fantastic, comical, and yet commanding figure to his immediate watchers, and to all those others, far and near, who continued to watch him through another unobtrusive camera eye, set on the balcony rail above.

At last a happy smile crossed his narrow, swarthy face.

"Nice and hot," he rasped appreciatively.

"Careful—you could get yourself nicely sunburned," Ron warned.

"I don't think so," Barlow denied. "Even at a greater distance from the sun, ultraviolet light comes through the thin Martian air stronger than here."

Penny finally did manage to take his arm. He let her lead him forward, until he jerked back at the flagged-terrace edge.

"Is it truly okay to step on the—lawn?" he questioned.

"Well, sure—certainly!" Ron replied in the mild wonder of one confounded by a query too unlikely to believe. "Oh—outside these walls, there are signs on many lawns. But, here . . ."

"Uh huh—I've seen on video," Barlow said. "Only —at this gravity? Crushing life? Back home, we try to respect anything that manages to grow in the open. It deserves consideration."

"Barlow, what a character you are!" Ron snorted. "Walk on the grass, and it springs right back up. It grows like hell. Ever hear of lawnmowers?"

"Yuh—I guess. I've seen pictures."

"Take off your sandals, Tim," Penny urged in sudden inspiration. "Try it barefooted. It's better like that."

As he hesitated, she knelt down impulsively, and unfastened the straps, as if he were a child. Part of his drive to retain personal independence seemed to have slipped his mind; anyway he didn't protest.

"Now, kick! Okay . . . ." Penny sluffed off her own sandals, picked up both pairs, and took his arm again. "So here we go. Fun, huh?"

"Hey—yuh! Cool, prickly, soft! Hey . . . ."

An expression of beatific happiness crossed his gaunt features.

From far off, as if at a sports stadium a couple of kilometers distant, a triumphant game play had just happened, there was a prolonged and tremendous cheering, whistling, and clapping. It wasn't very noticeable here in the walled garden. Barlow himself could not have related it to his barefooted adventure with the grass, and how a tiny portion of his television audience —as a sample—was responding, while they watched and heard him in the large screen and associated sound system which had been set up in the actual stadium of the university nearby.

He shuffled on with as much joyful fascination as— say—a storybook Aladdin, on first entering the caves of treasure. Now he bent over roses. Next, an intermittently hopping robin, hunting earthworms on the lawn, caught his rapt attention. Then his head cocked to the trill of another bird—a distant dipping and soaring of notes.

152

"A meadowlark, I think," Ron Lorenz stated.

"Where?"

"Who knows? Too far to tell . . ."

Barlow was a little afraid of going under the first great tree—a copper beech with huge, spreading branches. But he shuffled on, resolutely. He scrutinized the smooth, gray bark in minute detail. This, before he reached out his calloused hand warily, first to touch the trunk with a fingertip, but at last—with the same slow doubt and wonder—with his entire palm.

*"Man!"* Barlow pronounced.

Into that single, spontaneous syllable, he seemed to concentrate all the joyful appreciation of natural things of many lifetimes.

"Hello, Tree!" he added. In his whispery, intense tone, unmistakably, there was both humor and love.

Once more, the far background crowd applause lifted and lingered.

Barlow leaned against the great trunk for a full minute, alone with the copper beech, of which he didn't even know the name, meditating and communing, as if he were at the goal of an old longing and a colossal pilgrimage.

At a five-meter remoteness behind him, Ronald and Penelope Lorenz stood close together, inspired to a private whispering: "So what's your devious comment, Elder Brother?"

"Just now I'm liberated from all that, Pen. We could all borrow some of this guy's artless enthusiasm. And not just for grim old Mars where heroes struggle, or for cozy and pleasant cylinder planetlets. Or even for strange, lovely worlds in other solar systems."

"You think I'm not borrowing? Such a huge child! Still, he's hard and bright, and he knows and can handle such a lot that we don't and haven't. But is this the kid that drove some kind of car all the way around

153

unexplored Mars—*alone?* It's confusing . . . . Ronnie —look—here I am, holding his sandals! Am I his mother? I feel old!''

"Oh oh! You couldn't be gone on him, Pen?''

"Haven't I said right out that I was? Ever since we first saw him in the desert.''

"No, you're not, Penny. It's just the vast novelty. I can't imagine *you*, Sister Dear.''

"Touché—perhaps. I won't argue *that* point, now. But, on another subject, what do you, as a good PR man, think, from what you've observed so far? Is he still the Big Hope for pushing the cylinder worlds idea, which, from every common human viewpoint, makes the most sense? Though, elsewhere, there's a regret . . . .''

"More than ever, certainly, Pen. It's a little oblique, considering his probable Martian loyalties. But his doing was what really got the drive into space fired up again—recapturing public attention with his legendary courage, individualism, and just enough freakishness. Damn, I kind of love that guy myself! And there's Agnes Frost, who just might have even bigger appeal. It depends a lot on what this pair say and do, not only in the next few hours, when they're supposed to meet the public directly, but a couple of months hence. Will interest in them have staying power, or will too many people think again that they're being asked to support too much? There are a lot of delicate imponderables and uncertainties, including what to do about those poor wretches left on Mars.''

"Um-hm, Ron. Barlow and Frost . . . . They're being manipulated. And studied like bugs. Is that nice?''

"Here we go again, Penny. I suppose we all get manipulated, one way or another. Maybe we shouldn't ask so many half-rhetorical moralistic questions. They have too many conflicting facets of opinion for me! Of

154

course Frost and Barlow are being studied, not only from the brain-wave patterns and other data the medicos took, but from every gesture, sound, or movement they make—by everybody! Because people are curious and interested, naturally. So what's wrong with that? And if these two fantastic strangers were told everything we feel and know, right out from the start—if there was even time for that—they'd probably freeze up, go inhibited, so that even their own simply joy would be spoiled. Besides, they might be less help in what we believe should happen."

Pen Lorenz proved much of her brother's words with her own social instincts, when she whispered urgently: "Ron—sh-h-h!"

# 22

Tim Barlow had turned back toward them. Now he was scowling, as if some portion of their thoughts had reached him. Actually, it was only that, from under the mass of fascination that had been thrust into his senses and wits, a deep, personal concern had finally managed to emerge.

"What happened to Agnes?" he demanded roughly. "Isn't she somewhere here? Why don't I see her?"

"Calm it, Tim," Ron Lorenz told him. "We can't imagine things being any less than fine for Agnes. She was flown out to California—west side of the continent —for fair distribution of our two major celebrities. It wasn't hers nor our decision, but don't you agree it's right? You can probably talk to her and see her in a minute, whenever you want to. Right now, though, I'm reminded that you haven't had any solid nourishment for more than a full day! So shouldn't we go back in the house and see what's for lunch?"

Barlow nodded, amiably now. He was visibly tired, as if the strong gravity was wearing him down. He reached inside his shirt, tore the *Exofact* receipt from its adhesive fastenings to his bare shoulder, took it out, glanced at it, shrugged, and stuffed it in a side pocket of his slacks. It was as if the *Exofact,* now in competition with other concerns that had been thrust into his mind, had lost much of its importance to him.

Pen Lorenz had taken his arm again, but neither said anything. Ron had hurried ahead to see about food; but now he came back out on the terrace.

"Yes, a call for Tim Barlow!" he hailed cheerfully. "Agnes Frost is on the visiphone! She seems in a hurry!"

Barlow was shoved gently into a small room beside his bedroom, and the door was closed behind him, perhaps for privacy. Agnes' grin was there in the phosphors of the videotube.

"Sit, sit, Timmy," she urged. "Talk to me! You *look* okay."

"I'm fine, Ag. I was worried about you. Then they told me—California—"

"Oh, I'm absolute A-one-plus now, Timothy! After all those tests and the sleep, and not knowing what was going on! But—dust devils!—it's all turned super! I was up before dawn—the clock reads earlier here than where you are—and how lovely everything was—is! What a marvelous planet to be on! It's hard to walk far yet; but Maggie and George McKay—I used to talk to them some from Olympus, after you got Earth-folks wanting to do that—are officially looking after me, besides being my friends! They tell me I'm going for a drive to Los Angeles in an hour, to see all the crowds, and speak to them, even! Oh, I'm frightened, but it's a thrilling fright! And George and Maggie have a big, tough, nice, handsome associate named Len Ross!"

"Ag, should I come to you? Or do you want to come here?"

"Timmy—I—I'll come to you—if you want . . . . Or you could come this way. But I'm told we're more useful, and better situated for all these Terrestrians, if we're separated for a while. I want you close—only—"

"Yuh—there's this Len Ross," Barlow prompted in wry anger.

157

"Well—yes—a little. Dammit—you're jealous, Tim! Ha ha! I think I enjoy that! I hear there's somebody named Pen Lorenz! Also, that she's something extra . . . . Look, Timothy—I'm speaking plaintively—neither of us have had a chance at any exciting social life before! So, perhaps . . . . But, beyond that, we're alike —the only two there are! So we need to hang on— anyhow, I to you . . . . Still—Just at present . . . ."

"Sure, Ag." Not very deep down, Barlow was relieved. "I know. We gotta stay in touch. But you keep out of serious trouble—hear?"

"You likewise, Timmy. Don't let anybody . . . Tim, they want me now. 'Bye."

Barlow grinned crookedly to himself.

A minute later, Ron Lorenz drew him to a table and chairs in a bright dining room, and spoke quickly, "Dr. Henry Thorne just called too, Tim. You can call him back right now, or whenever you're free. He just wanted to report that they've been working on the fragment you brought from Moeris Lacus ever since it arrived at the lab yesterday. They agree that it must be from some other solar system. From atomic ratios, they rate its age at about seventy million years. It will take at least a month of intensive testing and tracing just to begin to construct a schematic of its inner structure. But they think they might get a modulated signal out of it, by passing a slight current through one pair or another of its leads. Thorne said they've already gotten a very slight chirp. He was quietly excited and anxious to keep going."

Barlow felt an eager questioning. But being involved in so much else, himself, he pushed it aside.

"Then I shouldn't bother Thorne now; let him do his job," he said. He sniffed the air. "Smells good! Our promised lunch?"

Barlow found he was ravenous. Knives and forks

158

were familiar to him, of course. But the heavy gravity after so much zero-g in space, on top of his lifelong acquaintance with only 0.38-g on Mars, was making him inept in the manipulation of tableware. Well, he was getting over his sensitivities. He was glowing to himself again, inside and out. The food was great, far beyond any criticisms his very limited experience could have provided, and not too unfamiliar. All of Earth, and being on it, and getting along all right, helped. And there was Penny—minute by minute, more and more, she was seeming the best of many wonderful things. Her smiles, the friendly shine that seemed to emanate from her, even though she spoke little, the memory of the touch of her lips, and some things she had said, then; it was all getting plainer to him, softening his wary harshness, pushing—without pushing!—at his own simplicity.

"It's good wine, Tim Barlow, you seem to like it. But maybe three glasses are enough. You have a heavy afternoon just ahead."

# 23

A helicopter swished and whistled down onto the garden lawn. The party of three boarded and lifted off. Barlow was all eyes, looking down on fields, highways, and fantastic, green woods. The little towns were dustless, clean, bright, and they seemed big to him. Wondrous! After thirty minutes, they landed at a small aviation field, and switched to a car—a black, official limousine —with four motorcycles escorting.

"Couldn't I drive?" Barlow asked naively. "It doesn't look very different from what I've done a lot of."

"No, Barlow; not here, not you, not now," Ron Lorenz said firmly.

"We should refresh your memory about Earthly history, Tim," Penny stated. "Yes, we have a beautiful world, I think. It's true that circumstances have been much improved for people generally, since that mini-nuclear holocaust, some years back. Sometime, you must tell us how it seemed from Mars. But we were here! I still get nightmares from that time; how I left the City with Ron and our parents, and was too terrified even to cry! Somehow, reason got scared back into place. Ocean resources were internationalized and jointly developed, instead of various countries trying to stake out claims, as they had done. The Inter-Nation Congress is about as fair and impartial as any such body

160

can—realistically—be expected to be. And it's tough against polluters and wasters of what must be conserved, as every country knows and wants, so there are few offenders.

"So far, fine. But there's always that memory and danger hanging over us. It's not that people are basically evil; most are not. Yet among so many billions with differing viewpoints, it is mathematically certain that conflicts of opinion will develop, and sometimes become threatening, particularly since human nature has always been excitable. So the cry must always be for *peace*. We're sure you agree, Timothy. The uses of courage and fury have to be in constructive—not destructive—directions."

Barlow did not notice that Penelope Lorenz seemed to speak as if from a prepared script, withal a very benign one, or that Ronald Lorenz now took over in a second phase of the same earnest process. "And it is right and natural that mankind should be fledged from the nest of Earth, Tim. Bunched together on one world, we could become extinct in a single blast. But there are wider reasons, even poetic ones—and not only to find room for our increasing numbers. Maybe our ultimate destiny is even to spread across the Galaxy. A beginning has been made on Mars. You know all about that. It should continue. Yet, an easier, simpler, less costly, more-appealing means has been planned to operate concurrently. You know what it is, too. A new, small prototype cylinder world is in preparation. To accommodate only five hundred inhabitants, when a full-scale type will take twenty thousand. It is an old but magnificent idea. People will live in an entirely Earthlike environment, but with total weather control. There would be lush, beautiful gardens all around the fantastic, upward-curving landscape. The centrifugal gravity will approximate the terrestrial, so there will be no problem

161

of bone-and-muscle weakening. Distance from the sun will be approximately that of the terrestrial orbit—not too near or far—not giving too little, or too much, warmth.

"It is a great solution for many things, Barlow. The prototype will be built in Earth orbit from Earthly materials. But survey teams are already on the Moon, to prepare a tapping of that easier source. There could be any number of these cylinder worlds—planetlets, as we are beginning to call them—providing more and more living room. One can even imagine that, in some distant age, *all* of the substance of the natural, solar planets and their satellites will be converted into these separate habitations. They will form a vast, discrete ring, flowing around the sun as Saturn's Rings circle Saturn. They will support a population of many trillions. Sure, that is only a dream, now; but we must make a start. That much is within our powers! Our youth, in particular, is sick of negativism and stagnation. And I suspect that any kind of beings must use constructively whatever knowhow it has, or there will be mischief. Scientists who understand all aspects of this plan agree that it is not only the wave of the future, but of now. I hope that you will also agree, Tim Barlow. Your support would be a big help."

Barlow had listened to his companions with only a fraction of his attention, and with no adverse reaction. To him it had seemed a kind of gentle, background babble, suggesting large and thrilling images, while most of his mind was avidly on immediate Earthly marvels: houses and trees flicking past, the sudden emptiness of the road ahead, the increasing numbers of persons shouting and waving from its sides, the gray outlines of huge buildings getting nearer, and, presently, to the right, the glitter of water.

"The Hudson River," Pen said.

162

Soon, the car was moving along slowly between walls of structures and massed people. Panic stirred in Barlow again, because of the crush and noise, and the running, crowding, shouting figures. His own age, his own kind? They were shaggy, sort of, and bold. Built squarer, broader—even the slim ones—than he was. And there was power in them. Slapping the car's hood, flanks and windows with their palms. Though they let the vehicle go through, until it reached some central square that police had, so far, kept open. But then they closed in, for the moment almost with an ominous quiet.

Eyes were level with Barlow's own. Strange eyes. Close. Meeting his gaze. Girl eyes among them . . . . And the shouting became truly immense: "Skyclimber! Big Voice—welcome! You're *home*, Marsborn! We brought you *home!* Hey, Skyclimber! Are you going to show us the way even to the stars? Open up! We love you, Big Voice! You belong to us! We're yours! Open, Skyclimber!"

Gripped by a spasm of agoraphobia, Barlow might have fled, had there been a place.

"It's all right, Tim, I think," Penny said tensely from beside him. "They're for us, especially for you. They mean what they say. If you could talk to them a little? Maybe it shouldn't be much! A few calm words. There's that little lever on the door."

Barlow moved it. The window rolled down, and hands reached in, touching, grabbing. The door was unlatched and pulled open. Half of a sleeve of Barlow's shirt of Mars-grown linen was torn off. For an instant, he almost had to flail out with his fists.

"Easy!" somebody in the crowd forefront shouted. "Goddammit, Vinnie—stop! Give him a chance to get his legs out! Back, you buggy souvenir snatchers. You crapheads, give him room to stand! There you are, Skyclimber!"

163

A girl in vivid green-and-gold shorts and halter, tried to buss him on the mouth, missed, got his ear instead.

Amid the whistling, shouting cheering and clapping, Tim Barlow remained placid only because he was dazed —and pinned in the press of people. Yet he was—in some way—happy!

"Back, everybody, back!" the impromptu leader was yelling. "Timothy David Barlow, you don't have to walk, here! Or ride—except on our shoulders! Hup, men, hup! Across to the rostrum!"

A band played some weird, fierce, jingly-jangly music.

Barlow's hand was shaken by some older, stolider men. Mayor, President, Senator? He didn't really listen to the words.

Then he was at a microphone on the platform. Pen and Ron Lorenz were somehow standing behind him. The numb euphoria of being honored primitively, furiously, almost savagely—of sudden, huge, noisy celebrity to which he must somehow respond—pushed down hard on Barlow, and became his worst spasm of dread, as he heard the thundering applause, and saw the awesome expanse of faces. He was of the empty wilderness of another world. He had never seen a real crowd before, and this one seemed beyond mere crowds. It was more like an infinity of human force—a juggernaut that could crush him or anything. Barlow's body was quivering. He couldn't be an utter fool and run; nor could he, anymore, remove this horde from his sight and hearing by snapping a switch. So he *must* face up. That was his way, wasn't it? Or at least his code and legend; certainly his brag! He had to make it true!

Ron Lorenz whispered at his shoulder, as if afraid of what he might say, "Tell them, Tim. A phrase or two will be enough. Nothing furious. Your honest feeling about Earth, now, maybe. Though there's something

164

mighty in front of you, and not altogether good, you're mostly among friends.''

Far in the background, a small group was yelling, "Mars fools, die on Mars . . . ." But these thin cries were almost submerged.

The showman in Barlow became subdued. And his fright sank away, beneath a self-anesthetizing glow, as if he were chief priest at some primitive orgy. But his feelings were very sincere.

"My shouting is over," he said. "Yes, I'm Barlow. You brought me home. So I'm here with you—rescued. My thanks should be spoken quietly—for all you have given me. Home. My long dream. Earth, the Blue Star in the Martian sky. You can't know how beautiful it looked from there. Or how much more beautiful and miraculous it is to me, now, even after less than two full days of being here. Trees, grass, sky, sound; smell of growing things. Vital colors; new friends I begin to know. A world where I can at last walk about naturally —belonging here. Do you understand what it is like, always to wear an air helmet while afield, just to sustain one's breath?

"Believe me, I have known a more difficult planet, and am surely one who can appreciate the difference and the marvel of Earth. I didn't ask to be born on Mars; though I appreciate it, too, it is now my lost past. I am where I belong. I am here to catch up on all that I missed. And to study and learn—attend a university. To blend, become one of you, not strange or special, but like anybody from anywhere.

"Let's cherish our Earth. Let's keep it, conserve it, love it, not defile it, or trouble it with terrible angers, as has often happened in the past. When it seems so easy to be at peace in such a beautiful world, to calm silly rages in friendship and cooperation. My eyes have been opened to Earth, as perhaps yours now are, a little

165

more. Though it is less easy to honor what one has always had.

"I am told that there are big, renewed plans for going into space. I am glad. It is right that we should do this. The adventurer in us must be served and satisfied, or it may turn sour and destroy us. And we are too much for just one world—even Earth. But I am also told that, in the planetlets, Earth will be the pattern of the way of living. We will copy its beauty, and take it with us. That reassures me. It is also right. Friends, let's do it!

"So—always in peace—I guess that's all I want to say, now."

Barlow stood there, a great, gangling, fantastic figure, under the early-afternoon sunshine. His simple, final line, had a note of special and startling humility, and its honesty projected outward to the throng. He had mouthed much of the promptings of the Lorenzes, because he believed in them as they did. But the essence of what he had said most, had surely also been brewing in his mind for years on Mars. His throat ached with the depth of his emotion, and its center remained gratitude for being on Earth, and now for a hero's huge adulation. Gratitude—warm, enormous, stunned, simple, wondering, yet uncorrupted, perhaps terribly innocent.

Now, there was an infinitismal instant of silence. Until somebody broke it by yelling: "Skyclimber! Lead us! Strength! Strength!"

And the multitude roared and moved.

If there had been any thought of a question-and-answer sequel to Barlow's speech, it was slammed out of existence by the massiveness of audience size and enthusiasm in expressive action toward its strange idol and his raspy earnestness. Fortunately, this had been foreseen; an escape route had been prepared. There was a short run, with the Lorenzes pulling Barlow, to a small

166

doorway and up a back elevator to the roof of a tall building.

As the helicopter clattered northward, its three passengers listened to a radio-news commentator: "The messages of Barlow and Frost, from their separate locations, were essentially the same. Peace, and endorsement of the cylinder-worlds project. Both speakers were very effective. Agnes Frost had a funny little doll from her childhood. It was made from the husks of corn, grown on Mars. She did a humorous and charming pantomime with it, saying that Terri—for terrestrial—was also glad to be on Earth at last."

Barlow's grin struggled to become even happier. In these last minutes he had been smiling so hard that his cheeks ached.

Back in the quiet of his refuge, Barlow tried calling Agnes at once. It took a while to get her on the visi, and when she was finally there, she poured forth with an ecstatic word flood:

"Timmy—hi! We've got a funny kind of faithfulness going, haven't we? I rush to call you, and things get jammed because you're calling me at the same time! We did it, didn't we? One media guy said we 'sent 'em spinning'! And now Maggie and George McKay and Len Ross want to show me the Pacific Ocean! For tomorrow—guess you know?—you went all the way around Mars, so they figure it's appropriate for you to go all around Earth as well! But it won't be just you— I'm included! Except I'll go west—Tokyo, first— while you'll go east to London. Dust devils, Tim! I've got to run in a minute, and wash my face before— Tim, are you all right? Truly having fun? Timmy, say something!"

Barlow spread his hands, helplessly.

"Yuh, I was meaning to, Ag," he laughed. "If you gave me a chance. I'm doing okay, myself. Yes, the

167

Lorenzes just told me about the trips. Just so you don't . . . . Ah—what the hell, though, eh? We might talk tomorrow. Anyhow, very soon."

"Sure, Timmy. Remember! 'Bye."

Barlow had a lingering moment of amazement and concern about her. Was his warm admiration somehow laced with pity? His ache of jealousy was dim and fading. He hadn't noticed whether she was wearing his gold-nugget necklace. But she hadn't mentioned seeing that his shirt was torn. Agnes Frost. Tall, tough, serious girl from the slopes of Olympus Mons. Now a magnificent, ecstatic, frivolous transformation! But wasn't it far too fast, maybe? Scattering her wits, as perhaps his own were scattered? Too much else was in his head; the couldn't hold onto the thought.

As he left the small room where the visiphone was, Penny touched his arm. "Whiskies and soda to celebrate. Ron is bringing his. Wait . . . ."

"Sure, Pen. You know what? Ag just said they were going to show her the Pacific Ocean. Here we must be very close to the Atlantic. A long-time yearning of mine —to be right on the beach of a real ocean."

Penny frowned, then brightened. "Guess we can manage that. Though even private beaches in summer aren't such good places for anybody so completely in the public eye. But up the coast, there's a big stretch of sand reserved for oceanographic research. For you, Tim Barlow, I'm sure it can be arranged. So, tonight when it's quiet? Now, after our drinks, you ought to rest."

# 24

So it was done. There were just the two of them, and the unobtrusive helicopter pilot, who landed them on the deserted beach, and then lifted his craft away to wait at the oceanographic station's landing platform.

Barlow stood staring, and sniffing the wind. Before him lay the splendid, craved, dreaded mystery of lonesome ocean, under the high-riding, bizarre Moon—nothing like the little, chunky, hurrying Phobos, or the dim, laggard speck of Deimos. He looked out over the wild surf. All was new to him. Those great, slow, rustling, sobbing, foam-crested waves.

Plus so much more, besides, that was hungered for—that he should have had!—clotted together in another kind of wave of thought, feeling, poetry, and muted song, until maybe it was too much catching up for all at once. Making, in spite of joy, a sickness in his gut and head.

Barlow wouldn't remember all of that night. Only the disjointed—yet joined—lovely, achieving fragments. With lovely Pen the focus, the personification of it all. On beautiful Earth.

"Hurry along, Savage!" she urged. Then, as he broke into a kind of shambling run, "No—not so fast!"

Sandals chucked, they walked to where the water came to ankle-depth, and then receded, like slow pulse beats. And then on to a stretch of sand between Moon-shadowed rocks, where cool wetness and the smell of sea called to him like billions of years of lost ancestry.

"My first chance to swim," he rasped. "I'll try it now."

"But you can't," Penny protested. "Anyway, it's too soon; you haven't acclimated nearly enough. Tim—don't! You could drown! You should be afraid!"

"So I *am* afraid. But I've been much more scared, and have done crazier things before."

He was remembering the misty, cryogenic cauldron of the Martian antarctic. There had been a stubborn, defiant urge, then wild triumph. In the sensuous summer night of this far gentler planet, he sloshed on, into deeper water.

"Tim, we're wearing clothes. Oh, well—how can that matter! At least let me show you . . ."

The ocean bore him up, buoyantly but insecurely. He gasped, sputtered, coughed, flailed out. Then her hands were on him, guiding.

"Relax, Tim. It's really easy. Extend yourself. See—you're floating. Now, next . . . ."

They went to shore once, to shed their thin but encumbering garments. Back in the sea, they laughed, sputtered, played.

"I'm absorbing moisture into my dry bones," he said.

Then, a little later: "Pen, you're more than anything. Where are the words, even? Damn! I love you!"

The raspy rustle of his voice had also taken on the hoarseness of lust and tenderness. He touched velvet flesh under velvet water. Curve of breast and inner thigh. Close, close . . . . The all of her in suave moonlight. A momentary vision as they hurried to the damp shore. For the necessary, the imperative . . . . With no one else around.

Cry out silently, reach, clutch, plunge, penetrate,

cling. Penetrate again. Fury and delight for self, trying to find greater depths or heights. Or an end of loneliness ages long. In her—Penny. Yes—nice name—Penny Lorenz . . . .

Until, in tiredness and somewhat alone again, though he still mounted her, he raised his eyes and noticed the arrangements of narrow, wire-linked slats, rolled out and mounted vertically on the higher, dry beach, to inhibit and check by friction the wind-blown movement of dry sand and prevent its encroachment on the water's edge. A sand fence.

"Pen," he said. "That fence. It's just like what is used at Arsia Base to keep the dust back."

He let her up to see. She looked long at it as if trying to reach and grasp a fragment of his past. Then she searched the sky.

"There, Tim!" and she pointed. "Your Red Star. Mars."

The Earthly air was quite clear tonight. But its density, and the Moon glow, made that ruddy spark, and the stars, seem faint to him. He studied his birth world quizzically, meditatively. This was the first time he had seen it from here. It was like many memories shrunken to a remote speck, as if there was no connection.

In contrast with the vividness of Now, it was an effort to grope back: Gotch. The Thorgersens. Marie. Leon. Everett. Bessie. They were like hazy legends. Loved and admired, but fading in his mind. As the idea of making a sort of second Earth of Mars was fading: It was an obsolete, overambitious scheme, offside from the reasonable path of future history. Mars was too harsh, too far from the sun. The planetlets were a gentler, far better way.

Still, those old friends must be taken care of! Though their changed flesh and bones obstructed their return to

171

Earth. Still they must be plentifully supplied with what they needed to make them free out there! Everybody would agree that this was right. It would always be done. But then Barlow had a chilly insight. The past ups and downs of the Mars Project proved something. Public support was uncertain. And if there were other, more urgent, more reasonable, more exciting demands on attention and funds, it was easy for people to forget. Nor could there be too much blame, crying out of stinginess. Taxes hurt. And what were a hundred or so fools and fanatics, way out on a worthless planet? The effect and cost were too great, too fruitless, the distance too large, the occasions for contact still too intermittent. And now, perhaps, there were even the stars to dream about! Oh, some supplies would be sent, but never enough, and in diminishing quantities. Slowly those friends would die off out there. The domes would fall; the dust would drift over them; the Martian desert would conquer. Barlow quivered. Rage and sorrow were in him. But then, in love with this new life that had come to him, he rationalized. What should he do? Waste his days in futile weeping? Bah! That was not the way, on Mars. They had gambled high by going there, with full knowledge that they might perish. But everybody died. Mars had not been his choice, as it had been theirs. He had escaped it. Life was unbelievably good to him now, and—by Red Tharsis—he would live out whatever more it gave him! Let the memories fade, if they must.

Penny Lorenz had felt his momentary trembling. "Tim—what?"

"Eh—not much," he laughed. "Even thinking back is difficult."

"I love you, you crazy, wild, *strong* stranger."

"Not any more than I love you! And you're also strong, Pen."

172

"Yes—I s'pose I am—in my terrestrial way. But we have to look to you for special strength. Hold me a minute more, Tim, because privacy might come hard from now on. And we'd better find our wet clothes soon, and get out of here. Because tomorrow, early . . . ."

# 25

The special plane was swift and quiet. In London, Paris, Rome, Berlin, Athens, Cairo and onward, Barlow spoke out his gratitude for being on bounteous Earth; he exhorted for peace, and for the taking of the terrestrial environment into space, in the advancing and ambitious cylinder-world project, which, thanks, largely to him, and to Agnes Frost speaking elsewhere, was winning international support. It was all a fine, popular theme; Barlow was very earnest about it; the crowds continued to be huge and enthusiastic. If Barlow often had to repeat what he had said before, in other cities, did it matter much, yet? With unabated eagerness, people still wanted to see in person this weird, forceful being from another world, and to feel that they took an active, on-scene part in the romantic outward drive he represented. Barlow had his narrow—but thrilling!—escapes from their adulation. He wasn't displeased.

And in Athens, he had a telephone call from Dr. Henry Thorne, chief scientist at the Marspro lab in Texas, that pleased him very much. Thorne spoke with that absolute, casual calm which, of itself, may indicate extreme excitement in prominent researchers who are proud of their cautious restraint before any discovery. "We have been trying again to reach you, Mr. Barlow. We have at last found one input lead in the *Exofact*,

174

which, when a minimal voltage is applied, delivers a definite and repeatable signal at another lead. It is as if, between these two more-than-spiderweb-thin terminals, in the body of this broken shard of something, there is a fragment of a—recording. Or, should I even suggest—of a memory? The signal is modulated, and can be converted into sound. It is not human, of course; our vocal cords could never voice it accurately. It is closer to the buzz and chirp of an insect or other wild creature. I would not think, though, that its origin is likely to be that simple or unintelligent. Now will you listen, please? From our own recording."

Barlow was suddenly, avidly interested. And ashamed of himself for not having gotten around to contacting the scientist before.

"By all means, Dr. Thorne!" he said. "Thank you! I'm all ears!"

It came then—an eerie stridence, with a musical quality mixed in. It was like Thorne had told him; Barlow wished that his phone had a visi-attachment, so that he could better judge the scientist's own reaction from his face. The sound was in three syllables. And Thorne was making it repeat.

"What do you think of it, yourself, sir?" Barlow demanded.

"You found the *Exofact*," Thorne answered. "You should be better able to speculate than anyone. Certainly a thing from many millions of years ago, and light-years away. A machine noise of some kind? Or a word or phrase in some spoken language? If they—it— whatever—had such language? Our groping minds can get caught in their own familiar clichés, and be totally, inconceivably wrong, when trying to grasp such separateness. An echo of some sort, left in a broken scrap of a robot brain? But that's another cliché. I'll stop there."

175

"Is there anything more to tell me, Doctor?"

"Nothing startling. There are still many details of the *Exofact* to probe, but I feel we may have come to the end of surprises, and up against the unrevealing blankness. Of course, you can have our report anytime you want it. Already it is a thousand pages."

"No—Dr. Thorne. Not now. Only if there's something that stands out. But thank you. Let everybody know what you have found."

"And thank *you*, Skyclimber. I call you that, not lightly, but with honor."

It was Ron Lorenz who had hailed Barlow to the telephone. Turning from his chair, Barlow now found both Lorenzes close beside him.

"We sneaked—we listened on the other extensions, Tim," Penny admitted, with an odd confusion of humor, contrition, and awe showing in her face. "We were tempted. We couldn't help it."

"Haw!" Barlow scoffed. "Did I ever say I've got secrets you shouldn't hear? Damn—I wish we'd made a recording so we could play back that sound! It's not so much, maybe, but it's better than—whatever those few, supposed-to-be-numbers-signals were—picked up by radioscopes from star-deep space! Almost—a voice?"

Barlow's hide was tingling with happy excitement at the dark mysteries his efforts had touched further. It was he who had discovered the *Exofact*. And here was more small movement toward the grandest of goals!

"We don't need a recording," Ron said. "The sound is already on the news broadcasts."

They listened. They tried to bend and wrap their tongues and throats around those alien, buzzing chirps. They laughed, they coughed. It was much more difficult than imitating a coyote howl or a frog croak. It was impossible! But they did achieve a vague approximation. Barlow did it best: *"Tzzarr-rrichh-het! Tzzarr-*

*rrichh-het!''*

Three notes, or syllables. The middle one accented—made more forceful than the others—and throat-deep guttural at the end. The first one buzzed at the beginning; the trill at its termination carried over into the start of the second.

When Barlow quietly gave his spiel there in Athens—with a simultaneous translation booming out over the multitude—he found many young persons also imitating, making that eerie sonic-imponderable an emphatic part of their applause, along with English words that everybody had picked up:

*"Tzzarr-rrichh-het!* Skyclimber! Big Voice! Peace! Peace! Barlow! Planetlets . . . even stars! *Tzzarr-rrichh-het!"*

Athens was perhaps the high point—his most joyful day—in his journey around a second world, this time, Earth. But as he moved on eastward, that adulating hail of *"Tzzarr-rrichh-het!"* followed him with undiminished enthusiasm.

So what did it mean—if it meant anything at all? Nobody knew. Except that it was from somewhere in the deep sky. A hint that told almost nothing, but suggested the immeasurable. It was the barest edge of remote enigma, that challenged, puzzled, and put the fire of romance and adventure in the blood. So, naturally, all of that, and more, was what *"Tzzarr-rrichh-het!"* came to mean.

# 26

Small flaws had begun to creep into Timothy Barlow's exalted sense of well-being. The theme of his speeches remained effective; but, for him, his delivery was seeming somewhat stale. He attempted improvements, but didn't come up with much. Routine was wearying him. Faint, insulting cries, such as "Mars freak!" had been with him all the way, and were no trouble. But his favorable popularity was! It confined him largely to hotel suites. Such, as ever, was the affliction of extreme fame; he could scarcely step into any street without being mobbed by shrieking, joyous fans. It had been a big thrill the first few times; but it grew irksome, and it *was* dangerous. Better to sit in his luxurious quarters, with a comfortable glass, and meditate.

It was these meditations that made him feel guilty and neglectful, again. So he began adding a few lines—a sort of footnote—to his public orations. "Of course we must never forget to supply those valiant friends on Mars with whatever they need. They have a hard life on a hard world . . . ."

"Thank you, Tim, for saying that," Penny told him, when he had done it for the first time. She smiled at him.

She didn't have his cynical foresight, based on clear, hindsight experience. And he didn't want to pain her with enlightenment. Well, his extra words might do some good. Help ease his occasional qualms of conscience, for example. But, dammit! They *had* chosen a tough, risky course, which was turning out to be obsolete!

In a city a long way east of Cairo, a sniper took a shot at Barlow. He wasn't hurt; he wasn't even troubled very much; he was learning more about the risks he faced. It might have happened elsewhere, earlier or later, or not at all. The Lorenzes were much more disturbed than he was. He even laughed over Ron's serious suggestion that the sniper might not hate him at all, but admire him very much, and had only sought, in his cracked way, to be honored by his attention.

After he got to Delhi, and had spoken there, he realized that he hadn't talked to Agnes Frost at all, since the start of the trip. He knew that, in her westward course, she had passed north of him, via Vladivostok, Peking, and Moscow.

Penny and Ron were out of the hotel, fronting for him on some news details. He was feeling fine, except for a minor, down-deep irritation or two, one of them being that Agnes hadn't communicated with him either. Now he poured himself a small Scotch—Pen was worried that he was getting a bit much of that. Then he picked up the phone.

"Yuh, Barlow here," he gruffed. "Where is Frost now? Stockholm? Copenhagen? I don't really care where. Just contact her for me."

"We will attempt it, sir," answered the respectful voice. "A few minutes. We will ring you back."

Barlow sat waiting, beginning to fume. Fifteen minutes. Sixteen . . . . The phone rang at last.

It lacked a visiscreen, but Agnes Frost's personality and mood came through with her voice and tone, almost as if she were also visible. Still breathless and excited, with a childlike overreaction to small wonders. Would

179

she ever get over that?

"Timmy, hello! You got ahead of me, calling, again! The phone folks found me in this big, wonderful department store—in Copenhagen, I guess it is. It's full of fine furniture and elegant clothes and jewelry and just about everything! There are all kinds of nice people to wait on me, and all is free, as far as I'm concerned, and I'm being very greedy! Len Ross laughs and says I'm beautiful, though ridiculously frivolous!"

There already were some slivers of crossness inside Barlow's skin, and the way Agnes was bubbling added more.

"I'm beginning to admire your Len Ross a lot," he interrupted, roughly. "He's sure right about the 'frivolous,' Ag."

"Oooh! You don't love me anymore, Timmy!"

"I do, but maybe I shouldn't," Barlow lunged on, as if he couldn't stop. "I wonder if it would bother you to think about your parents a little bit? You, having silly fun like this, when they're coming closer and closer to more hardship, and, likely, eventual death, if somebody neglects to send stores out to Mars sometime."

Now it was Agnes who flared.

"You think I haven't been worried as much about my folks, and everybody else out there, as much as youh have, Barlow?" she snapped. "You think I haven't urged as much that they be always looked after? Well, you're way wrong! I have! And, as for having 'silly' fun, I've only been on Earth for fifteen days, and I do mean to have all the enjoyment of whatever sort I find to like, and not be dragged down by any gloomy, useless worries, even if they are in the back of my mind! About Len—I'm glad to hear you admire him! He is quite a man at that! Big, broad, vigorous, and clever! Professionally, he's a psychologist, dealing mostly with the problems of athletes. But hear this, Skyclimber Timothy

180

Davis Barlow! *Len Ross doesn't entirely reciprocate your admiration!* Not in the least! When this double tour ends, and both our parties join up for the finale in Chicago, you'll probably find out why directly from Lennie!"

Barlow was very startled and contrite.

"Hey, Ag," he stammered. "I never intended—"

"Go lose yourself, Timothy," she told him cheerfully. "I'm busy having silly fun!"

In a minute, though, Barlow wound up chuckling to himself. He'd deserved what he'd gotten. When Penny came back to the hotel suite with her brother, he hugged her appreciatively, and with something like tender apology. Along with Ron, she'd been a self-effacing doer of chores, in a performance of which he seemed to be the center.

"Penny," he urged wryly, gently. "When all this fury has quieted down a little, I'd like for just you and me to get away some place a while."

"We'll see," she answered. Her smile made him miss the shadow in her eyes.

Manila, Sydney, Auckland, Honolulu, and Chicago were Barlow's remaining stops.

# 27

The two around-the-Earth parties had arrived in the same hotel in Chicago at last. The two adjoining suites had had their connecting doors opened to make one. Frost's Maggie and George McKay—Mr. and Mrs.— and Barlow's Lorenzes had known one another for years as fellow radio scopers. Both of these pairs knew Len Ross, another scoper. Now there were brief words and touchings of hands as Frost and the Lorenzes and Barlow and the McKays were mutually presented, in person, though everyone present had, of course, seen all of the others, at least fleetingly, in audio-visual news programs. Similarly, Agnes Frost and Penelope Lorenz, and Timothy Barlow and Lennie Ross, were introduced. These were cheerful, momentary procedures; any possible flickerings of conflict had to be postponed a little.

For now the separated, Marsborn pair came together in a quick, affectionate hug. She was tall; he towered higher. There was hardly a memory of the small tiff between them, though they still had to grope for words, past all that had happened since they had last met.

"Love me, though I've changed, Tim?" she asked, unseriously.

"Always. And we haven't changed that much, Ag."

"Uh huh—you're almost the same old desert spire, Timothy . . . ."

He didn't get the differences in her in great detail. He wasn't attuned to that sort of appraisal. Yet she had certainly smoothened! Her blond hair shone, but retained a loose and pleasant simplicity. And she was in something Earth-green and practical. Her face and skin were more beautiful. She smelled, just slightly, of flowers. And she wasn't gushing with enthusiasms; her poise had settled. And no souvenir grabber had gotten her nugget-necklace; she was wearing it.

Len Ross and Penny Lorenz had been chatting amiably, but now they drifted close.

"Hi, Skyclimber!" Ross said with a broad and friendly smile. "Could we take a minute now for better acquaintance?"

"Hell, yes, Lennie!" Barlow responded in kind.

If a recent buildup of Ross, made to Barlow when Agnes was angry with him, still did anything to prejudice Barlow against Ross, any such effect faded now. For Barlow had the intuitive impression that Len Ross and he were considerably alike; though Len was a foot shorter, a good deal broader, and several years older. Lennie's tanned skin was almost as brown. He had a vitality, a controlled intensity. They shook hands again. Firm, but not too firm. Eye-to-eye; good guy-to-good guy. With possibly pleased and startled liking on both sides!

Only something happened within that handshake. Who made the first spoiling move? To Barlow, it seemed to be Ross. Len's clutch on his fingers got a little tighter. So he tightened his grip, too. Then the tightening continued in alternate steps. Meanwhile their facial expressions darkened in response to some primitive law.

Ross put words into the contest. "A little crude melodramatics, Barlow? Is that what you want?"

He added further pressure. So Barlow added more.

Till, in seconds, they were straining mightily. Barlow wasn't aware of much pain, but he wondered if his finger bones would be crushed. He struggled to squeeze harder.

"Barlow, you're a ridiculous, Martian freak!" Ross growled. "Worse—a self-important, empty bluff! Windbag, fake, phony! From a useless, dead planet! You were actually *brought* here to Earth to promote the Planetlet Program, as a strong leader? Incredible! Where is there any strength in you? You bi-worldly cradle hero—before you could more than scream and mess yourself up! By chance of birthplace, and the tendency of the public to get massively attracted to the sweetly sentimental! Oh, it's very nice of you to express your appreciation for finally being rescued to Earth, and to make some mildly approving remarks about our getting back into space—which you're too timid to mean very much! Now you've been bought off further by milksop-soft living, and a lot of poor slobs kow-towing! You rotten, stupid, bragging Martian deformity! Deserting those fool fanatics you came from, too!"

Ross jerked his hand away with a fierce grunt and a shove that was more like a blow. By now, Barlow's fires were fully lit, and roaring. Here was combat, battle, war, thrust on a peaceable person, though the only armament available was of the most basic sort.

Barlow had his unique background of experience. For instance, a sudden rip in an air dome had been like an enemy to be attacked as quickly and emphatically as possible. But with calculation. How best? And with what adverse circumstances to be countered? Thus, reasoning was ingrained into him, along with watchful habit, making it all a quietly on-guard process, forever ready to move at once, yet without too much time-wasting thought. The present situation, however, didn't

184

involve factors of nature out of control, but another man, obviously muscular. The problem was how to translate his abilities into similarly effective responses to meet the difference. What reserves for this special emergency, stored far back in some minor skull reservoir, did Barlow have? Only some rough-and-tumble exercises and play with Leon Bonard.

Shoved or hit by Len Ross, he hesitated for an imperceptible instant, during which those long-put-away tools of his brain, nerves, and muscles were found and assembled into method. Thought did not go beyond this primitive level, into the higher areas of mind where diplomacy and good sense dwelt so bravely. He was threatened by a hostile presence, much more powerful than himself, who had already flung enraging insults. The only way to overcome the menace to his pride in himself and his native world, and perhaps to his life, was by complete, swift surprise, and unconventionality of means, for he was thin, light, and still weak in this gravity.

Instead of merely shoving back at Ross, he leaped as best he could—and it was not so bad an effort. This fragile other worlder, disguised and gentled by a veneer of terrestrial ways, reverted—to the consternation of all —becoming as one fighting to stay alive in his own deadly land. Ross seemed too startled and off-guard to counterreact, as he was otherwise well able to do.

A bony knee on a long, narrow thigh, arrowed into Ross' belly. He grunted and then thudded heavily backward, with Barlow kneeling on his gut. His "What?" of wondering protest was slurred, for long, calloused thumbs were in both of the corners of his mouth, and were bearing down hard, until he felt the flesh of his lips beginning to tear. But Ross' big hands were free, and he had ample reserves of both strength and courage. His own hard fingers locked onto those fragile wrists, and began to squeeze. So again there was deadlocked struggle, force of will against force of will, with motion limited.

Barlow felt a grinding in his left wrist, as something gave. But he pushed a pain far off—as a trifle. The other wrist was about to go . . . . No matter . . . . Bear down harder . . . . Perhaps Barlow's dimming wits were again in a must-do fantasy from his past. In numerous ways, he had superior training in determination. The lips in his thumb crotches were tearing further. A lot of blood was on his hands, and on his enemy's beard.

And Barlow knew that he was rasping out words: "Put down me, my birth planet, and my first people, will you?!"

It was only then that the others unfroze from startlement, and dragged Barlow off Ross. Total combat time had been a few seconds.

"Len! Timmy!" This from Agnes Frost.

"Fer Chrissake, Tim!" This from Ron Lorenz.

"And you, Len!" George McKay growled. "What twisted machismo notion was in *your* head?"

"Yes—bugging Barlow like that!" Maggie McKay put in. "He probably doesn't understand such kidding around! So you both need patching!" She went to the phone to call a hotel physician.

Strangest of all, Len Ross was now sitting up on the floor, bleeding and laughing. Second glances from everybody around, assured them that this wasn't from hysteria. The laughter was genuinely humorous. Also, it was wondering, friendly, and someway triumphant. Part of this wasn't at once apparent to the others. Ross spat into a tissue that Agnes had given him, and looked up at Barlow.

"I suppose I've just pulled an idiot trick," he said. "But I've been worried. Yes, promoting the planetlets continues to be my main purpose. Also, it's great to

186

dream about going to the stars, provided we don't get carried away too much by the thought because of excitement about the *Exofact*. Mostly, though, I don't want even the planetlets publicly emphasized so much that it causes a neglect of major importance. So I remembered I'm supposed to be a psychologist. Well, maybe a little psychology? I knew you were no phony, Barlow. But did you have to half-wreck me to prove it?"

Still furious, Barlow was only half listening. Ron Lorenz and George McKay, both vigorous men, were having trouble holding him back on the divan.

"Ross called my friends on Mars fool fanatics!" he raged with whispery intensity. "And our world dead and useless! None of that is true at all!"

"I know!" Ross stormed back at him. "So hooray now for my screwy success! I just wanted you to realize, and assert, the truth; I thought if I riled you with insults, it might happen! We didn't care to prompt you too much; we preferred that you spoke out sincerely from your own convictions. About building up Earth to itself, you've done splendidly, and likewise for the cylinder worlds, though they're much more attractive than your Mars to the luxury concepts favored by the average joe and his family! Yes, Earth is a nice planet. But, Barlow, you've gotten so goddam Earth-struck that even what little you say, so mildly, about just keeping your oldest friends alive out there on Mars, makes them seem like worthless beggars, and what some of them have spent well over a score of years at as a mistake.

"I've never been on Mars, but I've kept up with the reports, and know the ups and downs they've suffered. I certainly think that anything that has come so far should continue to have a chance, even though in competition with perhaps better things! Yet you know from the past, better than I, how it'll be for them, unless

187

somebody speaks out very soon, and with real force, in their behalf! Already they're too insignificant-seeming, too far off, too out of step with the favored course of action. This condition will probably get worse. You haven't been an effective representative for them and what value they stand for, Barlow. Nor has our Agnes here, for that matter. But you're the one with the larger legend. You're Skyclimber and Big Voice; probably just now you're at the peak of your popularity, which may wane. Maybe it's not too late. I won't say any more.''

Ross had lost all of his laughter. His bleeding lips were swelling up, making his words slurred at the end.

But his odd method was doing its work on Barlow: From proud rage at insult and threat, down to shame and a harder look at himself. Ron Lorenz and George McKay had stopped restraining him, Penny was keeping his injured wrist straight. Agnes had brought a towel for Ross to hold against his mouth.

A physician and four attendants arrived. Ross shrugged, and allowed himself to be put on a stretcher.

"I think they want to carry you too, Tiger," Penny told Barlow.

Both men were kind of glad that newspersons and audio-visual cameras had usually been kept out of the living quarters of the two around-the-Earth parties as a concession to privacy, and that, in their own present condition, they were hurried, with only the medical persons around them, up a service elevator to the hotel infirmary.

"This afternoon, I'll try what you said, Ross," Barlow rasped on the way.

# *28*

The packed stadium and the stare of TV lenses were nothing new to Barlow. Except for a small, brown brace around his left wrist, he was outwardly the same person he had become—still fantastically dry-stalk tall, gaunt and tawny, but civilized now. The strong terrestrial sun of late summer brought out every detail of him, as he loomed on the high podium—the flowered-pattern of the Earthly shirt he wore, the vertical lines in his narrow face, the flash of his perfect white teeth, as he grinned genially.

And, in the sudden hush of the multitude, he began to speak quietly, as usual—never shouting like a mad prophet as once, it seemed, very long ago. He did not want to command; calm reasoning was always the sensible, civilized way. Had he sometimes forgotten that, a little?

The first part of his speech was much as always; though he shortened it somewhat. He urged peace; he extolled the cylinder worlds as the best solution to many problems. But then, more subtly, he shifted his emphasis toward the subject that he had previously relegated to footnote level.

"I love this Earth," he said. "It remains my beautiful Blue Star. I am very grateful for having been brought here. But let me confess this: I was dreadfully afraid to come to Earth, though I wanted to come even more desperately. What is outside of one's experience must often seem more awesome than it deserves.''

Barlow paused.

"Then let me confess another thing: In my wonder at being here, I haven't sufficiently pointed out that my birth world is also beautiful in its own way. I love Mars too, and the more than a hundred courageous people on it. With scant and uneven help, they have build a great beginning on Mars, and have survived there for many years.

"Until less than five terrestrial months ago, when I left Mars' surface, I was always there. About twenty years. Do I look so misused or abused?

"I believe that it is in our guts and souls and our natural, biological destiny to expand beyond Earth, our original home, instead of being clotted dangerously together on one sphere. Though I disagree entirely with some people that Earth is doomed. The cylinder worlds —the plantelets—may be the best means of accomplishing this wise dispersal; but Mars is not, and has not been, a lost cause as a place for extensive human habitation. Far from it.

"Yes, Mars still is a harsh planet. Often I thought I hated it. I knew less than now. And I am told that youth usually wants to travel to distant places, see marvels it has never seen, learn what is beyond its acquaintance. To me, Earth was gentle and different—if I could get used to it—and as far from dull, familiar home— wherever that may be—as any creature of our kind has yet gone. I wanted to choose my place—not be born to it —become that free.

"Looking back, I admit that I had a fine childhood on Mars—probably better than many here—full of friendships and interests, before the hardships of our being neglected, and the distant marvels, took me.''

Again Barlow paused, and, unlike during his previous

190

speeches, there was no approving roar from the audience; there was only a questioning murmur at the different tack his words were taking. Now he continued: "Yes, people can die suddenly on Mars—as can happen here. Yes, you must be watchful and cautious for your life there. You could never survive out of doors without a vacuum suit. Otherwise—at best and as yet—it is true that you are confined to a few acres of free-breathing, biology-compatible ground, under plastic.

"On the other hand, have you seen cornstalks grow four meters tall in that lesser gravity, beneath a covering dome, as, not very long ago, I have seen? Have you heard bees hum, there, over clover blossoms? Have you marveled at such things in pride at having helped accomplish what some would call impossible on such a world?

"Have you plodded your boot prints into the pink dust of slumped crater walls? Have you watched a great spinner—whirlwind, dust devil—ruddy and towering, pass in the desert, knowing that, if your domes were new and stout, such awesome magnificence could do you no harm? Have you winnowed presently useless gold from the dryness of an ancient riverbed, which might hold a living river again, if, perhaps, simple reflectors of megnesium-alloy foil, weightless in space, were placed in orbit around Mars, to concentrate more sunshine on its surface, warm its climate somewhat, evaporate all of the frozen carbon dioxide and melt the plentiful water-ice, some of which would become vapor, and help raise the air pressure? Hardy, Earth-type plantlife, growing under the open sky, might then even reduce most of the gaseous carbon dioxide to free oxygen, perhaps providing a breathable atmosphere for large lungs.

"Much of this remains a distant dream, of course. Due in part to the low Martian gravity, the present per-

191

unit-area mass of atmosphere would have to be multiplied by a factor of 45 to achieve an external air pressure of three hundred and fifty millibars—standard within the domes—which is a little over a third of the terrestrial norm.

"But enough is very real and practical. They out there know, as I know, for they have done much to shape their environment, and with full, proper, and short-term assistance can complete their start to a viable, self-sustaining level, and open their world to sustained immigration by persons of vigor and vision.

"To accomplish this, there are some gaps to be bridged. For instance, have you wished, as they have, that you had a few more goats to eat more grass that you could grow, to give you more fresh milk? And that you could do this if you had better machines and a better processing for a certain organic mineral, not found on Earth, so that you could roll it out into more dome material to cover more fields and gardens? Have you ever wondered by what chance—or nameless pre-planning—the days—sols—of Mars are unnoticeably so little different from Earth-days in length? Is this fact, in itself, a silent call for more people?

"Have you dug down to the nickel-iron alloy of great meteorites—not oxidized or sulphidized ore—needing no smelting, and wished that you had more electricity to melt, mold, and shape it to your needs? And that, similarly, there is native—metallic—copper. Also various minerals containing other, necessary metals in quantities comparable with sources on Earth. All this while being aware that energy to produce the electricity for processing is available, if only you could set up the equipment to tap it in quantity?

"I am not thinking of uranium for nuclear fission or heavy water for nuclear-fusion power, though both of these substances are available. Rather, I am concerned

192

with a simpler, less dangerous energy supply, unique to Mars. Oh, you may say that Mars has no active rivers to turn water turbines and generators; that it does not have enough atmospheric density for effective wind power; also that, at its greater distance from the sun, solar energy is less than half of what it is, per unit area, on Earth.

"But have you stood, as Frank Gotch—whom you will remember—and I have stood, in the midst of a huge, natural power reservoir in the Martian antarctic? During every winter there, uncounted millions of tons of atmospheric carbon dioxide congeal to dry ice, and evaporate again in the southern summer; while, in alternate sequence, the same process goes on around the north pole: gas to solid, solid back to gas—an enormous change in volume. Have you imagined how many water-power stations on how many rivers would be needed to equal the millions of megawatts of electricity—for industry, heavy and light, for heating many more domed gardens and fields, and for towns and cities—that now goes to waste there?

"Have you wished that you had the means, and the numbers of able and skillful hands to tap a portion of this uncomplicated, pollution-free energy source, and a population big enough to use it effectively to improve your planet? There are those who have so wished and worked.

"But I am not urging that much now. What I do urge is only enough to complete a beginning. I should have said so more emphatically before; my neglect has been pointed out to me; I must have thought it was right and obvious enough to happen by itself.

"Those hundred-and-some settlers on Mars must not be allowed to fail and die! An effort which has been carried so far forward must not be discarded here on Earth merely because another way into space for mankind seems better, and less wearied in the public eye by familiarity. It is there, real and proven; the groundwork is laid.

"One last, more massive thrust of supply and research, well chosen for economy of weight and completeness of basic need coverage, must be made to put what has been accomplished on a firm, self, sustained footing, from which it can go forward on its own. Forty loaded ships should be enough, making up in part for the eight years when no supplies were received at all. To hurry is necessary, because only a year and a half remain to prepare, before the next window time. But the really critical requirements now are only three: One, the means to make dome plastic successfully and in quantity, on Mars, and from Martian materials; Two, more advanced basic tools, and the technology to build locally, or to improvise, such devices and their spare parts as may be needed to maintain what is, and to advance Martian industry into a larger, more complex form, in a small but growing society. The things particularly involved here are Mars suits and their life-support packs, vehicles, and construction and manufacturing equipment; and Three, most important, skilled, adventurous people, eager to tackle another world, and to work and dream hard. Such folks have been easy to find in sufficient numbers in the past, nor can I imagine that they will be less easy to find now, or in the future. Obviously, they should be granted the privilege of parenthood, on a planet that ultimately can support a large, productive and forward-looking population on a wide-open frontier.

"I doubt that Mars could ever become fully a second Earth. It is a different place, and I think it is best that it retain much of its own character. But I also believe that our kind should have a second large and true world, instead of merely the planetlets.

"More is involved here than human survival and natural expansion. There are elusive elements, like poetry and song. There is a reaching for enigmas. Yet there is the simple pleasure of planning, sweating, and doing for the primary urges toward having a home and family. There is the vision of rest and love, rewarding difficult work. There is admiration for a new and savage scene, yet the hope of conserving—not spoiling—it. The factors are simple, yet imponderably complex. Maybe there is something both empty-handed and full? In journeying so far, there are surely danger, excitement, uncertainty. But adventure is the driving force of manking at its best. That one can love both the Blue Star and the Ruddy Star is part of the intricacy. The fragment of almost imponderable design that I found in Moeris Lacus fits into all the many deep and groping factors that human life includes—outward drives of puzzlement, curiosity, wonder.

"My attention now, however, is on a far more immediate and urgent concern—that final, massive thrust to establish our kind firmly on Mars. Shout out for it—even join it—if you believe you should. You may be among those selected to go. I don't tell you what to do; I only declare what seems right to me. Now I will stop talking, and leave what is to be done to you."

Timothy Barlow waited there on the platform.

There was almost silence. This wasn't like the thunderous applause of his every public appearance up to now. But he had never spoken like this before.

Now there were murmurings, as the throng questioned itself about what was different. Then there was scattered clapping. Merely polite? And more hisses than usual? At last there was rising sound: yells, whistles, cheers, stampings of feet. Thousands rising. Another standing ovation for the great, tawny, stalk-thin stranger. A little less? Or more?

"Barlow! Big Voice! Skyclimber! Show us! Lead us! *Tzzarr-rrichh-het!*"

He would have had to flee again, or be mobbed—except that this was not the end. The spreading of his arms for attention, and to hold back the rush, was superfluous. For Agnes Frost now appeared, up a little stair, from a concealed place behind the podium. This was a designed withholding for heightened drama. As the two Marsborn stood smiling, arms across each other's waists, the thunder multiplied itself. They were tall, exotic, legendary. She was in a costume that glittered, but with a ridiculous, grinning little doll, Terri, contrived of corn husks, pinned to her shoulder. And she was wearing the Mars-gold necklace.

Barlow bowed, and then sat down at the back of the podium. As Agnes raised her hand in a small gesture, the abrupt silence was like another huge crash of adulation. Then her pleasant, husky voice was washing against Barlow's senses. He consciously heard only fragments of what she said. She didn't urge much, as he had done, but talked of ordinary matters.

"So what do I remember? Watermelon . . . A pet chicken . . . . The day I was five years old by the Earth-calendar. There was a big party, even a cake, entirely from Mars-grown ingredients, and with beeswax candles. And my mother had made me Terri—named for Earth, which I love, though I love Mars too, and those I left behind. There must be a Mars for me to revisit sometime. I remember the time we watched the Blue Star in fright, thinking that Earth would end. I remember the thrill of learning to drive a Wanderer . . . also how to grind and shape metal in the shop . . . spinning and looming flax . . . I remember Sven Thorgersen playing a fiddle, pieced together from the wood of a cherry sapling that died. As if, in spite of recordings from Earth, we had to develop our own

196

Martian folk music. Music to match the red ground, extending away to the yellow sky—and yet the apple and clover blossoms on a sunny morning, when there were frost patterns on the dome curve above. Yes, though I love Earth, and will stay, there is something good on Mars which is not here. It should not be lost.''

When Agnes finished thus, there were a few, swift touchings of hands to the yelling, surging multitude. Then Barlow and Frost took their prepared escape route, down a stairs and out of sight. A little sad that they must keep on doing this.

"We wowed them, Tim!" Agnes said briefly, as a heli returned them to their hotel. "Or did we?"

Behind her excitement and happy smile, was there a hurt shadow of something corrupted—too humanly self-centered, insincere, staged, contrived for a purpose? Though the purpose remained very good.

"We'll have to wait and find out," Barlow commented wryly.

"You both did well," Len Ross said from behind his mouth bandage. "Though one always hopes for something better. So now do we all hasten to Washington to help implement details for the two intensified space programs, while public enthusiasm is also highest."

# 29

Barlow met top executives, including the topmost. He sat and talked with them briefly, in cordial, knowledgeable fashion, as he had done with others elsewhere and before. They responded with lively interest. But somewhere his own mind lost them; they passed before him as so many shapes and presences in review.

Matters seemed to be going well. Primary emphasis remained with the planetlets, but attention to Mars was much increased. The McKays and Ron Lorenz got their assigned tasks, relating to both of the interlocked programs. They would split up as liaison with contractors, out on the West Coast and elsewhere. Len Ross would go back with Agnes to her place in California. Pen Lorenz would return to upstate New York with Tim.

Barlow was feeling temporarily tired and relaxed. But he was beginning to get an odd impression. And at the last meeting of the group in their Washington hotel, Agnes grumbled at him: "You know what, Timmy? Maybe you and I are being sort of left out and ignored now? For me, though, it's rather a relief. If I don't want to rest, I can always stir up something that will help."

So Barlow stared around, rather bewilderedly and truculently, at his other companions.

"Hey, yuh!" he complained. "What am *I* supposed to do?"

Ron Lorenz answered him, "Tim, look, along with

198

Agnes, you've been the key to restored enthusiasm for space—the planetlets and Mars. That was the most important part. You've even gotten the promise of those forty ships. So can't you relax a little? Oh, there'll be plenty more for you to do. Speaking briefly everyday, to keep the action livened. Helping with lists of things to go to Mars. Maybe you'll train new Mars immigrants. Otherwise, frankly, you're still not well enough versed in the devious aspects of terrestrial psychology and customs to function very effectively in critical areas— if we're not to fail—when nothing is ever quite sure. I'm afraid, Tim, honestly. I'm sorry, but the rest of us can do a better job. Worse, you and Agnes are too visible, too known and loved. Everywhere you went to help get something done, there would be an interrupting furor. I hope you can accept this? Please?''

Barlow managed to shrug genially.

"Okay, if you say so, Ron.''

So Barlow retired to his refuge, with Penny and a few household personnel. He made his daily spiels in front of audio-visual eyes and ears, urging what he had urged before, for Mars, while not forgetting the cylinder worlds. Here he practiced restraint, because neither subject should be made tiresome by overemphasis. And there were always visitors: media people, scientists asking questions, politicians, university professors. Barlow enjoyed it all. But soon it became more than he wanted, while it left too much out. And was the aspect of the most important consideration no longer quite as firmly optimistic as it had been?

"Penny," he urged. "Now's our chance to escape for a few days. I could leave recordings behind for broadcast. There's a whole, big, open-sky Earth all around, especially the wilderness parts—the Canadian woods, or the ocean—even way down in its deeps! Let's go

199

tomorrow—or today!"

They were lying on lounge chairs on the swimming-pool terrace, and he was sipping his third drink of the afternoon. The autumn weather was unusually warm. He loved the walled garden, with its vivid-hued leaves falling. In the domes at Arsia Mons Base, he had become used to a similar confinement. But was this quite right on the world of his ancestors and his choice, which offered infinitely more? Pen touched his arm, and her look had tenderness, pain, and wry humor in it.

"A fine idea, Tim. Only not very workable—at least now. We'd be spotted, followed, ganged up on, no matter where."

Barlow was coming to realize this blunt truth fully. Other persons before him had become the prisoners of their own celebrity. For him, this effect was multiplied. Not only was he too known and honored; his appearance was too odd—too tall, thin, and freakish-looking. For all of his life, even in the decline of his fame, countless persons here would remember him. He couldn't get five steps most places, without having a shout go up—even if, by improbable luck, nobody had ever heard of him, wherever he happened to be. He was, in this sense, condemned by circumstances.

"I'll tell you what, though, Savage," Penny pursued. "Tonight and other nights we can go somewhere in the heli for an hour or so, like we did once to the ocean. To a lake, or some other unfrequented spot. But that's about all that's easy—except being right here—which many people wouldn't consider too bad. You've got the pool to swim in. And large grounds with trees and grass —Earth in a small form. And your bicycle to ride on."

Barlow gave his wry, rustly chuckle.

"Sure, Pen, you're right. Besides, you're here."

200

# 30

So that was how Barlow's life became in a former rest home. For him, the kid who had first girdled Mars alone, in a decrepit Wanderer. Here he couldn't even drive his own car, except for a few times in deep night, and on remote, unlighted roads where he would not be seen and recogized.

Otherwise, in many ways, it was a pretty good existence. There was excellent terrestrial food, quite in contrast with the frugal fare of Arsia Base. And an attractive, affectionate girl as his companion, with a dozen acres of the best loveliness of Earth all around him. Also a bike to fall off of; he never became very good at riding it, maybe because of his leg length and structure, or because, in the massive gravity, his sense of balance went a bit wrong. But there were those short, agreeable sneakaways after 11 P.M.

Other aspects of what was happening were less pleasant. Some newscaster stated that there was a rumor that the number of ships for Mars might be cut from forty to thirty because manufacturing schedules were in difficulties through shortages and bottlenecks occasioned by other demands. Though others spoke against the irresponsibility of such reports, it was a familiar story.

But then some firebrand used the phrase "this Martian demagogue" to describe Barlow. "Employing his own questionably eminent position to dictate an obsolete course of action favoring a Martian clique, for which he had a natural and obvious loyalty, a course which, long ago, has proven to be a wasteful failure.'' Such remarks were perhaps hardly stronger than similar ones which had always been in the background. Nothing, then, to be greatly worried about. Or a somewhat more graspable edge for a growing opposition to grab hold of, and pull at?

Barlow himself was diverted from deep concern by other exciting evidences in space—jet flames to watch for after dark. Going upward out of the west to meet a steady cluster of lights that, every 128 minutes, crossed the sky from west to east. The jet flames were those of shuttle tenders taking prefabbed constructions into Earth orbit. The cluster of lights was from the orbiting assembly point, where the structural skeleton of the first new cylinder world was already being put together.

"Pen, this is great!" Barlow husked, the first time they saw this action clearly from their garden.

And, for just then, his own thoughts about his native planet were shoved out of his mind by this new thrill of progression. People all around the Earth saw too, and reacted similarly. Though it was inevitable that billions of watchers would see what was going on, it is very likely that particular proponents of the planetlets were well aware of the psychological effect; here was visible, substantial propaganda which heavily favored their cylinder worlds. This, while the tiny, ruddy spark of Mars, timelessly ancient, marched unnoticed across the firmament.

Barlow could wince sharply and guiltily about that, while remembering. But then, had he fully believed in Mars as a place for people? Had he lied a little—forced himself somewhat, when he had spoken out—thinking sentimentally more of his friends at Arsia and Olympus, than of the fundamental worth of the idea itself? It was an agonizing quandary. Why couldn't he be left just to roam over, and enjoy, Earth? That had been his old, driving vision.

He sensed the decline of his own popularity, not great, but palpable. He had nothing new to offer, to grab refreshed attention from the historically roving public eye. Well, good! Maybe this brought him a little closer to becoming an average person. And the people of Earth had minds of their own, after all. They were not just followers, a mass to be led. Good, again! They had judgment. Their attitudes were slipping sideways from where his words tried to guide them. Outward into space, yes—a fledgling from Earth, which was right— but in the best way. By the beautiful, Earthlike planetlets. Cheaper, easier, less troublesome, they seemed.

Some group had even brought him a large model to set up in his workroom. Everything in lovely miniature, around its parklike, inner curve, where the artificial, centrifugal gravity of axial rotation would be established: Villas in beautiful, landscaped settings; trees, flowers; shopping and cultural areas; a lake; factories as neat and charming as all the rest. In the larger, final versions, there would even be clouds, floating high around that inner curve, toward the axial center, where the air pressure would drop under the centrifugal action. In this model, the clouds were represented by little bunches of cottony floss—mostly white, but with some denser and darker, to indicate controlled rain. Yes, lovely! Magnificent! Utopia.

Yet something intrinsic to it all kept rankling faintly in Barlow.

"It looks so right, Pen," he commented. "For the future of mankind in the solar system. Thousands of these constructions. Someday millions and millions, circling the sun in a great ring. The Moon to be torn apart first, to build them. There are already engineers on the lunar surface to determine the best way."

"I guess it *is* right, Savage."

She sounded tired, too.

"But Arsia and Olympus, Tim? They also have meaning. Not only because of your friends. Well, we shouldn't worry. The best reports show that the parts for ten ships are already being fabricated. And that those for ten more will be started very soon, when engineering changes for improvement get a firm cutoff date, with reasonable assurance that no further serious bugs will turn up to be corrected. Meanwhile, there are those two hundred people, eager for Mars, who are under intensive training."

"Yuh, Pen. Only, it feels like the old, familiar yarn. Slippage. Mounting excuses. Understandable economies. Now, drift of interest away from something considered second rate, outdated. Forty ships down to thirty. Maybe, in the end, twenty—or less? Not enough . . . . And, in three and a half years, at the following window time? Even the Planetlet Project will probably have lost considerable drive by then. Mars could be gone—forgotten—same as before. Never enough support to finally make out. They'll still die slowly out there. End of a great try."

"Maybe not, Savage. You can keep arguing. If it doesn't work, well, maybe populating Mars is the wrong way."

Barlow winced. Then he shrugged and grinned. The Mars settlers had chosen their course, knowing that they might lose. While here over his refuge garden, the autumn air was crisp and bright. If he felt rather helpless, still he could enjoy. And he could still urge, in front of TV camera lenses and microphones. Even if his mild words were becoming a routine to be only half heard:

"Mars is a whole world. Small but vast. All of it land —as much as all the land on Earth. Can we risk losing it? And the lives of those who dared?"

## 31

To attend a terrestrial university had been part of Barlow's aim for almost as long as he could remember. Now it was being realized. But not as he had always happily pictured it. He didn't go to classes with other student companions. That would have been difficult and disruptive. Instead the professors came to him, pleased that they were so honored. Of course, they had to give him top marks. Maybe he deserved this; in many ways he had picked up as much knowledge as they possessed—often more. However—wry circumstance! —dared they have done less? He was still Timothy Davis Barlow, and they were awed.

Now he often communicated directly with Arsia Base on Mars, the audio-visual impulses being projected and received via a radio telescope 1,500 kilometers away. He saw faces he remembered, heard matching voices speaking in monologue, as they must, over the time lag of light speed across interplanetary distance, which made short-sentence, conversational exchanges impractical. He saw the heads hunched together, sometimes blurred and wavery, and the voices sounding likewise. Leon. Everett. Bessie. Homely old Gotch.

A typical contact, maybe with Everett Holsten, would go like this: "Hi, Tim, good to see you! You ask what we can still cut from the list. Well, overland electrical cable. Ten tons—not fifty. If we need more later, we might make it ourselves. But try to hold the line on vehicles. And the specials, of course!"

Into a short pause, after such words, Barlow would throw a wryly cheerful comment: "Yuh! So maybe I can trade off the reduced cable weight for more attention to the special stuff. I'll keep chewing their ears."

There was that one particular happy time when Bessie Blythe spoke up with good news:

"The Memnonia-Gum problem is getting licked, Tim! Engineer Mort Lovan, and his woman, Helen Miller, and the other chemistry and industrial products crew here, did lots of the work. Leon Bonard, now hitched to widow Ruth Parkins, chemist, rigged test apparatus. But smart folks in the Texas lab did more. Most of the solution isn't chemistry, but physics—very precise heat control; here, Tony's Lida Sturm got into the act. During the rolling process, heat has to be varied according to an exact curve, in order to get large, even sheets for the domes. It looks as though the Gum can be spun and woven too for fabrics. But all of the first workable machinery will have to come from Earth—since it'll be complicated. Also heavy . . . ."

Then had come Gotch's gravelly growl. "Uh huh, Tim, with thirty shiploads of carefully selected stuff, we still ought to do all right. The special tools and jigs for custom-building whatever we might need are the important items, along with the kind of folks to do the jobs. Keep pushing for that much, kid! It's not as big a deal as it can seem. Hey, you look sort of frazzled, fella. Ease off a bit, when you can, and stop worrying . . . ."

Gotch looked tired and worn, himself, as did the others.

"Sure, keep talking up, too, Frogface!" Barlow answered. "You know that you're coming in on general-broadcast TV right now."

It was true that many persons on Earth would still be watching and listening to those Mars dwellers—with

206

sympathy and otherwise. But, to other many, were their voices becoming a tedious thread, to be ignored?

Thirty ships? Would the actual number be even twenty?

Barlow would make himself another drink, and try to relax, with a lopsided shrug, into its glow, wondering what else might be cut from the lists. Not the minimal quantities of a few rare metals—useful in electronics and in fusion-power systems. Their weight was slight, anyhow. Then what? Less of the few luxuries usually sent? Less Earth beer? Less beef? Huh! Almost, but not quite, a joke!

One bit of information bugged him somewhat. Newscasters stated happily that Dr. Thorne had gotten a substantial government grant for further exhaustive study of the *Exofact*. And the populace seemed very pleased, as if—in a common tendency to overreact—they imagined that interstellar travel by humans was somewhere in the immediate offing. While the real chance on Mars slipped.

But Barlow did get a sense of involvement. A small barracks was hastily built within the walls of the refuge. For two weeks at a time, groups of ten young couples would come to sit at his feet on the lawns or, when the weather turned wintry, on the floor of the barracks assembly room. These were the new crop of candidates for the Red Planet, all with their skill specialties complete and their fundamental training. They were a selected lot—rugged, serious, alert, very intent on their purpose—and to him, at least, almost compulsively polite and obedient, this though many of them were older than his own not quite twenty-one years. In their private talk, which he sometimes overheard, he was referred to by the ancient honorific: The Old Man.

His function was to give each briefly sojourning group, in their blue Mars coveralls, a final polish—a

207

contact with the fact of a world that, hopefully, at least some of them would be going to—in the form of meeting him—He-Who-Had-Been-Born-There—and of hearing his casual, raspy, almost person-to-person talk, variable and rambling, while, also in a blue coverall, he ambled around before their rapt, ground-sitting or floor-sitting figures:

"Hey—Red Tharsis!—good to see you all! So you chose your possible future, and worked and stayed with it. Of course, you remember that if you stay there too long, your bodies will adapt, so that it might be tough for you ever to come back? But you know, and you've made up your minds. Just keep your cool and your friendly outlook, and you won't usually need any more than that. There'll be some rough times, but also some great moments, days—sols . . . Sorry that all of you pioneers may not get to go. We must keep rooting to get a possible transportation shortage corrected. Some folks ask me, am I returning to Mars, myself? Well, no, not for quite a while; I haven't been on Earth so very long. It was tough getting here. I'm supposed to be going to school. Besides, Earth is a pleasant place, as I hope you realize . . . ."

For all that kept frustrating him here, Terra remained Barlow's preferred and lovely world. Except for deep-down feelings that twisted and haunted him. He was turning moodier for various reasons.

He enjoyed talking to those trainees for his birth planet. They were the most adventurous cream of the crowds that had hailed him with such vigor. Yet even among these selected ones, he suffered a where, who, what-the-hell-am-I, and where-do-I-fit confusion. Though he loved them, he never reached them as age-group equals; it hardly even occurred to him to try. He was on some other level than they, too obviously. They wanted to touch him with their fingers—"For luck,

Prof, okay?'' Besides, none of them were around long enough to become his close friends. Unless he wanted to include Penny among them, since she usually sat in on his talks to successive groups.

Oh, they were kind to him, picking him up gently and solicitously, whenever he fell off his bike again. They smiled in tolerant amusement at the sometimes-odor of his breath. No, not Martian pungence. And wasn't it quaint and comical that the great Skyclimber got his kicks from bourbon or Scotch whiskey?

The worst part of his tension still lay in what he could see happening in the sky, contrasted with reports about a competing matter. It was claimed that construction of the prototype cylinder world planetlet was lagging by several weeks, which hardly seemed of vital importance, when, through a small telescope, he could see it taking shape very nicely—metal-sheathed ceramic skin going on over the light girder skeleton. He could be pleased about this progress, also remembering that, in a remote way, it was part of his doing—though nobody asked him whether he wanted to be shuttled up there for a close look. And if they—that always elusive, hard-to-identify "they"—didn't want his disruptive presence, he wasn't going to insist for himself!

The thing that really annoyed Barlow was that the imperceptible setback in the work on the planetlet was being accounted for thus: "Of course preparation for the Mars Mission must also go forward." As if *that* was being called a senseless obstacle!

And what was actually being accomplished in that sector? The prefabbed segments of the first ten ships were declared to be ready; the status of parts for the second ten was vague. So far, there was no sign of any ship being assembled in orbit.

"Dammit, Pen!" Barlow rasped one morning at breakfast that she had prepared; they had come to

209

prefer this more intimate and private way of living. Trying to do two huge jobs at once! "The planetlet should have been set aside! Now I'm getting this clearer and clearer! Twenty ships are not near enough—if there will be that many!"

Penelope Lorenz—the aggressive young woman who had lately assumed more and more self-effacing role while trying to calm the increasingly tense and disgruntled Skyclimber—was now at a weary point where she couldn't be less than totally frank.

"I'm afraid that's the way it is, Tim," she said quietly.

But she thought of his people out there: Gotch, Doc Pharr, the Thorgersens and all the others. She had seen and talked to them briefly, sometimes. They were her friends, too. Mars, itself, was almost her friend. She shared Tim's worries. Besides, he had related problems. His life here continued to hold elusive promise; eagerness still showed in his dark, squinted eyes. For himself, he was probably glad that his public appeal and power were waning, except that it diminished his effectiveness. But he was contributing to this in a way that she couldn't control—here he became the blandly immovable object. Veiled hints were on several newscasts, maybe with studied intent from some quarters, to downgrade Mars further as a habitable world: That the Great Inspiration, Barlow the Skyclimber, was crude and weak—one who drank too much. So, should his urgings be listened to anymore?

Finally, Penny said, "We haven't heard from my brother, or the McKays, or Len Ross, or Agnes, for days. We should call. Helpful ideas might come up."

Barlow gave his one-sided shrug.

"Except maybe Ag, they're all very busy with their jobs," he said. "Besides, they know. And what can they do? As for Agnes, she'll just be amusing herself someplace.''

Pen could see that, in spite of his outward cynicism, her man was as taut as the legendary hair, trying not to break under the weight of the heavy, legendary sword. And for reason. He hadn't been talking for TV lately, either—as if he felt that continuing with that might actually do more harm than good.

She watched him get up from the table, and stalk around the bright room. He had brought in another bottle. He took it from the sideboard, then set it down again with careful effort; Barlow still had his capacity for discipline. He sighed heavily, and grinned. Pen wondered what he, she or anybody else could do about a vast failure.

Just then, a bell tinkled in a traditional function. Penny lifted the phone.

"It's Agnes," she said. "By parallel thought, I guess. Better take it on visi."

"Okay, you too, Pen," Barlow gruffed.

They went to the little room where the visiphone was.

Agnes Frost's face wasn't quite as cheerful as usual. But she was excited, and her words rushed out as during her first days on Earth: "Timmy! Let's skip the preliminary remarks. Difficult times, hey? But look, I've got a small notion. The Mars gold you brought. It's in a New york bank—as I bothered to find out—Tim, would you officially release it to me?"

"Huh? I might," he grunted amiably. "If it's mine to decide. But what's this all about?"

"I want to call a special public appearance," she answered. "To start an auction—nugget by little nugget —getting, Len thinks, at least a hundred times what it's worth as just gold! Because it's gold from Mars! Not just to raise funds, but much more to perk up interest and public support for getting enough stuff, and immigrants, out there. I could make a nice beginning out here

211

in California. Then, elsewhere. you could get in on the procedure, Timmy, be top member—unless—well—you don't wan't to? But I could still handle it on my own. It's a small effort—it might not be enough. But it should help a little. Otherwise it'll maybe be only ten ships, according to what Len knows.''

Barlow's gaunt visage had lighted up.

"Okay, Ag,'' he rasped agreeably. ''Go ahead. Record this. I'll repeat it as often as your attorneys, or whoever, require: 'I release the Mars gold to Agnes Frost.' Otherwise, the show is all yours. You'll probably do better without me.''

"Come to notice, you *do* look a bit peaked, Timothy,'' Agnes commented. ''All right, my super-thanks. And—hey—wait a sec—don't cut contact. Len Ross wants to say something to you.''

Ross' broad features replaced Agnes Frost's, in the visi. Barlow didn't notice the small, white scars at the corners of his mouth, but he did read anger in his narrowed eyes and controlled tone: ''Hello, Barlow. I don't know about you, lately, but let that go. There's a wild, crazy, improbable chance, based on something which everybody seems to have missed. It's the separation of programs, and the way matters get chaneled, each bunch selfishly concerned with its own. I accept part of the blame, since I'm involved in both things, and should have caught on. What little that can be attempted this late—besides Agnes' try—depends on *you*, how much *real guts* you've got! And whether you can make an audio-visual appearance without sounding and looking drunk!''

Barlow's narrow jaw went grim. Was this damned Ross character determined to enrage him—like once—again? And now!

''Hold on, Barlow!'' Ross snapped. ''Till I tell you about it.''

Penny was still right there, too, and heard everything Ross said. When the visi blanked, she looked at Barlow anxiously.

"Is he nuts, Tim?" she asked. "And what will you do?"

"I dunno, Pen. But I'll go think . . . ."

# 32

Barlow didn't take the bottle from the sideboard. Instead he got one from his office room. He had been trying to restrain his growing dependence. But being who he was, and thus able to get most anybody to fetch whatever little thing for him anytime . . . . This, though there were healthier wants that he couldn't seem to have fulfilled at all . . . .

He stepped out of a side door, ambled to the nearest big copper beech, and crouched down under it. Summer had come again, and a light rain was falling.

To hell with Ross! He fiddled with the cap of the bottle. But so much rage was boiling up in him that he forgot what he held in his hands. He was feeling as frustrated, cornered, helpless, and totally desperate as on that Martian afternoon, way back, at Arsia base, when he had stolen Gotch's decrepit Wanderer, and had taken off on a vague, madman's venture that promised him little more than uncaring death. Perhaps now his consciousness clouded, so that, in a sense, he was back there again, wanting to howl at the sky, like a deranged holy man in the Martian wilderness. Nuts to the milk-and-water words of so-called civilization. They didn't fit his proper image or what he had to do today! He didn't like to throw his weight around. But if he must!

He placed the unopened bottle on the ground. He didn't need it. He stood up to his full, stalky height, and absently patted the smooth bole of the great tree, as if in love for all of his ancestral planet. As he ambled back toward the house, a young couple passed him on the walk; they belonged to the latest bunch of Mars candidates, likely without any such prospects, now. To the girl's easy "Hi, Prof!" Barlow only nodded brusquely, and passed on.

He picked up the phone in his office, and pushed a red button.

"This is Barlow," he rasped. "I want to break in on all public audio-visual networks. Right now."

"But, Sir, Skyclimber!" a male voice protested. "We couldn't—at once . . . ."

"You've got it right—Skyclimber!" he growled back, a shade more sharply. "I won't wait because of any small or large excuses. I've got some very important things to say. So get moving. If anybody objects, let him answer to me."

He did have to wait, but not very long. It gave him a chance to better find the focus points of his thoughts and rages.

A cue light flashed beside the camera eye and microphones. Except for the difference of scene and his light, colorful clothing of terrestrial summer, Barlow now reverted to being that savage, alien of another world. Some might believe, in shock, that he was not only drunk, but gone truly insane.

"Blue Star!" he yelled. "I am Timothy Davis Barlow! Shame on you, wonderful Blue Star! Inhabited by lazy, soft, gutless grubs!"

He paused a second for the jolt effect of this preposterous effrontery to sink in.

"Blue Star!" he repeated yet again. "I used to speak quietly because I thought your people understood. But I see they don't! So, once more I must shout out truths!

"In the sky, what do I see? A habitable cylinder,

nearing completion! Forerunner of many others! Good! It took courage of imagination, mind, and body to design and build such things! Beautiful, neat! Fine, luxurious places to live—and perhaps work a little! I admire them! They are a dream of rest, luxury, and peace realized, after ages of struggle. A much deserved outcome!

"Still, in your planetlets, Blue Star, isn't there a flaw? Something not for every human mood and urge? Not for the fierce, searching, adventurous part? Something unreal? Too sweet a prettiness that would soon cloy in and bore our lusty natures, which were made as they are through ages of struggling up from nothing?

"Or are we humans suddenly made different by some weariness, or some imagined—or legislated—law? So that we can fall, with resigned contentment, into a dainty stagnation, and rot there? Bah! I am sure we could not stand it for long! The thought, itself, is disgusting! Are our tired yearnings to lead us into the trap of petty comforts? Are we never again to cross a wild region, sweat, endure and be joyful for having accomplished something that seemed impossible, that demanded daring and much effort? Are we never again to accept responsibility for what others have well begun, but lacked the means to finish alone?

"Not without purpose do I mention here a small fragment—since known as the *Exofact*—which I picked up in a desolate place. Perhaps its strangest property is its suggestion of distant origin. But right away, small, cool Blue Star—shining only by reflected sunshine—do your people imagine that they also, will soon cross the light-years, to at least the planets of the nearer, flaming stars? How quickly and glibly do some believe this, on the small assurance that other beings have crossed inter-stellar space; therefore it can be done, and will also be done by—*or for*—them quite easily, as well! Ah,

216

yes . . . .

"To dream mightily is brave and cheap; to actually *do* is another matter! Oh, I don't doubt that humankind *could* reach the stars someday—for more room, for the gut adventure of it, and to probe more of the mysteries —thus to worship, by clearer understanding, Whatever-It-Is-That-Controls-The-Universe—as any person does, too, when he examines an Earthly flower, or a micro-fossil or the *Gelucipulae* of Mars! But the means for journeying so far still remains uncertain! Somehow, at crawling light-speed? Or even much slower—asleep for centuries? Or will some usable chink in the structure of space and time—not yet found—somehow appear, providing a shortened, transdimensional path? Or by a supra-light-velocity? Who knows? Do *you*, Blue Star?

"But there are some clear challenges—and doubts! First, the estimated age of the *Exofact. Seventy million years ago,* other intelligences, or their devices, seem definitely to have come to our solar system. In spite of innumerable reports of other visitations, solid evidence to substantiate these, has been, at best, scant and inconclusive. And those beings of the *Exofact* appear not to have stayed, not to be here now, or to have ever returned, as far as is known! So *once in seventy million years—back to the era of the dinosaurs!* Does that suggest that interstellar travel will be easy for humans to achieve? Something to devote extensive attention to, now, when a far simpler challenge—though in the same direction—is immediately in front of you, Blue Star, and is well within the present ability of your people to accomplish, if they act quickly? As they *must!*

"I of course refer to the complete and entire fulfillment of the promises made to the Martian settlers! Their courage and determination are *not* obsolete—I hope! If ultimate human destiny is truly toward the stars, then my birth world is a far better training ground

217

for the qualities of strength that will be required than the dainty planetlets! Mars is a whole world, a place for adventurous vigor! How can it be casually shoved aside in favor of artificial toys, fine and useful though they should certainly be?

"One thing I know most of all, Blue Star! Either your people will help those on Mars to stand tall, at last free in what they have so well started among their wild, desert hills—either your inhabitants will recognize them as themselves—of the same Earth blood and vision—or your Mankind is of the *walking dead!* Then it is a mass of cowardly nothings—fascinated by an illusion of luxurious indolence, and not a people at all! If it does not honor and help its bold ones, then it is doomed to extinction by its own decay! Yes, this I know most! It is the repeated lesson of history. It is the dangerous way of biology. True, rest is necessary. But stagnation is fatal! Movement is life; only death is still!

"Fortunately there is a means—which we should have seen sooner! Some did, but they did not speak up firmly enough! So hear this well, Blue Star! No, not forty small rocketships to Mars! Instead, one large one! The planetlet! Intended for five-hundred inhabitants and all their goods! It lacks only a propulsion system for achieving a trans-Martian trajectory! Let it be borrowed for a few months! Let it be fitted with the needed propulsion! Let it be loaded with what is needed! Let it go far out, to orbit Mars! Let there be means to unload it! Let it then return homeward, perhaps to assume its original, intended purpose! With nothing lost!"

Barlow paused to draw breath into his capacious chest. At the last, here, he had been shouting sonorously, somewhat beyond the manner of inspired holy men, and more like a barbaric divinity in an act of creation. Now he roared on.

"Blue Star—your engineers say that the planetlet was not designed for so long a journey? That there are deli-

218

cate balances, technical problems in attaching a powerful driving system? True! But therein is the challenge! Let your engineers ply their wits coolly, swiftly, and with care! Let them see what they can use that is already in stock for the small ships! But let them move fast! There is still most of a terrestrial year! Halt the small-ship building! Save the parts that cannot be used now for a later time! This is a better, less costly approach! Let them try! Try, I say!

"There is a choice between greatness and weak folly! For, if they do not try, Blue Star, then—I repeat!—your Mankind are the *walking dead!* The zeros! The deserters of life! Less than cowards and bastards! Less than insensate dust! And so be it! For it will be justice! I am Timothy Davis Barlow, and need I say more?"

His voice was a whisper at the end. His slim, tawny hand moved, shutting off the communications equipment. He sat panting for a moment, with his long chin on his chest.

He turned, and found Pen beside him. Her eyes were huge—with fright and worry as much as anything.

"So the original Skyclimber came back," she remarked conversationally. "I wondered what the yelling was."

"Yuh, Penny," he responded dryly, shifting his tone back to that of simple, sane talk. "Skyclimber, the legend, the great myth. Now we wait and see what happens. The psychomedics could be coming to fetch me away."

"Or you shouting into the microphone again in a couple of hours, Tim."

"Uh uh—not if I don't have to, Penny. I've shot my bolt. The media will have recorded it for repetition. And Ag Frost needs room for her Mars-gold auctioning—just as important for grabbing attention as my part, and taking much longer, and so, holding on better, time-wise. Pen, I need a drink. Maybe now I deserve one."

# 33

On TV and radio, there was almost a stunned silence for a few minutes, while minds fumbled dumbly to rearrange themselves before a new jolt. Then came the floods of voices. There were angry declarations of Barlow's insanity. But these were battled by a rumble of cheers. This happened yet another—a final—time.

"Big Voice! Skyclimber! Returned! We *do* have courage! Lead! Lead! Mars Girl! Agnes Frost! Mars gold. Gold from Mars! The planetlet to Mars! We insist!"

It was a colossal, grass-roots surge that worked in its steps upward, through hurried legislation to top executive. Then on to the engineers and the factories. Still risks, uncertainties, problems, blockages. Nothing ever quite sure.

Meanwhile, Barlow reverted to what he had recently been. He lectured to his swiftly passing and now even more eager Mars candidates. He swam. He fell off his bicycle. He roamed his beautiful, walled prison garden, touching and greeting great trees happily, and feeling Earth's seasons and weather in their enchanted cycles. It all remained wonderful. Yet he still knew that much in his personal life was not right. He didn't even slip away very often at night by helicopter with Penny anymore; it seemed a repetitious waste. And if he walked too much, his hips, knees, and back ached, with the pain tending to linger longer and longer.

So, one morning at breakfast—was that his time and place for bringing up critical topics?—he asked diffidently, "Pen—tell me true—do you want to go to Mars?"

They had talked about this before. Now she had an expectant light in her amber eyes.

"You know I wouldn't object, Savage. But you're stubborn, and I think you still want to stay here? What you'd rather do counts with me, Tim."

"I *do* want to stay on Earth, Penny," he insisted. "Look, it keeps on being as though I had just arrived. I haven't climbed a mountain, or even a low hill. Nor have I been to the bottom of any ocean, nor into a jungle or a terrestrial desert. Once I walked in a little town after midnight, when the heli landed close by, but never down a city street, like most anybody else could. I can't go into a bar, order a beer, and make a casual friend. The Skyclimber bit can die down some, but how can any plastic-surgeon shorten my legs, and otherwise change my shape and appearance enough, so that I could get lost and blend in, like anybody? It wouldn't work; there's too much, Pen. Nuts, though—what am I grousing about? I've had it very good here on the Blue Star! It's nice right here inside these walls. And maybe somehow, someday . . . ."

Penny Lorenz considered again the idea of spiriting her man off to an empty region. But such places, where he wouldn't be spotted and followed, were getting extremely scarce on this planet.

Poor Barlow! Yes, maybe *poor,* in that sense, forever. He was denied the elbow room of anonymity, in which to adjust to his beloved Earth. His Big Purpose here—and there remained some doubt whether it was going to be fulfilled successfully—had been accomplished in so far as he was able to affect it. He had gotten a

221

couple of dozen honorary Ph. D. degrees, but what did they amount to? So he spun downward slowly and rather gently.

Ron Lorenz and George and Maggie McKay showed up singly or companionably now and then during the busy months of preparational activity, and tried to help Penny straighten Barlow out with arguments and kidding, but what could they do with such a genially obstinate guy? Besides, who wants to love, or be a friend, by denials?

Barlow slipped away from Pen one chilly, sunny afternoon.

Soon, some of his Mars trainees found him under his favorite copper beech. He was very well sozzled. They carried him into the house.

"I don't need your group medic," he kept insisting.

Timothy Davis Barlow had long ago proven that he was a man. Lately, he had been proving another side of the paradox that was himself—that he was partly a lost child, made that way, perhaps, by his contrasting fortunes.

In half an hour, under his mate's ministrations, his head was contritely clear. He sat up on the edge of his bed.

"Hear me, Penny," he rasped earnestly. "I said that folks might let themselves rot. Well, it's me that's rotting here. You understand that Mars is a rugged place, and it's a little late for you to start training, but you've soaked up a lot of knowhow already. Will you go?"

"Yes, Tim, I will."

For a moment she cuddled up to him, then said further, "Besides, it's really out of my hands, isn't it? I have to get you home—to where, maybe, you can function again. Don't worry about my training—I'll accomplish that. But, look, you big, long dummy!

222

You'd better get over a bad terrestrial habit you picked up, or you—*yes, even you!*—are liable to be declared unfit to be sent out! Then, what would you do?"

Because he was feeling an older love than for Earth— the pull of the harsh grandeur of his native scene— like the light at the end of a dark tunnel, it seemed to him just then—what Pen had just said truly scared Timothy Davis Barlow.

# 34

Compelled by his own rather haunted sentiments and curiosity, Barlow contacted Agnes Frost by visi the next evening. After he had made a few agreeable remarks and queries, her response rushed back at him:

"Yes, Timmy, I've heard. One of us should go back. I'm glad it's you, if that is your choice? You ask about me, so I say no—not now. After just these few months? Isn't it just and right for one of us to stay? The McKays are taking their crash training, like your Penny and her brother. Len Ross wanted to, too! Only, he has a heart problem—me! Nice. of him—huh? Though I'm generous—I would have let him leave! But then, I'm fickle—you know that! Everybody is so damned nice to me, and I'm enjoying myself! Tim, the nuggets have been auctioning wonderfully, unbelievably! I *like* Terrestrians! And look at me now, here in this big studio where you've caught up with me, wearing your necklace, and Terri. Yes—I'm gonna be an actress, Timothy! I'll visit home sometime, I hope, but who knows when. Give my parents and everybody my love, when you see them. Take care of yourself and Penelope. Gosh, what's the matter with me? I sound as if you're leaving tomorrow, when it'll be a good while yet—and we'll be talking often before then! Now, excuse me, Tim —they want me—I have to be at the auction. So 'bye!"

"Sure, Ag—goodbye," Barlow muttered tolerantly.

But after the contact ended, he kept thinking about her: Different from himself. A woman. Softer, easier, less furious inside. She was getting more and more beautiful, smarter, cleverer. If she still remained part great, gangling, rawboned, awkward girl, there was an offbeat charm to this too, which people obviously liked, along with her spasms of bubbly eagerness. She hadn't been affected, as he had been, by his jagged, lonely adolescence, which still could strike back at him sometimes, with mixed pain, pleasure, and pride. She was always in a hurry for the excitement of the moment; being a top celebrity seemed an everlasting, happy surprise to her.

# 35

History has often proven it: Outcomes aren't always as large-scale as first plans try to make them. Mostly because of weight-and-safety considerations, there were—in addition to a ten-member operating crew—only 106 settler couples and nine unattached persons, 221 settlers in all—not twice that, as once estimated—who were to be lofted to the orbiting planetlet. In its originally intended function, it was supposed to sustain 500 inhabitants; but now it had become a different thing; room had to be made for much freight; besides, there hadn't been enough time to fully train more Mars immigrants.

While supplies and equipment were still being stowed aboard, the passengers were shuttled up in four successive groups; Tim Barlow and Pen Lorenz, newly married as were others, were among the last of these.

Solid-fuel boosters, originally meant for smaller ships, were steel-strapped in a single sheaf around the circumference of the great cylinder. For some minutes, the huge, hybrid craft, its hatches sealed, showed no outward movement except its orbital progression and its stately, axial rotation. Until the boosters flamed. Accelerating, it staggered slightly at first; its balance was short of perfect, because, after all, it was a mating of incongruous parts. But it accomplished what was expected of it. At rocket shutdown, it was on the desired trajectory.

The journey was a month longer than previous ones—five months on a slower, far bigger craft—almost a jury-rigged hodge-podge. But it was not a bad trip. Yes, it was made in almost Earthlike comfort. Conditions were somewhat cramped for that comparison, of course. This prototype planetlet was much smaller than the full-scale cylinder worlds, intended for 20,000 inhabitants, would be. So feet felt heavy and heads light under the tighter rotation of a narrower diameter. The sharper, inner curve made little dwellings, lashed stacks of supply containers, a small, rectangular lake, and planted saplings hung precariously overhead with a dizzying abruptness. Also, much of the workmanship was sloppy; even new paint on some of those dainty cottages had already begun to peel in spots, as in some hurriedly slapped-together housing development back on Earth. No matter, surroundings were still kind of nice.

"Agnes would go all rapturous over this!" Maggie McKay declared while the emigrants were first looking over their travel environment.

"I know," Pen agreed. "I almost do that, myself!"

Ron Lorenz shrugged in mild noncommitment. But the pretty, brown-eyed girl, Myra Froman, a power systems engineer, with whom he had just wedded, spoke up quickly, "So we can use some of our spare time re-touching the bad spots. If they left any paint? We don't want to go into our own small stock for Mars. Anyway, we can fix the gardens better for whatever more-or-less permanent inhabitants there will be!"

"And play tennis, swim, and have parties," Pen laughed. "A last fling at such frivolities, eh?"

"I hope not that finally!" Barlow chuckled back at her.

"So how do you like it here, Tim?"

His guarded gaze was still roaming around him. "Okay," he answered. "The trees are kind of spindly,

227

though. But they'll get bigger.''

Yes, even here he was already feeling divested of an importance he didn't want anymore; he was almost one among many who were more his own; this brought him a kind of peace. Still, his thoughts went deeper and darker than that. But why should he try to say them aloud, and chance disturbing anybody? True, he liked what he saw here; yet, for part of himself, because of his strange birth, and how his early years had bent him, it still looked small, petty, and rather shoddy and bleak.

Old eagerness stirred in him. Was he going home, after all? This was only the transit interval. There was a chilly, not unpleasant ache in him. Nothing was totally sure, of course—not even that they'd get to Mars alive; this too was a gamble.

"You'll do all right out there, Pen," Barlow said. "You're one who fits."

"I'll try to be that, Savage," she answered him, with pioneer spirit showing in her amber eyes and the set of her jaw.

So Barlow didn't watch and wait alone for the cold, red deserts and towering Olympus Mons and Arsia Mons. Besides Penny, there were all the others, chosen and tested to be of the same rugged kind, daring to seek a rewarding future in such scenes.

Time passed. Mars changed from a ruddy spark to an ochre bead with swirled dark markings, and the white dot of its south-polar cap at one end. Because of the cylinder world's rotation, it rolled dizzily around the sky. Then, after jets flamed to check speed for orbital placement, Mars was an enormous bulge, forbidding, yet beautiful with detail, and still seeming to tumble. Often, there were wide grins or tense expressions on faces. Barlow had long ago had extended conversations from space with his old companions; so neither he nor they seemed to feel any need to add to this contact until they actually met. In general, they were a hard-bitten, laconic lot, and to talk too much beforehand might detract from a pleasure.

Because of the low density of the Martian atmosphere, winged shuttle craft remained impractical for debarkation and unloading operations. As always before, parachutes must be used, with retard rockets firing at the last moment to slow descent further for contact. First over Arsia Base, and two sols later, over Olympus. But for each base, there would be a refuelable Lander for multiple orbital return. The primary function of these special vehicles was to carry weight upward, not down. Descent of most passengers and supplies would be much simpler, by parachuted, retrofiring capsules bundled into two clusters of ten each, one cluster for each base. Just before atmospheric entry, the clusters would disperse. But their ten units would still touch down close together.

Along with ten other persons and many containers and boxes, Tim and Pen came down in one of these capsules. After the thud of contact, there was a rush to unfasten restraining straps from around bodies clad in new Mars suits, and to be out and viewing and busy. This was not haste but eagerness, plus organized efficiency. The newcomers stumbled some in that 0.38-g. Still, they knew their work.

"Easy, you characters!" Barlow laughed. "There's enough time!"

Drawing Penny with him, he stood aside, to put memory back into place with reality. His gauntleted hand swept upward and around the yellow-hazed horizon, over the rocky, dusty ground, until he pointed to a massive shoulder of lava rock in the nearer distance.

"So there's Old Hunchy, Pen," he declared with loyal emotion. "Our local volcano. Not so much smaller than Olympus Mons."

His arm swung further, to an extensive clump of

229

cord-lashed, somewhat lopsided domes, not much more than a kilometer off, across the dunes.

"And there," he said with benign sarcasm, "is our regional metropolis—Arsia Base, itself!"

Maybe she still looked slightly self-conscious, about her attire and some other matters, as she met his gaze and chuckled uncertainly from behind the transparent front of her air hood.

"Give me a chance, Savage, I'm still finding my feet," she told him. "Now . . . . Hey! I smell what you always talked about!"

He sniffed, and there it was, seeping inside his own sealed air hood, somehow—the burnt, dry odor of home!

Seconds later, he was putting his whole, stringy body to the task of unloading solid objects. It was great to be doing simple, useful labor again. He wasn't clumsy here, but much lither and quicker than the others, who were just finding their way, and didn't have his life-long adaptation. For kilometers around, other parachuted capsules were coming down, disgorging people and then freight.

"Hey, fellas," Barlow joshed cheerfully to those immediately around him. "Guess you've noticed that handle-with-care is stenciled on some of those cases?"

A young engineer—his name was Hollis Tillburn—smirked back at him. "We know, Prof," he replied confidently. "And we *are* compensating for our awkwardness with care. We'd better! Inside are tools, jigs, instruments, shapers—you name whatever you want to. They're our specialty—real lab stuff, to make just about any essential device or thing that could run short, or be needed. And somebody among us will know how."

At this reassurance of freedom attained, Barlow chuckled again. He helped the guy lift down a large case from the landing capsule. "Just kidding, Hollis," he said. "Thanks, though . . . ."

230

On her own, Pen Lorenz had joined a group who were spreading out a big parachute; in a couple of hours —well before the deepening cold of nightfall—it would probably be the inner skin of a general-utility dome, inflated with bottled oxygen, and ready for "camping" use.

Barlow might have grabbed an edge of the parachute, too; but veteran Mars dwellers had come out from Base, some in an old Wanderer, but most afoot. So there was the interruption of greetings and glove-touchings:

"Tall spinners! Isabel Perez and Steve Majorski!"

"Us—college boy! You flunked out, hey?"

"Something like that . . . . Bessie! Sven! Doc!"

"Couldn't stay away, huh, Skyclimber?"

"Stick me with my own bluff, will you? Well, it helped. Here we're all skyclimbers . . . ."

"Come on, Tim! These new folks know what they're doing. They've got procedures all planned out for the area maps. Give 'em room! See, they've even got a new Wanderer unlimbered. No matter—this old wreck'll do. Let's go—we have stuff to show you!"

"Wait! You have to meet Penny!"

"Wups—yeah—your girl! We're dumb rustics! Hey-y-y!—welcome to *you*, Pen Lorenz! Where do we find your small luggage?"

In a cloud of red particles, Tim and Pen were borne away toward the dust fences of Arsia Base. The first thing they were shown was a rectangular pit in the ground, lined with carefully cut and cemeted blocks that were coated with a silicous sealant, devised in the Base Lab. All around the pit's perimeter was a similarly paved area. Since the last ship contact, the Arsians had evidently strained even harder to be constructive.

"It looks familiar," Penny commented. "So what is it?"

She was beginning to sort out the responding voices.

"A sort of symbol of everything else we most want,"

231

Leon Bonard answered her almost solemnly. "A real town, a school, the good life."

"Yes, we got the idea from what we heard about Tim's doings on Earth!" Lida Sturm, Tony Mancuso's physicist mate, piped up. "Sure—it needs a dome over it—the spare dome plastic and the parachutes from the last group of ships had to be saved to fix up the old domes. Also, what we've got here needs water, but that's no problem; there's still our large deposit of fossil-ice nearby."

"This is gonna be our first public luxury facility," declared Isabel Perez, the hydroponics specialist who companioned with Steve Majorski. "A heated swimming pool."

Penny stared around at the gaunt Arsians in their patched and dusty Mars suits. "A swimming pool?" she pronounced flatly. "For cold, desert Mars, that's as dreamy as anybody can get! Do I laugh or cry?"

She did laugh; perhaps she wept a little too—inside. In succeeding minutes, Barlow lost her to the Old Timers who were all around them, greeting and joshing, as they entered the Number One habitation dome.

In the crowded, noisy mess room, Barlow clasped Marie Manning's papery hand in his gloved one. She seldom wore outdoor garb.

"Timothy," she said. "That you're back with us is part of our thankfulness. To them on Earth—to the way most people are, everywhere. I don't know how to say it all. A riddle . . . . Even kind of nice—sometimes—eh—Tim? So it seems we're free and clear at last. I guess this is about the best moment I've ever had."

"Sure, Aunt Marie," was all Barlow could answer to this.

He hugged her fragile shoulders. She had remained the same—frail and whispery, semi-invalided by old hardship, but durable and useful still. Not like Deva Corliss, his and Agnes Frost's teacher—younger, but

232

less fortunate. He had been told of Deva's death while he was still on Earth, but under the pressure of events, he had almost forgotten.

Almost as a pleasant diversion, he said suddenly, "I haven't seen Gotch. Is he holding back, as usual?"

Marie Manning smiled. "Uh huh—likely. You know Frank. I think he's Outside, somewhere. He figures he'll get more of your attention by waiting till the last."

"He'll turn up," Barlow chuckled. "Will you excuse me, Aunt Marie? I should go back out for a minute."

It wasn't to look for Gotch that Barlow left the dome briefly. There were five new graves on the cemetery knoll, since he had left for Earth. One of them was Deva's. Almost the oldest of all were those of his never-known parents, who remained more of a haunting puzzlement than an actual sorrow—a legend—part of the whole human phase, until now, of Martian history. As were all of the persons under the little mounds of rocks, with names painted on sheet-metal rectangles upheld by magnesium-alloy rods. For some seconds, Barlow stood, contemplating. His stalky shadow was very long in the muted sunlight of late afternoon. Here on the slope, the thin, frigid wind swept the mounds clean of encumbering dust. He read a name: Aldo Carlyle. He shrugged, finding relief. Nobody here had died in vain.

He re-entered the habitation dome, returning to the greater importance of the present. He saw Penny's auburn head, as she wandered off, laughing, with Bessie Blythe and several others, perhaps to tour more domes, or to go to receive some of the new arrivals, coming across the desert in their sleek Wanderers for a hospitality visit. Though, due to their numbers and the straitened economy of the Base, until now, they would have to feed and house themselves, except perhaps for a small offering of algae cakes and honey. No matter, they were prepared.

# 36

Leon Bonard, widowed and remated, latched onto Barlow again.

"I've got something to show you, Tim. In the shop . . . ."

So, with his removed air hood under his arm, Barlow stood before it, looking: a busy, mechanical combination. Primitive—like an antique. But gleaming, quiet, beautifully made. Half of it resembled a small, reciprocating steam engine, with spinning, well-balanced flywheel. This much directly shaft-attached to an electrical generator, on the brushes of which blue sparks purred.

"Meteorite steel and local, native copper," Bonard said. "Even Memnonia-Gum insulation—not as difficult to fabricate as sheets. Before she died, Arelle urged me to start building it, and Ruth, her friend, has helped, and kept me on the job, when there was time. Every bit here is Martian. Especially the power source. Outside, there are two blackened tank boxes, surrounded by polished-copper solar reflectors to increase warmth absorption. One tank is filled with dry ice, sealed, and producing pressure. The other is opened for reloading. What we wanted, Tim! We didn't have to go to the polar regions for the dry ice. There's a deep fissure a short ways up Old Hunchy—very cold, where sunshine never reaches. Lots of frozen carbon dioxide has collected there. Enough to start tapping the big Martian power supply! The juice produced by this little plant feeds into the local electrical system. As soon as possible, we want to try a bigger turbine generator up the mountain. Then, before too long, maybe the antarctic.''

Barlow had to let his own eagerness, his firm handshake, and some banal phrases of congratulation, be enough of a compliment for tired Leon Bonard. But Leon surely knew what his feelings were.

They went back to the habitation dome through an interconnecting tunnel. Mingling with the crowd in the mess room, Barlow looked for Mort Lovan, engineer, or Helen Miller, chemist. He found Helen. She, too, had agreeable things to tell and reaffirm.

"Yes, I just came back from the landing site, Tim. My Mort is still out there. I was afraid we'd never find the four big containers; they were all in different freight capsules. But the new hotshot kids helped us look, and we found them and opened them to check. Everything for processing Memnonia-Gum was there: grinders, softening vats, heaters, the all-important multiple-stage-controlled-heat rolling machine, even a spinner and a weaver! Mort is hauling the last load into Base; it'll all be under a new shelter dome in an hour. We have to wait till tomorrow to set things up and maybe make a trial run. I'm scared, but I'm fairly sure everything'll work out fine. If not, we'll fuss around till it does. Then we'll have the stuff to build as many domes as we can use.''

Barlow kissed Helen's cheek, and then got attracted away by the young engineer, Hollis Tillburn. With everett Holsten and several more veteran settlers, he was now discussing a development map spread out on a mess-room table.

" . . . Here in the east hollow, away from the domes,'' Tillburn was saying. "This might be a good place to establish the metallic ores and chemical facilities. A complete, small-scale operation . . . . What do you think? Some things I believe I know, but you people have lived here . . . .''

Barlow listened with interest. But then he looked up at an old TV camera with attached microphones, still bracketed on a bulkhead. He could see that it had been activated. Well, they on Earth had a right to watch and hear. He went close, and said clearly, though not very loudly: "Thank you, Blue Star. For your gifts to us. Thanks to your people. May the gifts also be to themselves. For we are part of them, and have helped open this new frontier for the good they can make of it."

As he stepped away from the camera, he noticed that persons from the crowd moved up to emulate what he had just done, as probably he had emulated others from before.

He made his way to his old quarters. His and Penny's gear had been taken there and set down. From his luggage he extracted one of two bottles, took it back to the mess room, and set it on a table for anybody to pass around. Good bourbon. He snorted in a kind of elfin satisfaction. He had had three drinks of hard stuff in the last five months. Restraint had been a little difficult at first, but the causative strains had already been dissolved; he hadn't needed any bracers. Still, right now, he kind of wished. That was when Gotch came up behind him.

"Hi, kid," he graveled. "One for me—one for you. Two beers."

"Frogface! So where the hell have you been?"

"Where do you s'pose? Out where the manna has been falling. Got there just about when you left the landing area. Been helping—and helping myself a little. That's how I got these two cans. Your redhead Penny is back out there. Says she has to earn her keep. Told me you must still be here. So I came to look. Soon as we drink up, maybe we'd better drift back."

Briefly they stood near the dome skin, where they found some foot room.

"Beer—one thing I kind of missed," Gotch said.

236

He looked good, wrinkled, brown, tough, the tiredness drained out of his face by the broad improvement of general fortune.

"Did you ever go get your old Wanderer back?" Barlow asked with a ground-level sort of curiosity.

"Sure, Tim. Went for it when we could. Towed it in from where you left it busted, you thief. Fixed it up. It's out in the assembly-square now."

"I haven't driven hardly a damned thing since I left here, Frank. Could I?"

"In a minute. Soon as we finish. Skyclimber!" Gotch gave his gravelly chortle.

"Okay, you want to rub that in, too, Frogface? One of the best things about being back is the end of most of that rubbish. People know me here—what I am and am not. Same as anybody, and no faking. On Earth, there are lots of two kinds of folks around, Frank: Those who want to lead in a big way, and those who have an ache to be led. It may be necessary sometimes, but—embarrassments aside—it can get damn dangerous."

There were pebbly rattlings in Gotch's throat again.

"You weren't all fake, kid. Sometimes your fakery turned nearly solid—even sublime. A fleeting evanescence. Agghh!—shoot!—I like to *think* rhetoric, but saying it out loud can feel mighty silly. Folks need leaders—as part of their jagged, uneven movement—I hesitate to call it progress though maybe it is."

"Be a prophet, Frank. How are things gonna be?"

"Here on Mars, Tim? Like anywhere—like always, probably. Building up a place. Thinking that today circumstances aren't so bad—next year they'll be better. Maybe pounding comfort out of what seemed an unlikely place, and saying, this is ours—see what we did! For ourselves and our children! Include some big vision or mystery to go after—like Sven and Ilga Thorgersen—looking for, and probably finding, a bit better contact with the Great Ultimate Presence—what-

237

ever it may be—in their *Gelucipulae* and microfossils. Don't quote me, but of all such is the elusive stuff of happiness made, as far as I know. Wups—beer's ended. Let's take that ride, kid.''

So Barlow was driving the old Wanderer out of Base, well away from the landing site, which was too close for more than a minute of this enjoyment; he would loop back to it later. Just now let him feel the remembered bounce of speed, and the wheel in his hands, with his own lonesome hills before him.

"Best time for me is now, though, Tim," Gotch offered further. "The worst sweat, the hardest, rottenest part, finished. Just steady work ahead—for what I half want, like anybody—but still plenty of wild country around that I don't care to give up. Uh huh— my paradox—though others own it, too. It'll last here as long as I do. Before the million domes spoil it. And it ought to be a couple of centuries at least, before they start breaking up Mars, like they plan to break up the Moon to start making their big, solar ring of neat, little, make-believe worlds. If we Martians ever let it happen here at all!''

Barlow drove on, feeling very good indeed. They spoke intermittently.

"Still got that contra-implant under your hide, Tim?''

"Yep. Even with the ban against births lifted, most of the newcomers are also holding back for a couple of months. Commonsense. And to give some of the oldsters a chance. Though a whole planet is waiting. We'll get started soon.''

Gotch snorted wistfully. "Yuh! Marie and I will have to pass. But you and yours will be around.''

Here, Gotch changed the subject, "Hey, another thing we did. Whenever we could, some of us went out to that gully, tore up the ground and winnowed a lot more gold—three hundred kilograms, Earth-weight of

238

it. Funny—gold was the first Martian product valuable enough to be worth its shipping cost. And now there's this second, bigger batch, to be sent when the planetlet and its crew start for home. A small down payment for favors.''

"On top of the gift of an entire world as a new frontier and population outlet—not to mention an exercise ground for many lusty urges!" Barlow quipped back. "How much is all that worth, and what does it weigh?"

Gotch only gurgled in deep satisfaction. But he wasn't done with expressing some of his rambling thoughts.

"Before long, kid—when things quiet down, you and I have got to take another trip. Say, toward the north pole this time.''

"Hell, why not, Frogface!"

Barlow had ruminations which he didn't express aloud.

Old Gotch, here. He loved Mars as some had loved war. But Mars wasn't the basic name for what was meant. It was any strange place in any age. There had always been folks like that. Hopefully, there always would be. He was one himself.

A few of the veteran settlers would no doubt be going back to Earth soon on the big ship. Taking their chances —for bold pleasure—another look at the human birth world. But some would also be going because of tiredness. And he, himself, was physical evidence that there would be a Martian race.

He thought further. About the strange, jagged, human course and reaching. The intricate soul of Man. Biological, dangerous, contradictory—often seeming aimless. But outward bound. Whence and whither? As with other beings—where and when? Millions of years, with distances to match. Stuff around which the human imagination was probably too limited to bend or guess.

239

Earth, long studied, still had mysteries, as humans, even within themselves, had mysteries and terrors. Mars had mysteries that would last long. The triangular pyramids. And those three trenches at Moeris Lacus. Supporting niches for the triad of tail fins of some great, interstellar ship? Bah! Maybe a hopelessly naive and wrong cliché? And the *Exofact* . . . . For Man—the stars? In five hundred or a thousand years? Please, let it be not too easy, for that would cheapen and narrow something beautiful. The Universe, and the Ultimate Enigma . . . .

Barlow circled the Wanderer back toward the landing area. A small dome had now been fully inflated there; it would serve first as temporary habitation for the new arrivals. Other domes would be erected closer to the original Base. Barlow drove slowly among the busy crowd, searching.

"There's your Penny," Gotch graveled.

She was with a half dozen others, unloading cartons from a freight capsule. When Barlow stopped the vehicle, she turned, her arms around a box.

"Hey! What are you two doing?" she puffed and laughed, not quite crossly. "When you could have been hauling provisions into the new dome for supper?"

"Riding, talking, thinking," Barlow answered, as Gotch and he got out of the Wanderer to help.

"About what, you sluggards?"

Barlow glanced up into the west, where the Blue Star was just beginning to be visible above the setting sun.

"About—well—there's just one phrase deep enough to say it all, Pen," he answered.

Then he voiced a poor imitation of strange sounds. Who knew what they were for, or what they really meant? Except that they were from somewhere very far off, and long ago.

*"Tzzarr-rrichh-het!"*

Some of the gang laughed. Everybody began piling cartons into the old Wanderer.